PENGUIN

AUSTRALIAN SUMMER STORIES

PENGUIN BOOKS

Penguin Books Australia Ltd
487 Maroondah Highway, PO Box 257
Ringwood, Victoria 3134, Australia
Penguin Books Ltd
Harmondsworth, Middlesex, England
Penguin Putnam Inc.
375 Hudson Street, New York, New York 10014, USA
Penguin Books Canada Limited
10 Alcorn Avenue, Toronto, Ontario, Canada M4V 3B2
Penguin Books (NZ) Ltd
Cnr Rosedale and Airborne Roads, Albany, Auckland, New Zealand
Penguin Books (South Africa) (Pty) Ltd
4 Pallinghurst Road, Parktown 2193, South Africa

First published by Penguin Books Australia Ltd 1999

10 9 8 7 6 5 4 3 2 1

Cover design by Glenn Thomas, Penguin Design Studio
Text design by Leonie Stott, Penguin Design Studio
Typeset in Sabon by Midland Typesetters, Maryborough, Victoria
Printed and bound in Australia by Australian Print Group,
Maryborough, Victoria

National Library of Australia
Cataloguing-in-Publication data:

Penguin Australian summer stories.

ISBN 0 14 028307 2.

1. Summer – Fiction. 2. Short stories, Australian.

A823.010833

CONTENTS

THE FELLOW PASSENGER   1
Elizabeth Jolley

THE TURTLES' GRAVEYARD   19
James Bradley

THE HOTTEST NIGHT OF THE CENTURY 29
Glenda Adams

COME WALK WITH ME, MY LOVELY   42
Matthew Condon

THE FERRY TO MANLY   61
Amanda Lohrey

THE BOOSTER SHOT   68
Peter Goldsworthy

SAUSAGE SIZZLE   79
Nick Earls

CANDELO   96
Georgia Blain

THE SWIMMER   104
Liam Davison

RIVER PICNIC   117
Kristin Williamson

THREE WAYS   127
Gerard Lee

AT MEREWETHER BEACH   144
Marion Halligan

THE SEA BREEZE   155
Larry Buttrose

DUST SLAPPED   166
Nikki Gemmell

THE IMMOLATING NUN   174
Raimondo Cortese

ANZAC DAY   184
Matt Dray

THE LAST DAYS OF SUMMER   206
Penny Flanagan

THE BOY, SUMMER 1961   211
Nicholas Jose

POSTCARDS FROM SURFERS   232
Helen Garner

THE MUNTA-GUTTA   251
Herb Wharton

HELLFIRE IN NEW HEAVEN   263
Phillip Scott

THE WITNESS   271
Amy Witting

NOTES ON THE CONTRIBUTORS   285

ACKNOWLEDGEMENTS   291

THE FELLOW PASSENGER

ELIZABETH JOLLEY

Dr Abrahams stood watching, for his health, the flying fish. They flew in great numbers like little silver darts, leaping together in curves, away from the ship, as though disturbed by her movement through their mysterious world. Nearby sat his wife with her new friend, a rich widow returning to her rice farms in New South Wales. The two women in comfortable chairs, adjoining, spoke to each other softly and confidingly, helping each other with the burden of family life and the boredom of the voyage.

'Who is that person your daughter is talking to?' said the widow, momentarily looking up from her needlework.

'Oh, I've no idea,' Mrs Abrahams said comfortably. And then, a little less comfortably, she said, 'Oh, I see what you mean. There are some odd people on board.' She raised herself slightly and, raising her voice, called,

'Rachel! Rachel dear, mother's over here, we're sitting over here.'

As the girl reluctantly came towards them, Mrs Abrahams said in a low voice to her new friend, 'I'm so glad you noticed. He does seem to be an unsuitable type, perhaps he's a foreigner of some sort.' She lowered her voice even more, 'And they do have such ugly heads you know.'

Their voices were swallowed up in the wind, which was racing, whipping the spray and pitting the waves as they curled back from the sides of the ship.

Dr Abrahams walked by himself all over the ship. The sharp fragrance from the barber's shop excited him, and he rested gratefully by the notice boards where there was a smell of boiled potatoes. The repeated Dettol scrubbing of the stairs reminded him of postnatal douchings and the clean enamel bowls in his operating theatre.

Whenever he stood looking at the front of the ship, or at the back, he admired the strength of the structure, the massive construction and the complication of ropes and pulleys being transported, and in themselves necessary for the transporting of the ship across these oceans. It seemed always that the ship was steady in the great ring of blue water and did not rise to answer the sea, and the monsoon had not broken the barrenness. Most of the passengers were huddled out of the wind.

When he returned to his wife he saw the man approaching. For a time he had managed to forget about him and now here he was again, coming round the end of the deck, limping towards them in that remarkably calm manner, which Abrahams knew only too well was hiding a desperate persistence.

Knowing the peace of contemplation was about to be broken, Abrahams turned abruptly and tried to leave the deck quickly through the heavy swing doors before the man, with his distasteful and sinister errand, could reach him. There was this dreadful element of surprise and of obligation too. For apart from anything else, the man had an injury with a wound which, having been neglected, must have been appallingly painful. It was something, if seen by a doctor, could not afterwards be ignored.

'All you have to do is to treat me like a fellow passenger,' the man had said the first night on board. He entreated rather, with some other quality in his voice and in his bearing which had caused Abrahams to buy him a drink straight away. Perhaps some of the disturbance had come from the unexpected shapeliness of the man's hands.

The Bay of Biscay, unusually calm, had not offered the usual reasons for a day of retreat in the cabin. Abrahams, excusing himself from the company of his wife and daughter, had again invited the man for a drink.

'What about a coupla sangwidges,' the fellow said, and he had gobbled rather than eaten them. A little plate of nuts and olives disappeared in the same way.

The two stupid old ladies, they were called Ethel and Ivy and they shared the Abrahams' table, were there in the Tavern Bar. They nodded and smiled and they rustled when they moved, for both were sewn up in brown paper under their clothes.

'To prevent sea sickness,' Ethel explained to people whenever she had the chance.

A second little plate of nuts and olives disappeared.

'That'll be good for a growing boy!' Ethel called out. Like Ivy, she was having tomato juice with worcester sauce. Already they had been nicknamed 'The Worcester Sauce Queens' by the Abrahams family.

Abrahams, with the courtesy of long habit, for among his patients were many such elderly ladies, smiled at her. His smile was handsome and kind. The very quality of kindness it contained caused both men and women to confide. It was the nature of this smile, and the years of patient, hard work it had brought upon him, that had necessitated a remedial voyage. For Abrahams was a sick man and was keeping the sickness in his own hands, prescribing for himself at last a long rest. He had been looking forward to the period of suspended peace, which has such tremendous healing power and is the delight of a sea voyage.

At the very beginning the peace was interrupted before it was begun, and Abrahams regretted bitterly the sensitive sympathy his personality seemed to give out. It was all part of his illness. It was as if he were ill because of his sympathetic nature. The burdens he carried sprang from it. That was what he allowed himself to believe but it was not all quite so simple. There were conflicting reasons and feelings which were all perhaps a part of being unwell, perhaps even a part of the cause. He tried to make some sort of acknowledgement, to reach some sort of inner conclusion in the all too infrequent solitary moments.

At the first meeting, Abrahams' feeling was, apart from a sense of obligation or the good manners of not liking to refuse to buy a drink for the stranger, a feeling of gladness, almost happiness, perhaps even a tiny heart-bursting gladness which could have made him want to sing. He did not sing, he was not that kind of man. His work did not include singing of any kind. There was not much talking. Mostly he listened. His work kept him quiet and thoughtful. He often bent forward to listen and to examine and to operate. He had good hands. His fingers, accustomed to probing and rearranging, to extracting and replacing, were sensitive and capable. If he frowned it was the frown of attention and concentration. It was his look of kindness and the way in which he approached an examination, almost as if it was some kind of caress, which made his patients like him.

In the bar that first night, he reflected, he had come near singing. A songless song, of course, because men like Abrahams simply would never burst into song.

Once he did sing and the memory of it had suddenly come back to him clearly, even though it had been many years ago. Once his voice, surprisingly powerful, it could have been described as an untrained but ardent tenor, carried a song of love across and down a valley of motionless trees. Throughout his song the landscape had remained undisturbed. He had not realised how, in the stillness, a voice could carry.

'Heard yer singin' this half hour,' the woman had said, holding her side, her face old with pain.

'Oh? Was I singing?'

'Yerse, long before you crorsst the bridge, I heard yer comin'. Thanks to God I sez to meself the doctor's on his way, he's on his way.'

It was during a six-months' locum in a country town. That day he sang and whistled and sang careering on horseback to a patient in a lonely farm house. He remembered the undisturbed fields and meadows, serene that day because he went through them singing.

The stranger's voice in the bar, and his finely made hands taking the glass from Abrahams, brought back so suddenly the song in the shallow valley.

On the track that day he thought he'd lost his way and he was frightened of his surroundings. The landmarks he'd been told to watch for simply had not appeared. There was no house in sight and no barn and there were no people. He'd been travelling some time. Joyfully he approached some farm machinery but no one was beside it. He almost turned back but thought of his patient and the injection he could give her. In all directions the land sloped gently to the sky, the track seemed to be leading nowhere and he was the only person there.

He came upon the man quite suddenly. He was there as if for no reason except to direct Abrahams, though he had a cart and some tools, but Abrahams, in his relief, did not really notice. The man's eyes shone as he patted the horse and Abrahams felt as if the intimate caress, because of the way the man looked, was meant for him. He continued his journey feeling this tiny heart-bursting change into gladness, which is really all the greatest change there is, and so he sang.

As he walked or stood on the deck he thought about loneliness. The crowded, confined life of the ship was lonely too.

'Give me some money,' the man said. 'It'll look better if I shout you.' So in the temporary duskiness between the double swing doors Abrahams gave him some notes and small change and followed him as he limped into the bar.

'What'll you have?' the man asked the old ladies. They were there as usual, before lunch, their large straw hats were bandaged on with violently coloured scarves. They sat nodding those crazy head-pieces, talking to anyone who would listen to them.

They were pleased to be offered drinks. Abrahams had a drink too, but it was accompanied by disturbing feelings. The thought of his illness crossed his mind. The man's hands had an extraordinary youthful beauty about them, out of keeping with his general appearance. As on the other occasions when glasses had passed between them, their fingers brushed lightly, but it was not so much the caress of fingers as of a suggestion of caress in the man's eyes.

Abrahams, with a second drink, found himself wondering had he been on horseback that time in the country or in a car. Had that other man touched the horse or merely put a friendly hand on the door of the car? With his hand he had not touched, only the expression was there in his eyes. This time, all these years later, it was a touching of exceptional hands together with an expression in the eyes.

In the afternoon there was a fancy-dress party for the

children. Mrs Abrahams had been making something elaborate with crepe paper. Already the cabin blossomed with paper flowers. Abrahams discovered his daughter sulking.

'Look, Rachel darling,' Mrs Abrahams persuaded. 'You will be a bouquet, we shall call you "the language of flowers",' she said, holding up her work. 'White roses – they mean "I cannot" – and this lovely little white and green flower is lily of the valley. It says "already I have loved you so long" and here's a little bunch of violets for your hair, Rachel, the violets say "why so downhearted? Take courage!" and these pretty daisies say . . .'

'Oh no, no!' Rachel interrupted. 'I don't want to be flowers, I want to go as a stowaway,' and she limped round and round the cabin. 'Daddy! Daddy!' she cried with sudden inspiration. 'Can I borrow one of your coloured shirts, please? Oh, do say I can. Do let me be a stowaway, please!'

Abrahams took refuge among the mothers and photographers at the party. He joined in the clapping for the prize winners, 'Little Miss Muffet' and 'Alice in Wonderland'. 'All so prettily dressed!' Mrs Abrahams whispered sadly. A girl covered in green balloons calling herself 'A Bunch of Grapes' won a special prize. The applause was tremendous.

'They must have made a fortune in green umbrellas,' the rice-farm friend said with delight.

'Spent a fortune on green balloons,' Abrahams muttered to himself, almost correcting her aloud. He was unable to forget, for the time being, his sinister companion who was somewhere on the decks, waiting with some further demand. Silently he watched his little daughter's mounting disappointment as she limped round unnoticed in one of his shirts, left unbuttoned to look ragged.

He thought he would like to buy her a grown-up-looking drink before dinner, something sparkling with a piece of lemon and a cherry on it, to please her, to comfort her really. If only she could know how much he cherished her. He longed to be free to play with her. She was old enough, he thought, to learn to play chess. But there was the fear that he would be interrupted, and she was old enough, too, to be indignant and to enquire.

'I am not quite well,' he explained to his wife after the first encounter with the man. 'It is nothing serious but I am not sleeping well.' He did not want her disturbed by something mysterious which he was unable to explain. So he had a cabin to himself and arranged for his wife and daughter to be together. Their new cabin had a window with muslin curtains and a writing table. Mrs Abrahams took pleasure in comparing it with the cabins of other ladies on board. Dr Abrahams called for her and Rachel every morning on the way to breakfast.

The children's fancy-dress party was depressing. The atmosphere of suburban wealth and competition seemed shallow and useless. The smell of hot children and perfume nauseated him. But it was safer to stay there.

The ship remained steady on her course and the rail of the ship moved slowly above the horizon and slowly below the horizon. There were times when Abrahams felt he was being watched by the stewards and the officers, and even the deck hands seemed to give each other knowing looks.

These feelings, he knew, were merely symptoms of his illness which was, after all, nothing serious, only a question of being overtired. All the same, he was worn out with this feeling of being watched. He avoided the sun deck for it was clear from the man's new sunburn that he lay up there, anonymous on a towel, for part of each day.

'You'd better let me have a shirt,' the man said. 'I'll be noticed by my dirt,' he said. He took a set of three, their patterns being too similar for Abrahams to appear in any one of them. He needed socks and underpants and a bag to keep them in. The nondescript one Abrahams had would do very well. It was all settled one evening in the cabin which Abrahams had said he must have to himself. The fellow passenger slept there, coming in late at night and leaving early in the morning. It was there in the cramped space Abrahams dressed the wound on the man's thigh with the limited medical supplies he had with him.

'Easy! Easy!' the fellow passenger said in a low voice.

'It's hot in here,' Abrahams complained. He disliked being clumsy. 'It's the awkwardness of not having somewhere to put my things.'

'It's all right,' the fellow passenger said. 'You're not really hurting me.' He seemed much younger undressed. His long naked body so delicately patched with white between the sunburn, angry only where the wound was, invited Abrahams.

'I'm not wounded all over,' he said, and laughed, and Abrahams found himself laughing with him.

'Easy! Easy! Don't rush!' the younger man said.

That laughter, the tiny heart-burst of gladness was a

fact, like the fact that the wound was only in one place. They could be careful. It was a question of being careful in every kind of way.

Abrahams knew his treatment to be unsatisfactory but there seemed nothing else to do in the extraordinary circumstances. If only he had not answered the smile in the man's eyes on that first evening; he should have turned away as other people do. Knowing the change and feeling the change, in whatever way it brought gladness, was the beginning and the continuation of more loneliness.

Incredibly the ship made progress, her rail moving gently up and persistently down.

Like many handsome clever men Dr Abrahams had married a stupid woman. She was quite good at housekeeping and she talked consolingly through kisses. Her body had always been clean and plump, and relaxed, and she was very quiet during those times of lovemaking, as though she felt that was how a lady, married to a doctor, should behave. Abrahams never sang with her as he sang in the cabin.

'Easy! Easy!' the fellow passenger said. He laughed and Abrahams put the pillow over his head.

'They'll hear you.' He buried his own face in the top of the pillow. He could not stop laughing either.

'And they'll hear you, too!' Abrahams heard the words piercing through the smothered laughter.

Always unable to discuss things with his wife, Dr Abrahams did not want to frighten her now and spoil her holiday.

'Your husband is a very quiet man,' the rice-farm

widow said to Mrs Abrahams. 'Still waters run deep, so they say,' she said. That was very early in the voyage after a morning in Gibraltar, spent burrowing into little shops choosing antimacassars and table runners of cream-coloured lace.

'Did you go to see the apes?' Ethel enquired at lunch.

'Plenty of apes here,' Abrahams, burdened and elated by discovery and already badtempered, would have replied, but instead, he smiled pleasantly and, with a little bow, regretted the family had not had time.

'You see Ethel and I have this plastic pizza,' Ivy was explaining to Mrs Abrahams and Rachel. 'At Christmas I wrap it up and go down to Ethel's flat, "Happy Christmas, Ethel," I say, and she unwraps it and she says "Ooh, Ivy, you are a dear, it's just what I wanted", and then next year she wraps it up and gives it to me. It saves all that trouble of buying presents nobody really wants. Thank you,' she said to the steward, 'I'll have the curried chicken.'

Rachel, accustomed to good meals, ordered a steak. Abrahams could not help reflecting that Ethel and Ivy had both the remedy and the method which simplified their existence. They appeared to be able to live so easily, without emergency, and without burdening other people with their needs. They could, of course, require surgery at any time, though he doubted that this ever occurred to either of them. Perhaps he too, outwardly, gave the same impression.

The fellow passenger's demand was both a pleading and a promise. At the beginning Abrahams had risen to the entreaty, but, as he understood all too quickly, his response was complicated by an unthought-of need in himself. Walking alone on the ship he was afraid.

The begging for help had, from the first, been a command. Abrahams knew his fellow passenger to be both sinister and evil. In his own intelligent way he tried to reason with himself what, in fact, he was himself. At the start, but on different terms, it was a matching desperation of hunger and thirst and an exhaustion of wits. The fellow passenger had certain outward signs. For one thing, he had a ragged growth of beard which in itself was dangerously revealing. He was dirty, too. He needed help, he told Abrahams, to hold out till the first servings of afternoon tea in the lounge, and until such time when the weather would improve and cold buffet lunches would be spread daily in the Tavern Bar and on little tables on the canopied deck by the swimming pool. To be in these delightful places, in order to fill his stomach, he needed to mingle in the company.

'It's dangerous,' he said, 'being alone. Being on my own makes me conspicuous and that's what I don't want to be.' A companion who was both rich and distinguished was a necessity and it had not taken him long to find the kind of fellow passenger he needed.

'I better have a bit more cash,' he said to Abrahams. 'I'll shout you and them old Queens. They know a thing or two about life, those two. I'll take care of them.' His words sounded like a threat.

They had, without laughter, been sorting out what was to happen next. The cabin had never seemed quite so small, quite so awkward. He had plans to alter a passport, he knew exactly what had to be done. He needed a passport and it only needed the doctor to produce one.

Like many clever men Dr Abrahams was easily tired. He had come on the ship, as had the fellow passenger, exhausted, already an easy victim. Now, more tired than ever, he hated the man and saw him as someone entirely ruthless. It seemed impossible to consider what might have been the cause. It was clear that there would be no end to the requests. Abrahams realised that soon he would be unable to protect his family and quite unable to protect himself. The voyage no longer had any meaning for him. Together, the two of them went to the bar.

Ethel and Ivy were there as usual.

'It's on me today,' Ethel cried and made them sit down. 'You must try my tomato juice,' she cried. 'It's with a difference, you know,' and she winked so saucily everyone in the bar laughed.

The fellow passenger drank quickly.

'Now it's my turn,' Ivy insisted. 'It's my turn to shout.' She watched with approval as the fellow passenger drank again.

'So good for a growing boy,' she declared and she ordered another round.

Dr Abrahams held his glass too tightly with nervous fingers. After the conversation about the passport he felt more helpless than ever. He could scarcely swallow. He should never have lost his way like this. Quickly he glanced at all the people laughing and talking together and he was frightened of them.

'More tomato juice for my young man,' Ethel shrieked. Her straw hat had come loose.

'Ethel dear, watch yourself!' Ivy shrilled. 'We're in very mixed company, you know, dear.' Their behaviour drew the attention of the other passengers.

'Steward! Steward!' Ethel called. 'Don't forget the-you-know-what-oops la Volga! Volga! It makes all the difference. There, dear boy, let's toss this off.' She raised her fiery little glass to his. 'Oops a daisy!' Her hat fell over one eye.

While the fellow passenger drank, Ivy retied Ethel's scarf lovingly. She rocked gently to and fro.

'Yo ho heave ho! Volga-Volga,' she crooned. 'Volga Vodka,' she sang, and Ethel joined in.

'Yo ho heave ho! Volga-worcester-saucy-vodka-tommy-ommy-artah – All together now – Yo ho heave ho-Volga-Vodka,' they sang together and some of the other passengers joined in. Above the noise of the singing and laughing Abrahams heard a familiar voice, but it was much louder than usual.

'Go on, dear boy! Go on! Go on! Don't stop now!' Ethel and Ivy cried together, their absurd hats bobbing. 'Tell us more,' they screamed.

It seemed to Abrahams that the fellow passenger was telling stories to Ethel and Ivy and to anyone else who cared to listen. Hearing the voice he thought how ugly it was. The ugliness filled him with an unbearable sadness.

'So you're wanted in five countries!' Ethel said. 'Why that's wonderful!' she encouraged. She bent forward to listen. Ivy examined the young man's shirt. She patted his shoulder.

'This is such good quality,' she breathed. 'Look at this lovely material, Ethel dear.' But Ethel would not have the subject changed.

'Rape!' she shrieked with delight. 'And murder too, how splendid! What else, dear boy? Being a thief is so exciting, do tell us about the watches and the jewels and the diamonds. You must be very clever. Ivy and I have never managed anything more expensive than a pizza and then it turned out to be quite uneatable.'

The fellow passenger did not join in the laughter. He began to despise his audience.

'Look at you!' he sneered. 'You two old bags and you lot – you've all paid through the nose to be on this ship. But not me, I'm getting across the world on my wits. That's how I do things. I've got brains up here.' He tapped his head with a surprisingly delicate finger. 'It isn't money as has got me here,' he said and he tapped his head again.

For the first time Abrahams noticed the ugliness of the head. He thought he ought to find the Purser and speak to him.

'It's all my fault about the head,' he would confide, and explain to the officer about the arching of soft white thighs and the exertion. 'It's like this,' he would say. 'When you see the baby's head appear on the perineum it's like a first glimpse of all the wonder and all the magic, a preview if you like to call it that, of all the possibilities.' The Purser would understand about the shy hope and the tenderness when it was explained to him. Abrahams thought the Purser might be in his cabin changing for lunch. He could find the cabin.

'What has happened?' he wanted to ask the Purser. 'What has happened?' he wanted to shout. 'What is it that happens to the tiny eager head to bring about this change from the original perfection?'

He walked unsteadily towards the open end of the bar. Really he should speak and protect his fellow passenger. He felt ashamed as well as afraid, knowing that he needed to protect himself. Of course he could not speak to anyone, his own reputation mattered too much.

He was appalled at the sound of the boasting voice and, at the same time, had a curious sense that he was being rescued. The fellow passenger was giving himself to these people.

Abrahams did not turn round to watch the man being led away by two stewards in dark uniforms.

'Mind my leg!' He heard the pathetic squeal as the three of them squeezed through a narrow door at the back of the bar. It was a relief that the wound, which he was convinced needed surgery, would receive proper attention straight away.

There were still a few minutes left before lunch. For the first time he went up on the sun deck. Far below, the sea, shining like metal, scarcely moving, invited him. For a moment he contemplated that peace.

'Yoo hoo, Doctor! Wear my colours!' Ethel shrieked. Turning from the rail he saw the Worcester Sauce Queens playing a rather hurried game of deck tennis. Ethel unpinned a ragged cluster of paper violets from her scarf and flung them at his feet. Politely he bent forward to pick them up.

'You must watch Rachel beat us after lunch,' Ivy shrilled.

The pulse of the ship, like a soft drum throbbing, was more noticeable at the top of the ship. To Abrahams it was like an awakening not just in his body but in his whole being. He stood relaxed, letting life return as he watched the grotesque game and, with some reservations belonging to his own experience, he found the sight of the Worcester Sauce Queens charming.

THE TURTLES' GRAVEYARD

JAMES BRADLEY

It has been fifteen hours since the boat left. Not long perhaps, in the greater scheme of things, but long enough. Long enough for the sun to wheel across the cerulean immensity of the sky. Long enough for the massing light of the constellations to rise and begin the long arc of their nightly motion. Long enough for this water, once warm as blood, to turn cool, then cold against my body. Long enough for my arms to tire, fall motionless to my side. Long enough for my skin to swell and pucker.

Have you ever raised your head, gazed upwards into rain? Seen that strange, perspectiveless world of cloud and tumbling water? If you have you will know there is a moment, as the world recedes, when the rain will seem to pause in its descent, like the motion of a stone's parabola at apogee. I say a moment, but that is not quite the word, for time itself becomes elastic, slowing finally to a point, before it begins again, and there is reversal, slow at first, but hastening like the stone falling earthwards, and all of a sudden the rain is no longer falling, it is you who is falling, or rather rising, upwards, against gravity, like flight, like breathing.

I fly like that now. Once this was water, but now I float in stars. Far beneath me the plankton dart and burn, phosphor-bright, cold meteors against the dark. Around me the light from the stars dapples the water's surface, motes of light that move with the water like leaves across the limpid surface of a lake. And all the while I am rising into the sky, falling upwards into the ancient deep of night, the stars passing me like rain as I rise.

Beneath the water's surface my watch's face floats, ghostly green. One hand on three, the other at four: 3.20 a.m. Eight hours since Jenny left, swimming steadily away across the shimmering water, growing smaller and smaller until her body vanished into the haze of light and all I could hear was the faint sound of her stroke, growing fainter, and fainter. Then nothing. Only the fire of the setting sun on the lapping sea.

At first I wondered whether I should have gone with her, tried swimming for the shore, but I saw how low the sun had fallen, and knew, despite Jenny's protestations, that once it set we would no longer know which way to swim across the featureless sea. I cannot read the stars, nor can she. There are no stars in the city of light. And besides, I still hoped that someone might realise we were missing, seek Gerhard or Chas out in their cluttered office and demand to know who had counted the heads when they climbed back on board. That Gerhard and Chas would feel the yawning space of their error open within them as they glanced one to the other, realising what they had done, and come racing for the boat. For us.

But Jenny was frightened, too scared and angry to hear these possibilities. She knew we would not last the night, and wanted to swim for the shore. When I refused she swore and wept and then finally kissed me, her lips cold with the seawater, so I knew at the end she did not mean her words of anger.

I wonder where she is. Perhaps she can see the land, almost hear the music from the beachside discos as it echoes across the water. Maybe it is not stars that play around her but the reflected neon of the town, slithering silkily across the waves. Or maybe she is lost like me, floating somewhere in the vastness of the night, too far from land to see the faint glow of the lights, needing the dawn and the sun to gauge which way to swim now. Or maybe she is dead, pulled beneath the surface by a shark, or just drowned, her corpse already puffy and bloating.

I know it is morbid to think like this. But I am not frightened. Instead I feel a strange calmness, almost a euphoria, which has grown in me as the night has passed. This is not how it was at the beginning, when the two of us broke the surface, excitedly laughing and talking one over the other as we pulled at our regulators, eager to share the delights we had just witnessed. Our first reef dive. The culmination of two weeks of training in that grass-walled hut with Gerhard and Chas, all for this. Not realising at first, as we turned slowly, looking for the boat, that they were gone, not quite believing our eyes as we turned once more, faster this time, only to see that it was no deception, no trick of the light, but that they had gone without us, back to the island, to the bars and lights and restaurants, leaving us out here. Alone.

Then, all of a sudden, we saw them, a receding speck in the immense blueness of sea, and although we knew it was futile we screamed and waved, using our fins to propel our bodies upwards, launching ourselves out of the water like dolphins performing in some wretched show, hoping that someone might turn and see us. But it was too late. Then, for a time, we waited here, telling each other that someone would notice, that they would realise there were too few of them, that some of the equipment was missing, that we had not been seen since they weighed anchor, but as the long day wore on that possibility receded too, and we were left, just waiting. Alone.

How strange that this should happen now. After Jenny and I saved and planned for this holiday, lured by the falling baht, by the promise of the beaches and the discos. For weeks we spent our lunchtimes planning where we would go, what we would do, until I could think of little else, my excitement as consuming as a child's. I do not remember when the diving course became part of our plans, but once it appeared it lodged, like a burr, and everything else receded, the discos of Koh Samui replaced by the more austere pleasures of Koh Tao, the sight-seeing by depth charts and equipment tests. Nor do I remember whose idea it was. I would like to think that it was Jenny's, but it might just as well have been mine. Not that it matters now.

This holiday was special to me. I'm sure it was special to Jenny as well, but for her it did not carry the weight of symbolism. Instead it was just another holiday, three weeks of sun and drinking and sex. Sex. Even now it makes me laugh to think of Jenny and sex. The men she took to her bed, without shame or guilt. I cannot do that, not yet, although I hoped that tonight, maybe Peter and I, we could have done it, high on beer and sun and maybe just enough grass to make me feel loose and distant from my stern, lonely flesh. For it frightens me, the idea of it, of a man I do not know taking his member and placing it into me. Would it have been like Roger? His face, pale and cruel and somehow earnest as he hammered away on top of me. I think it was the earnestness I hated most, more even than his cruelty, which was real, particularly since that afternoon at the doctor's. More even than his hypocrisy; his false tenderness before, the way he would roll off without a word when he was done. I am not even sure how other people, *normal* people actually do it. I saw a movie, at a party that Jenny took me to. I remember the way she grinned at the way I stared at it, open-mouthed, but I was surprised, there's no sense denying it. The size of his cock, the things those two women did with it. However joyless it seemed I could not help but be startled by the inventiveness of their frenzied panting. The joylessness I have experience in, the inventiveness I will have to improvise. Or would have.

I wonder where Roger is now. I imagine he is asleep,

alone in that bed we shared for six years. I can almost hear his breath, the choking rattle of his snore. It will be dawn there soon, and he will wake to the alarm, shower, dress for church. It is a while since I've been, but I imagine the services are still at six each weekday, seven on Sundays. I wonder whether he has met someone else yet. Maybe Hanny Crawford, or that new girl from Perth. He's not bad-looking, not like most of the creeps in the Church, so he shouldn't have too much trouble. I ran into his brother Mikey on George Street a month ago, and he told me the Elders had annulled our marriage because of my Godlessness, that they had absolved him of all blame. I think he thought I would be ashamed, but I only laughed, told him that I was pleased, maybe now Roger would get a new girlfriend and stop driving past my flat in the middle of the night. He didn't like that much, but I didn't care. Mikey's a jerk.

Roger blamed my job, said if I had never gone to work in the city I would never have met Jenny or Bill or Jodie, and I suppose he is right, at least partly. It was strange, my days spent with people who were not in the Church, men and women with lives that revolved around things other than prayer. People who fornicated, who smoked and drank and took drugs, men who loved other men, like Bill. Sweet, gentle Bill. Sinners, Roger called them. And worse things.

But it wasn't Jenny or Bill or Jodie. Nor even was it Roger. It was God. That afternoon in the doctor's office, when the doctor told me the infection had affected something within me, that I would never conceive. And Roger, white-faced, his sweaty palm wrapped around mine, so tight my hand turned white, then blue. That can't be, he kept saying, You're wrong, but the doctor just looked at him over his glasses, his fat face exuding sorrow, although in his eyes you could see he was bored, bored with us, with all these desperate women and men, bored with everything. I'm afraid not, he said, The tests are conclusive, and then he looked at me and said, There's always *in vitro*, and I said, What? and he said it again, *In vitro*, and Roger looked from him to me and said, No, we can't, it's against our beliefs, and I remember thinking, Our beliefs? I don't remember believing babies were wrong.

And afterwards, in the car, as the miles and miles of suburbs passed by outside, I remember thinking that this couldn't be right. Not in the way that Roger thought it couldn't be right, but that it couldn't be right at all, not if God was in the world, not if God truly loved us. I had done everything I could, I had been good, and now God took away my right to bear a child, and then forbade me to conceive one outside my body. How could He be so cruel?

For a month I carried these thoughts with me, too afraid to tell anyone. And then there was the night of Jenny's party. Roger didn't want to go, but I made him, and grudgingly, he went. We parked in the street at 8.00, winding our way up the stairs to Jenny's apartment, only to find ourselves the first ones there. Roger wouldn't take a drink, his eyes black as murder when I sipped at the beer that Jenny put in my hand. I didn't miss the way she watched his face as she closed my fingers around the cold glass of the stubbie. Then later, Roger grabbing me in front of everyone, telling me I had to come, he was leaving, his voice booming out into sudden silence, everyone turning. Now, he was saying, pulling at me, Now! and then Bill was there, between us, and Jenny was pulling me back, her arms around me. I thought Roger would strike Bill, as he did me, as he had that night after the doctor's, but he didn't, he didn't do anything, just turned and walked away without a word.

I saw him a week later, and he told me I was a whore in the eyes of God, then begged me to come back, and I said no, so he called me a whore again, and seeing the way his fist was tightening I looked him in the eye and told him that if he hit me I'd have a restraining order put on him. Jenny had told me to say it, and it worked, he went quiet. I love you, he said, and I shrugged. Don't you love me? he asked and I shrugged again. Is this about you and children? he asked, and I nodded, although I knew he didn't understand how it all connected.

On my wrist my watch still glows, the silent gleam of the hands reminding me that dawn is still two hours away. I seem weightless, as if I have slipped free of all that bound me, as if my life has no weight. As if I have become light, and I fall through the water in shafts. This morning, when we made the first dive, I saw the fish dancing, their myriad quick-silvered bodies rising in a spinning cylinder upwards, through a column of light, the sum of their motions like some liquid geometry. Back in the boat between dives I told Peter what I had seen, and he just smiled, told me it was like birds in flocks, that strange unity of movement, the way their motion flickers and changes as if they were one creature in many bodies. I didn't understand, and he said it was all a matter of maths, the fish keeping a certain distance between themselves and any other fish, so that when one moves they all move, but in unison. Nothing is truly random, he said, It's all a matter of discerning deeper patterns, and I said What? like God? and as soon as it was said I regretted the sharpness of my tone, but Peter only smiled and shook his head. I don't believe in God, he said, but I do believe the world has shape and meaning if you only know where to look.

And then he told me about flowers which have sums in the structure of their petals and patterns in smoke and the way the spots of a leopard can be drawn by a computer, and while he was talking I thought I understood what he was saying, although afterwards, when I tried to explain it to Jenny, all I could remember were the sums in the petals and the flocking birds. It seemed strange to hear a mathematician talk this way, but somehow, when I listened to him, and when I thought of those fish, I felt less alone, less adrift.

We were diving here so we could see the turtles' graveyard. A hole in the coral ten metres deep, five metres round, the sand at the bottom gleaming white. Swimming downwards the water grew colder, darker, until scattered across its bottom like some primeval ossuary we saw them; the bones of the turtles. Their great bony heads and jaws half swallowed by the sand, surrounded by the protruding serrations of their ribs and shells, the folded knuckles of their fins, all picked clean and white by the darting coral fish, the tiny, chomping plankton.

Gerhard told us that no one knows what draws the turtles to these holes, what invisible lines of force guide them onwards, but somehow they feel it when their time arrives, an impulse in their blood that pulls them here, and so they swim, sometimes thousands of kilometres, steady, determined, unwavering, their heavy bodies graceful against the shifting light of the surface, like great birds across a sapphire sky. Maybe that is where my bones will settle, deep amongst theirs, my flesh devoured by the fish and crabs. Will I know that then, will I remember me? As my body passes outwards, through the teeth and bellies of the fish, will I be like the schooling mackerel, one mind in many bodies? My matter part of some greater fertility, some greater whole.

On the horizon I think I see a light, the fading dark before the dawn. Maybe a boat will come, maybe not, but either way it will be too late. Am I sky? Or am I water? I no longer know. Maybe this is how the turtles feel it, the coming of their time. Maybe they too feel it like a waking, like breathing.

Like flight.

THE HOTTEST NIGHT
OF THE CENTURY

GLENDA ADAMS

I was born within the sound of the waves, in a house on a sandstone cliff. It was the hottest night of the century.

The night I was born my father went swimming. It was the last time he ever went willingly into the water.

My father put on his bathing trunks and climbed down the cliff path to the rocks below the house and dived into the sea. He was used to swimming in the ocean, and some mornings he even swam around the headland to the next beach.

While he could not clearly remember having decided to make such a swim that night, he assumed when he found himself in the water that he was heading south around the headland. When he had swum for some time and the familiar cliff and rock shelf had not appeared on his right, he stopped swimming and took stock of his surroundings. To his great surprise he found himself far out to sea, heading away from the land towards the horizon. He was even more surprised, when he resumed swimming, that it was not back to land that he directed himself, but along the course he had begun, towards the horizon.

After he had swum for several miles a small fishing boat spotted him and pulled him aboard, against his objections. He told the fishermen that he was not at all tired and intended to continue his swim. When they asked him where he thought he was going, he replied New Zealand, north island, and if possible Chile.

The men brought him back to the bay and handed him over to the police. He was placed under observation at the hospital for one day and then released.

After that, my father would go only to the water's edge. He refused to wear, or even own, a bathing suit, nor would he wear shorts or go without a shirt on hot summer days. Sometimes he took off his shoes and socks and rolled his trousers above his ankles and walked along the beach or around the rocks, letting the sea lap at his feet.

I never saw any part of his body except his head, his hands and his feet.

From three sides of our house we could see the ocean.

By the end of the day the windows were always clouded with salt, in spite of the fact that I took great care to wipe them clean every morning.

The ocean spray also corroded the gutterings and caused the window frames and doors to swell and stick.

The house was old and shabby, but very beautiful.

My father often stood by the window and watched the

sea. Some mornings he went to the phone box at the terminus down at the bay and called his office to say he was sick. Then he would stay by the window all day watching the sea, frowning.

I, too, watched the sea, and I was able to stay very still beside the window for long periods of time.

My father never liked me to come near him, especially when he stood by the window. I had to choose a window in another room for myself. If I refused to leave him alone, he would slam out of the room and often right out of the house, leaving rattling floors and doors behind him.

On occasion, however, he became so consumed with watching that I was able to move quietly into the room and remain near him for hours without his hearing or feeling me.

People often remarked that it was most unusual for a child to be able to stay still and quiet for more than a minute or two. People said I was an unusual child, and they were always very glad to turn to my little brother.

Everyone admired him.

He had good brown skin and very beautiful brown eyes and good, strong white teeth. He laughed often and was good-natured.

My father loved him greatly. He often said that the son would do all the things the father was being prevented from doing.

My skin was pale and the veins showed through. I was obliged to wear a large sunhat and something covering my arms and legs whenever I was on the beach.

I did not care for swimming. I hated the way the waves tossed me about against my will. I preferred to sit at the water's edge, on the sand or on the rocks at the foot of the cliff.

I sat just out of reach of the waves and they had to strain to touch me. They had to keep jumping up and falling back and jumping up again.

Sometimes, on calm days, I lay in a shallow rock pool.

My little brother loved to swim. He loved to dive and splash and laugh in the water all day.

In summer we went down to the beach every day, even during heatwaves. For protection from the white sun I wrapped an old cotton bedspread about my shoulders and legs. My brother played on the sand beside me, his skin and body welcoming the sunrays. Now and then he started up and dashed into the water and splashed about until he was cool.

'How long do you think the longest story is?' I asked him once.

'As long as "The Nose",' he said.

'Not how long a distance, but how long a time?' I said.

'One whole hour,' he said. 'Or perhaps even two.'

'I know a story that lasts until the sun goes down,' I said.

'No you don't,' he said.

I only smiled.

'Do you really?' he said.

I nodded.

'Tell it to me,' he said.

'You could never listen that long,' I said. 'It is only just after breakfast and the sun won't go down for a whole day. You are too young and can't stay still longer than a second.'

'I could so,' he said.

I said nothing. He got up on his knees and pulled at my bedspread.

'Please tell it to me,' he begged.

'It is a most important story,' I said. 'How can I be sure that you will stay still and listen?'

'I promise I'll listen, I promise,' he said.

I said nothing.

'Please,' he said. 'Cross my heart and spit my death.'

I waited for him to do so.

'Since you have sworn,' I said, 'I shall tell you. But I must warn you. If you stop listening, even for a moment, you will suffer untold tortures and great pain, and you may die.'

He lay down on the sand beside me on his stomach. He lay rigid and attentive.

And I closed my eyes and told a story that contained one sentence for every grain of salt in the sea.

I opened my eyes when my father grabbed my shoulders and shook me and slapped me many times over the head.

'You've gone and killed your little brother,' he said. 'Is no one safe with you?'

The shadow of my sunhat stretched out in front of me and was long enough almost to be touched by the water. The sun was on its way behind the houses on the hill behind the beach.

My brother lay on the sand beside me. His body was swollen and had changed from nut brown to deep red. His mouth had fallen open and sand was clinging to his lips and tongue. But he was not dead.

For two weeks my brother lay on his stomach in bed. The doctor came every day to treat him for sunstroke and dress the burns on his back.

When the wounds began to heal, it became clear that the sun had left behind dark brown spots and scars, all over his beautiful back.

I was kept away from his room for the first week. When they allowed me to visit him he turned his face to the wall.

I reminded him of the warning I had given him that day on the beach.

'You must have stopped listening,' I said. 'Otherwise you would not be suffering this great pain.'

'I never stopped listening,' he said.

But when I asked him to prove it by recounting something of what I had told, he could say nothing.

After he recovered he did not care to play with me.

Even when he was much older he refused to go anywhere with me alone and if we happened to walk down to the terminus at the same time, he would make sure there was always six feet at least between us, and he would warn me to keep my distance.

For company my brother talked to his cat.

He kept the cat away from the house as much as possible. In the winter he allowed it into the basement, but during the warmer months the cat roamed all over the headland, coming to the house once every evening to seek him out. After it had eaten, it would sit on my brother's knee to be searched for ticks, of which there were three or four every day buried in its skin.

Once the cat did not appear for four evenings in a row, and we assumed that it had wandered off. The following week, however, as I danced in the remotest corner of our yard, I found the cat lying in the undergrowth, beneath a eucalyptus. It was dead. I knelt beside it and counted seventy-two ticks hanging from its skin.

My brother brought home a new kitten, still very young and stupid. I was dancing among the hydrangea bushes and the nasturtiums when the kitten sprang out in front of my feet, and I kicked it. The kitten went flying across the ground and fell in the long grass. I knelt beside it. A colourless substance ran from its nose and from one ear, and it breathed noisily and with difficulty. I lay in the grass and placed the kitten under my shirt, against my nipple. But it did not revive.

I took it to the edge of the cliff and threw it over.

'You are a murderer,' said my brother, who had watched me throw the kitten away.

And then he suddenly started searching all over the yard, until he found the other cat under the eucalyptus.

'You murderer,' he said.

As soon as he was fifteen my brother left school, against the wishes of my parents, and went off on his own. Now and then he sent a postcard to say he was all right.

My father took me on a ferry ride across the harbour and back.

We stood at the back of the green and yellow ferry. I watched the foam churned up by the propeller. The agitated water was a pale, sickly green beside the dark bottle green of the calm. I had sweets, and I dropped the wrappers into the foam and watched them sucked under.

My father stood back, several paces behind me. When I turned around he was watching the sky rather than the water. His chin was lifted and his gaze passed over my head.

I went and stood beside him and took his hand, startling him. He shook his hand out of my grasp.

'I love ferries,' I told him. 'Just us and the water all around, and everything quiet and smooth.'

He turned and walked inside, jerking his head for me to follow. We leant against the wooden rail in the centre of the ferry and watched the engine.

The pistons, thick with grease, slid up and down, and as I looked down into the dark of the engine, I saw that every surface seemed to be coated with the same thick, dark grease, even the catwalks and ladders that the crew used.

'I hate it in here,' I said, and I screwed up my nose. 'How smelly and noisy and dirty.'

I watched the engineer checking the different parts of the engine and expected him to slip on the grease. The rag that he carried was black with engine dirt, and when he mopped his forehead or wiped his hands with it he merely redistributed the patterns of the oil slicks that coated him.

He was filthy from head to foot. My father talked with him about the engine and work, while I held my nose.

When we got back to the quay it was almost dark. All those on board, having taken their Sunday trip across the harbour, crowded to one side. They pressed forward and waited for the men on the wharf to set the gangplank in place.

The ferry was a small craft, and with everyone standing on one side, the deck inclined towards the wharf.

It was low tide and the deck was two or three feet below the wharf. After the engine was turned off it took a couple of minutes for the ferry to nudge its way into position.

Some of the passengers were impatient to be off, for they had connections to make with the buses or the train. Some men, their coats over their shoulders, jumped on to the wharf before the gangplank had been fixed in place, and then they turned around and leant back towards their girls, with outstretched arms, and called to them to jump.

Then there was a shout. One man had attempted to jump, but he had stubbed his toe on the edge of the wharf as he landed. He lost his balance and fell back into the water.

Someone quickly sat on the edge of the wharf and pushed at the ferry railing with both legs to keep it from bumping against the wharf, while the passengers on board fished the man out of the water.

He stood on the deck, covered with the slime of the tide, laughing.

I could take either a tram or a ferry to school. The tram went across the bridge and stopped almost at the gate of the school. The ferry stopped at the quay beside the docks. From the docks to the school were many stairs leading up the hill to a tunnel under the approach to the bridge.

One morning in the tunnel I met an old man. He had left the fly of his trousers open.

At home I watched for my father to come. I waited for him to put on his slippers and go to his chair by the window. I sat on his knee, quickly, before he could stop me. I put my arms around his neck and told him about the old man in the tunnel.

He pushed me off his knee and jumped up and raced from the house without bothering to change his slippers. When he came back several hours later his slippers and his trouser cuffs were soaking wet and had sand all over them. He would not talk to me or even look at me.

I told my mother about the old man in the tunnel. She sat down and wrote a note to my teacher. The next day the teacher took me aside and told me that it must have been a shock but I should try to forget what I had seen.

The headmaster announced that it was against the rules for any pupil to walk through the tunnel. Although he gave no reason for the new rule, the whole school seemed to know that it was because of what I had seen in the tunnel.

During class I received a note from some of the boys saying they wanted to meet me behind the observatory after school. I said I would meet them.

When school was over I went to the headmaster's office

and showed him the note. He and another teacher went to the observatory and rounded up the eight boys who were waiting for me.

The boys were caned and the headmaster sent notes to their parents warning them that their sons were a danger.

My father said I should go away to the mountains for a month for a change. I begged not to be sent away. But both my parents and the doctor said it would do me good after my experience.

I stayed at a holiday home for children. Since it was winter there were only two of us at the home, a very fat girl and myself.

The woman who cared for us made the fat girl and myself take a bath together every day. She stood over us to make sure we washed ourselves thoroughly. Then she supervised our drying, saying that she didn't want us breaking out in rashes and sores through leaving any part wet while we were under her care. She also said she would allow us to get into bed with her, since it was so cold at night.

I wrote and asked to be brought home. My father wrote back and said that I had to stay the full month. Nevertheless, the following Saturday he came in the train and brought me home, against his better judgment, he said.

The building inspector paid us a visit and condemned our house. He told us that the water falling from the leaks in the gutterings had split the foundations, and since the house was so old it might well collapse.

My father decided we should move to a new house, inland. He found a little house in a flat street that always smelled dusty, even in winter and when it rained. My mother liked the house. She said it could never deteriorate since it was made of cement blocks.

It was an ugly, horrible house. Its windows were large. But there was nothing to watch through them but the flat backyard and the tall, grey paling fence.

The sea was twenty miles away.

Every second Saturday I rode my bicycle to the sea, and often I did not get back home until nearly midnight.

I made a point of checking my father's shoes and trouser cuffs every night, without his noticing, but only rarely did I find traces of sand or the smell of the sea.

I met a boy with a car, and I was easily able to prevail upon him to drive me to the sea every Saturday.

Once, I stayed by the sea a particularly long time, and I did not arrive home until well after midnight. I knew that my father was not asleep.

Very early the next morning – I had only been asleep for an hour or two – my father came into my room.

'What do you think you're doing,' he screamed, 'staying out till all hours?'

I said nothing.

'You should be thinking of your studies and your exams,' he said, 'not boys.'

I smiled at him.

He strode over to my bed and shook me.

I only smiled.

He kept on holding my shoulders.

'You're enough to drive a man out of his mind,' he said.

He moved his hands to my neck. He touched my ears and my head. Then he put his hands over his face.

'I don't know why I try to keep on living,' he cried.

'So why do you?' I asked.

He drowned three weeks later.

COME WALK WITH ME,
MY LOVELY

MATTHEW CONDON

I'd always wanted to say one thing to a woman. Come walk with me, my lovely. I don't know why. It was pretty corny when you thought about it. Then again, I had a pretty good franchise on corny. Maybe I was just old-fashioned. Maybe I'd read too many romance novels. But it was more than that. Let me lay it on the line. Despite everything, I did believe in love.

'You're a dip,' Wilson often told me.

'A dip?'

'You know, dippy.'

'Ah,' I said.

'A dinosaur. A dumb dip of a dinosaur.'

'Okay . . .'

'A big, dumb, naive dip of a dinosaur.'

'I get your point.'

I hated it when Wilson decided to spread it on thickly.

Once he started he couldn't stop. Fuelled by his whisky sours, by the wave of alcohol, lifted by the wave, clinging to the thin raft of his exaggerations, he always rode it out to the shore.

'A big, dumb . . .'

'Will you shut up with that already?'

The good thing about Wilson was that he had the grace to know when I was unhappy with him. He clammed up then, sulked a little, ripped the edges off his coaster until he had peeled it away to nothing. It usually didn't last that long.

'What about Jenny?' I always turned the situation back to him during this sulky period. It brought him out of his pretend hurt. 'What did you say to her, you know, the first time, when you met.'

'Hi.'

'That's it?'

'Hi.'

I still hadn't brought him out far enough.

'Seriously,' I said. 'What was it about Jenny . . . what . . . how can I say this . . . did you know?'

'Know what?' he said.

'You know. Did you know that she was, you know, the one?'

'I can't remember.'

'You have to remember that, Wilson. Come on. You have to.'

'I'm telling you,' Wilson said. 'I don't know. What do you want me to say? Was there lightning? Sparks? Angels? Jesus, Ick. You really make me wonder sometimes, you know that?'

'I'm serious,' I said. 'They say that you just know, bang, straight off.'

'Horseshit.'

'I read it somewhere . . .'

'You read it somewhere. You read it somewhere. That's your problem. You got your head up there in the clouds, always reading something somewhere. That's your problem. You read all this stuff up there in the clouds and you wonder why you can't find it back on the ground floor. You wonder why your life's so cocked up.'

He was back. On another wave. Who knows how many others were lined up behind the latest one.

'You think so? You think my life's cocked up?'

He took his hands from the glass and opened his palms to me. 'Whadda you got?' he said. 'Tell me. What is it you got?' I didn't answer. 'Nothing. You got nothing as far as I can see.'

'Maybe we should leave.'

He shook his head. 'You had Jordan, now you haven't got her. Right? You had Melanie before that. Gone. Rachel. Gone. All of them gone.'

'There were reasons . . .'

'Julia. Gone. Becky. Gone . . .'

Here was the other wave. I let it pass over me, hunched on the bar stool, thinking of how to escape.

After a while I sat up straight. 'And you're so happy, right?'

It was a feeble defence, but I had to do something. We didn't say anything for a long while. More drinks arrived.

Wilson stopped tearing the coasters. He lost that coldness in his eyes. The waves had passed.

'Really,' he said, 'I worry about you. Jenny worries. We want to see you happy.'

'I am happy.'

'There's happy and there's happy.'

'That's a whole lot of happy,' I said.

He punched me in the arm. It hurt.

'Don't look for it,' he said.

'Okay.'

He was like a brother to me, my Wilson.

'And don't read so much.'

'Sure.'

'Something will happen. Something always happens.'

He was right, of course. I just didn't think it would happen so soon. Seven hours later, in fact.

I have tried many cures for hangovers. Dozens, both recommended to me and of my own invention. The best, I found, was an early morning swim in the surf, no matter what the weather or conditions. I got home that night at about one o'clock. By 7.30 a.m. I was down on the beach in front of the Parthenon.

It was the tail end of winter. The stalwarts were already there – an entire community of dawn walkers, joggers, swimmers, yoga practitioners, metal-detector sweepers, bums and dogs. They all seemed to know each other. It was like some weird club. It was, I realised later, the world as it used to be, right there on the sand, at the birth of each day. People talked to people. They left their wallets on their towels with no fear of theft. They let their children play alone in the sand. They bobbed in the swell of the ocean, watching the horizon light up. They laughed and joked. By the time the rest of the world had woken they were gone.

I was a bit of a stranger to them. They only ever saw me when I had a hangover. That made me a sort of honorary rather than a fully-fledged member. Nevertheless, what mattered was that I was there. At an ungodly hour. In whatever weather. Prepared to greet the day in the most natural manner.

I felt comfortable amongst them. I always thought – I must do this every day. Look at this. This is a whole new world. A beautiful world. See what I'm missing out on. I said that every time I carried my hangover down to the great Pacific Ocean. Not that I stuck to my philosophy.

But on this morning after the night before with Wilson, I was prepared to say it again. I did. To myself. I had to refrain from extending my arms above my head with the joy of it, despite my throbbing lobes.

I ran into the surf like a kid from the country. I dived straight in, straight under. I jumped up with a shriek from the cold of it and wiped the water from my eyes. It was this, always this, that gave me away as an honorary member. But I didn't care. On this morning my whole body tingled with delight. My hangover was already far away, receding, dissolving in the sea. I paddled out to the old boys and girls beyond the sandbank and the first line of breakers. I saw plastic frangipani flowers and daisies on the women's bathing caps rising up the front of waves.

I saw the deeply tanned and spotted bald heads of men submerge and rise. I said top of the morning to everyone bobbing around me. They all nodded. I was there, in the secret chamber of the club, loving life.

It was so beautiful, the water so glassy, I stayed too long. As the others drifted in like logs to shore, I continued to frolic. Maybe I had overdone it and embarrassed them with my somersaults and wild whoops from the crests of waves. Maybe the flicking of my hair put them off, considering I was one of the few male club members *with* hair. Before I knew it I was the only one out there, alone, my feet and hands wrinkled, with a decent deposit of sand in the crotch of my swimming trunks.

I didn't care. My headache was gone. I felt refreshed and all was good. I chuckled to myself thinking how Wilson must have felt by now. Like death, I hoped, out in his house in the Hinterland, dreaming bad dreams all foggy and dark, his mouth dry, his tongue furry, his stomach gurgling. So I read too much. Dreamt too much. How do you like that then, Mister Reality? Ha ha ha. I waited for a wave to take me in. I didn't wait long. The third was perfect, smooth and powerful and clean. I put my hands by my side and rocketed to shore, skimming, fairly flying, until the wave petered out a few metres from the beach.

Most of the club members had gone and the beach was in that strange transition period before the arrival of the sunbakers, the troubled hearts, the silly poets. Before the body builders and the triathletes and the nightclub barmen emerged to perform for each other. It was like a change of shifts.

I went to my towel, shook it out, wrapped it around my waist and started walking up the beach and back to the Parthenon. And that's when I saw her for the first time.

I'd hate to say now that Wilson was right. He wasn't. But he wasn't entirely wrong either. When I first laid eyes on Lauren, sitting back from the flags, at the foot of the dunes covered in whistling spinifex, there weren't sparks as such. No forks of lightning. No distant drum roll. I like to think it was better than that. She did, literally, stop me in my tracks. I was just passing the metal rubbish bin that swivelled on its flaked and weathered posts, a gang of gulls flapping and fighting for the overnight contents, when I saw her sitting on a giant red beach towel. I don't know how long she had been there. She may have been settled when I made my embarrassing spectacle out in the water. She may have arrived as I bodysurfed in to shore, my eyes half-blinded by the carnival of spray and foam and the surge of the water. I don't know. But when I saw her, when I saw her hair pulled back in a ponytail, her face open to the pale sun, her hands by her side, propping herself up, her eyes closed, her toes wriggling, I felt – what? – first a warmth. Maybe it was the after-effect of the swim, I thought, putting myself in Wilson's cynical frame of mind. It often happened after a dip in brisk water. Your body seemed to glow with heat afterwards. It was more than that, though. A warm sort of flurry of nerves perhaps. In the belly. Straight from the eyes to the brain to the belly in record time. It was this that made me stop, as if my legs had a disconnected wire, as if the circuit had broken. From a distance of about ten metres, too, I felt something about her. I could sense her honesty, her openness, her heart even (though I can hear Wilson chortling). But it was true. I knew, somehow, she was kind.

I don't know how long I stood there. Fortunately she had her eyes closed. Eventually, though, I moved off, the legs creaking into motion, and I didn't take my eyes off her all the way up to the wood-planked boulevard, until I could just see her, beyond the line of breadfruit trees and the gnarly spinifex.

And that's where I sat, oblivious to the time, to my job, to the position of the sun, and watched her. She had two quick dips during my observation, returning to the red towel and tipping her head to the same side each time, wringing out her ponytail. She straightened the towel. She sat down and leant back on those arms. After an hour, I think it was an hour, a child approached her. I had not noticed the child before. She was small, maybe four or five. She wore a little cane hat. She dropped on the towel beside the woman, who kissed her, rubbed oil into her tiny arms, produced a drink from a beach bag. The child came and went from the red towel to her sandcastle down by the water's edge. My rear was getting sore sitting on the picnic bench up amongst the breadfruit trees. I shifted from one cheek to the other. Held my hands in front of me. The salt had dried on my skin. My towel was almost totally dry. Finally she gathered up her things, took the child by the hand, and walked down towards Main Beach. I watched them. I watched them until they were little specks. They kept walking. For The Spit.

And that was it. She had already changed my life. The last faint traces of Jordan vanished from my mind. I tried to conjure Jordan's face but I couldn't. I can't say I was displeased. Every morning, from that morning on, I became a regular member of the early bird beach club.

She vanished. I went to the beach for a week straight. I had bags under my eyes. I had chafed inner thighs from all the sand in my swimming trunks. I was forced to wash my hair every day and it took on, just as it had in my youth, before the advent of gels, of wax, of sprays, a boofy appearance. In the office they called me sheephead. The gel, because of the constant washing, just wouldn't hold it. I was regressing into my adolescence.

That wasn't all. The more I thought of her the less I could see her. Her features faded from my mind. I tried and tried. I gave myself headaches with the effort, but I couldn't conjure her face. All I was left with after a week was a child's hat, the ruins of a sandcastle, and a red towel. Gradually everything evaporated except the towel. It was driving me dippy, as Wilson would have said, if I'd told him.

'Where you been?' he asked one day on the phone.

'Around.'

'Around? What's around? Come on.'

'Here and there.'

'Get outta here. Don't give me here and there. You're up to something. What is it?'

'Nothing.'

'You can tell Uncle Wilson.'

'Nothing to tell.'

'How about a drink tonight?' he asked.

'No thanks.'

'There's definitely something going on. What's her name.'

'I don't know what you're talking about.' At least I didn't lie. I didn't know her name then.

'You can't keep a secret from me you know. You know that don't you?'

I didn't answer.

'I'll be back,' he said in his silly chilling movie monster voice, and hung up.

I was getting fed up with Wilson. Not only had I lost the woman who, potentially, was the woman of my life, but I had to keep an eye over my shoulder for him. I should have told him to get a life of his own, or something, but I was too depressed about the mysterious woman. A red square of terry towelling. That was all I was left with.

I sat around in my spare time thinking of her. Working out what I would do when, or if, I saw her again. I didn't even know if she was single. There was the child. Perhaps she was a nanny, or something. Maybe it was her baby sister. But what if it was her own child? There would have to be a husband. A father. Then again, maybe not. What if it was her child, and they were alone? I had not fully considered this. If we got together, would that make me a father? An instant father? I was just a kid. I was thirty going on twelve. I didn't know how to do tax returns. I couldn't pay bills on time. I had only had a cheque book in the last year, and still I regularly sent them off without signing them. How could a man who couldn't sign a cheque become a father?

I went out to the Jersey and had a discussion with my mother while Roy was playing pool with his old buddies in the community hall. For the first time I told her everything about Jordan. Once I started I couldn't stop. I even described the matchbooks, flicking my Bic lighter as I spoke. She took it from me, and slipped it into her apron pocket. Then I told her about the woman.

'You've only seen her once?' she asked, preparing tea. We always had tea during a crisis. We always had tea anyway.

'That's right.'

'And you can't tell me what she looks like?'

'Correct.'

Hilda took her seat and swivelled the pot, as she always did, to hurry the tea leaves.

'Well,' she said, pouring. I took my cup and held it in both hands. 'She has a kiddy, you say?'

'I think, Ma. I think. Can't be sure on that.'

She sat back and looked to the ceiling, thinking, working out the peculiar puzzle I had presented her with.

'So tell me how she struck you? What was your first impression?'

I laboured over my answer. I looked into the cup. I avoided her gaze at all cost. We had never been great at these sorts of discussions.

'I felt ...' I began looking to the ceiling then. 'I felt ... comfortable.'

'Comfortable.'

'I felt ... at home.'

She smiled. I was embarrassed. I needed her help but I didn't want to be here. It was the same as it had always been throughout my life. I needed someone to tell me what to do. I couldn't make decisions on my own. Life was too big and complicated for a thirty-year-old going on twelve. I could never put my foot down. I could never take action and suffer the consequences.

'That's nice,' was all she said.

Nice? Nice? I looked at her now over the top of the cup. She started rocking a little in the chair.

'What do you mean?' I said. I put the cup down. I wanted her to give me instructions. To sort it out for me. To clear a path to logic and decision.

'Nice,' she said again, quietly now, rocking a little more vigorously.

'I don't ... what do you ... wha ... ?'

Tell me if I could become a father. Come on, Ma. Say it. Say Ick, you'd be a wonderful father. Or Ick, it's too much trouble, what with the world the way it is today, and you don't know why the husband might have left her, it might not have been him, though it was probably most likely him, gambling, you know, philandering, all that stuff that goes on today, and he would be part of your life, you know, with the child and all, the child would link him to you for the rest of your days together, you understand that don't you ... but she just rocked, quietly, rhythmically, and sipped her tea.

'Ma,' I said, 'what do you think?'

'You mean what should you do?' I hated it when she

did that, when she saw straight through me.

'No, no, that's not what I meant, no . . .' But it was.

She refilled our cups and started rocking again.

'You'll know,' she said.

'I'll know? I'll know? What will I know, Ma . . . ?'

'I think you already know.'

'Know? Know what?'

'You wouldn't come all the way out here if you didn't.'

'Sure I would.'

'It's Thursday,' she said.

'So? So it's Thursday.'

'You only ever come on Sunday.'

'Thursday, Sunday, Sunday, Thursday . . .'

'Best find her,' she said. 'Then you'll know for sure.'

She had that grin on again. She was rocking. I looked at her sweet face, all powdery and wrinkled, and thought back to when I was five, four. I could see her then, a young woman, younger than I was now, much younger. So what happened? How did it happen so fast?

She was right. I had to find the woman on the red towel.

'Hey, Ick, how you doing on this beautiful morning?'

'Fine Frank,' I said, waving.

They all knew me now. I had become a bona fide part of their ranks. They shared with me tales of their sun spots, golf games, financial deals, cooking tips and gardening methods. I was one of them.

A month had gone by and still I hadn't seen her. I sat in her spot, where she had draped the red towel, as a final resort. I would will her to return. That was it. With the force of my mind. I had started out on the picnic bench behind the breadfruit trees, then worked my way down the dunes, positioning my own towel, until I couldn't handle it any longer. I spread it out right there, on her spot. I saw what she had seen on that day. I saw Bob and Harold and Alan coming out of the surf, all wrinkled and dripping. I saw Mabel and Grace take off their floral bathing caps and fluff their hair. I saw joggers cruise by. But I didn't see her.

Bob, an old lifesaver who still wore those skimpy swimmers and didn't carry them off too badly for an eighty-year-old, came up to me one day and pushed the few remaining strands of his hair off his forehead.

'Care for a bite?' he said, and he started walking away. I said nothing. I just followed. Bob was like that. A strong man. With a deep voice. He was the sort who could fix engines, extract water from the roots of desert plants, build a house with a hammer and a bag of nails. He didn't say much on the way to the café in Tedder Avenue, just dried himself, slipped on a shirt, combed his strands, put on his loafers, flicked the sand off his towel and tucked it under his arm without stopping. Competent, I thought. That was Bob.

We took a seat outside under the poinciana tree. It was a pretty trendy sort of café. I usually went with friends to the one up the road, fifty yards away. This one, I thought, was for the mobile phone set. For the café crowd, the novelists scribbling in their pads, the letter writers, the experts on film noir. Bob didn't look a bit out of place. He didn't even look at the menu. He knew what he wanted. That was the thing about old people like Bob. They were beyond fashion, beyond embarrassment, beyond the strictures of the modern world. Old Bob was as timeless as leather, as oak.

'Bacon,' he said to the waiter. 'Two eggs over easy. Toast and black coffee.'

'And you, sir?'

'I'll have, let's see, a ham and cheese croissant ... no, sorry, some raisin toast, yeah, some raisin toast, and tea please.'

Bob just looked at me with those wise, all-seeing green eyes of his.

'What sort?' the waiter asked.

'Pardon?'

'What sort of tea would you like?'

'Oh,' I said, taking up the menu again. 'Umm, Prince of Wales, no, sorry, Russian Caravan ...'

He scribbled it down in his notepad and left.

'You eat like a bird, son,' Bob said.

'I'm not that hungry.'

'You got to eat good at the start of the day.' He slapped his hand down on the table and frightened the sparrows from the poinciana.

It was a nice breakfast, even though we didn't say much. You felt safe around old Bob with his big knuckles and bushy eyebrows. I fidgeted with my napkin.

'Something troubling you, kid?' he asked.

I could feel him staring at me.

'No, Bob. I'm fine, thank you. Fine. I'll get the bill.'

'Good-o,' he said, and I went inside.

Everything wasn't all right, though. Nothing was all right. Here was Bob, eighty, tanned and clear-minded, his life pared down to a beautiful simplicity, and me a jittery, complicated mess of a man, unable to concentrate at work, suffering broken sleep, buying red towel after red towel just so I could hold the only memory I had of her. I fidgeted in my velcro wallet. I dropped a few coins out of it. I bent down and retrieved them. I dropped my keys in doing so. Then my towel fell over my head. It was another one of those days, I said to myself. Yet another one.

I stood up, finally. I could feel that my face was red, full of blood, beaming, glowing. I was going to have a heart attack, at thirty. Bob was going to have to save me, pump my chest, bring me back.

Then I looked up, and there she was.

'Which table were you on?'

I dropped my wallet again. I felt the blood draining from my face. My mouth was open. I could feel my teeth drying.

She smiled. 'Which table were you on, sir?'

I pointed to Bob through the front window.

'Right,' she said. 'Number three.'

She took the bill down from the pinboard and added up the figures on the cash register.

'That's eighteen-ninety,' she said as the drawer of the register popped out with a ring.

I searched for my wallet. I couldn't find it.

'I think . . .' she leant over a little towards me and pointed down at my feet, '. . . you'll find it there.'

I snatched it up, took out a twenty, tossed it on the counter and bolted. I went straight out that door, under the arms of the poinciana and headed across the road. I could hear Bob yelling after me.

'Hey kid,' he said. 'Kid. Your pants on fire or something?'

I didn't stop until I got to the Parthenon. I had lost my towel on the way. I stubbed my toe on a gutter. I pressed the wrong floor button in the lift. I couldn't get the right keys in the door. I went into the bathroom, turned on the shower, stripped off, and sat there, my head on my arms, under the strong jets of water.

By the day I planned to make my move I knew a lot more about her through my contacts in the real estate office across from the café. Her name was Lauren. Her beautiful daughter's name was Phoebe. Phoebe was three. They had only been on the coast for three months. Daddy had not come with them. They rented at Main Beach. I could see the roof of their place from my balcony in the Parthenon. The reason she never returned to the beach outside Parthenon Place where I first saw her was because she and Phoebe were really regulars at Main Beach, a few hundred metres north, and had just happened to be there after a walk to Surfers. All the time I was sitting there waiting for her, she was up near the little yellow and blue lifesaver's tower towards The Spit.

I never went back to the café. I didn't want to talk to her for the first time there, in the café. She would have got that all the time, I guessed, geeks chatting her up, laying their lines, spinning their tales. No, it would be the beach.

On that morning I got up early, showered, shaved, splashed on a bit of aftershave and put on my best board-shorts. I polished the leather straps on my slip-on sandals. I took the biggest red towel I had and slung it over my shoulder.

But the closer and closer I got to Main Beach, the more afraid I became. I tried to pretend I was Bob. You have no choice, I told myself. You must go through with it. You must take the chance. You can only be embarrassed, and a little embarrassment never killed nobody. Sure, Bob. I felt a trickle of sweat move its way down the crease of my buttocks.

This is ridiculous. I didn't even know her. At this time in her life she might have wanted to have nothing to do with men, especially a stranger who strolled up to her on the beach, out of nowhere, cocky as all hell. I kept walking, though. I could hear Bob. Good on you, kid. Few more steps. That's the way.

I was close now and I could see Phoebe playing in the sand. She was right on the water's edge, and squealed every time the surf hissed up and over her tiny feet. I smiled then. At her innocence, her running around in circles, daring the water to catch her. I was fifty metres away, forty, thirty.

Then Lauren stood and came walking towards her daughter. I hesitated a little, slowed a fraction. What now? Bob? Ma? What now? Lauren launched into a light jog and surprised Phoebe from behind. The girl screamed with delight. She knelt down and hugged Phoebe and kissed her and held her tight, their reflection, both of theirs, wobbly and bright in the water that sucked back across the sand.

And that was it. That's what decided it for me. That image of them, together, mother and daughter, simple, natural, perfect.

As I got closer, twenty metres, nineteen, eighteen, seventeen, Lauren stood and faced me. She had her hands on Phoebe's mop of curls. The girl looked at me too, at the man with the bright red towel. Then Lauren smiled. She smiled at me. Lauren smiled at Icarus.

I repeated it under my breath, over and over, as I kept walking. Come walk with me, my lovely. Come walk with me, my lovely. Come walk with me, my lovely.

THE FERRY TO MANLY

AMANDA LOHREY

One day, out of the blue, Marita says that she would like
to meet Gareth. 'Invite him to dinner,' she says, but when
he suggests this to Gareth his friend is reluctant. Over the
past few months he seems to have given up going out at
night, perhaps because he is more and more fatigued and
is having to call on whatever reserves of strength he has
just to get to work. Instead he suggests that they come
over to see him at Manly on the Sunday. Marita agrees.
'It's a long time since Camille has been on a ferry,' she
says. 'The sea air will be good for her.'

The journey out of Leichhardt and across the harbour is
a trip to another country. It's humid and stifling along
Parramatta Road; exhaust fumes and flashy billboards and
a fretwork of black overhead power lines. But down at the
quay it's clean and clear with a light breeze coming off the

water. Camille skips along the walkway, making little forays ahead to the buskers and returning to pester her mother for change. She stops in front of a slim, dishevelled Koori playing a huge didgeridoo and selling dusty, unmarked tapes of his own artistry. She stares at him, then drops a dull gold dollar coin into his hat. *Pock*. Wherever she wants to stop, they wait, smiling, humouring her: it's her first trip on the Manly ferry, a special ritual not to be rushed. When, finally, they arrive at Pier 3 they are relieved to step into the shade of the iron roof. Camille wants to work the new electronic ticket machines, to fathom it out herself, which takes ages. Or seems to. Stephen is beginning to get impatient when at last the *Narrabeen* chugs into the pier and the incoming crowd filters across the ramp and on to the quay.

Camille wafts on to the ferry, ahead of them, and makes purposefully for the front. She wants to sit outside on the white plastic seats in the cool wind. No way, says Marita, not with your chest, and points to a seat inside. Camille sits up front, alone, the window open, her hair blowing blindly across her face. Every now and then she looks back and smiles at them unselfconsciously. After a while she stops this and stares ahead in a seeming trance. They know she is lost in the child's fantasy of travelling alone.

Stephen begins to think about lunch. He hasn't brought any food with him and he doesn't know why. He could have packed a nourishing picnic lunch; some brown rice salad, rice crackers with tahini, fruit, masubi, a thermos of mu tea and some ginger cookies with rice malt. He didn't.

Every now and then he has lapses of, for want of a better word, *address*. He finds himself just wanting to walk out of the house on impulse, without the lengthy premeditation that eating cleanly in a barbaric world calls for. He knows there will be nothing in Manly worth eating, that to put Gareth at ease he'll drink a cold beer on an empty stomach and feel querulous for the rest of the afternoon. No, he can do better than that: he can always buy some rice and stirfry vegetables from the Thai restaurant by the dock and fruit salad from the little canvas booth with the festive red and white striped awning.

At Manly Pier, it's lunchtime and the mall is congested with shoppers who mill around a jazz band that plays with a lazy even tempo. He hates jazz. They enter the cool dark lounge of the Blue Stag and look around for Gareth who, he knows, will have got there long before them and had two or three schooners to ease his shyness.

He spots him at a table near the far door, waves, ushers Marita and Camille over, makes quick introductions and leaves to order drinks at the bar, hoping that Marita will make an effort with Gareth. Sometimes she can be withdrawn, like him.

'Yeah?'

The barman is all of twenty, a bleach-blond surfer in a fluorescent pink and yellow singlet. The sort of person you never see in Leichhardt. Looking at the electric display of his Mambo shorts, Stephen feels a distinct presence: the Pacific Ocean. Outside, out there in that bright sunlight there are palm trees and the Corso and cake shops with sticky sugar bombs of pink icing and mock cream and matrons in bright pastels and young girls in tan moccasins, white socks and pale denim shorts and brown legs. And Marita and he look like a pair of pale, inner-city black-birds.

Back at the table it's clear that Marita is in a cool mode, but friendly. She doesn't say much but she gives Gareth her attention. He hopes that she will respond to Gareth's shy irony but just now Gareth is inhibited by her presence and doesn't offer any remark that's dry or witty.

Camille sips on her lemonade quietly, but is restless. 'Can we go to the beach soon?' she whispers to her mother, swinging her legs, knocking her heels insistently against the chrome in a monotonous clatter. He's beginning to learn that even when children are quiet they have a way of being interventionist.

But for the moment he's glad to be in the bar where he can adjust to the shock of seeing Gareth out of the office, and what seems to be a sudden deterioration in his body. Today he looks even thinner and more sallow. His skin is papery and dry; his fine hair even wispier.

'I'm *hungry*,' says Camille.

'We'll have to eat soon, Stephen,' says Marita. And they agree to buy some chips and eat them on the Corso.

Fifty minutes later they are sitting on the beach, staring at the water. Pacific blue. Gareth is lying prone on the sand. He had agreed, in the office, to let Stephen give him a Shiatsu treatment and when reminded of this just minutes ago he had simply smiled, shrugged and lay back on to the sand with his head resting on his hands and his eyes shut against the glare.

Stephen kneels beside him. The hot sun makes his head feel expansive, infused with the power of white light and blue water. Marita has taken off her shirt and sits in her bikini top. She lifts her pale face and neck to the sun, eyes closed. Camille paddles at the water's edge, entranced by the big surging dumpers that roar in and dissolve into frantic white foam at her feet. Stephen is aware of the woman near them who lounges in a white bikini. She has a low forehead, bleached hair, an unusually prominent mons and *that look*; brazen, receptive. They're different on this side of the harbour; they have an *expectation* of the sun. For a moment he wonders what it would be like to make love to such a woman, to enter into a kind of delirium of vacancy where there is only the body and yet the space of this body is somehow empty. Isn't that what he wants? Only the body? And yet, in the dazzling whiteness of her bikini he has an intimation of absence, of slipping into some kind of vacant space, which is not what he wants at all. Shaking his head to clear it, he leans back on his heels, closes his eyes and begins to focus on Gareth. Resting the flat of his hand on Gareth's midriff he presses firmly into the *hara*. Ah, yes, he might have guessed: heart deficient; a sadness, the heart swamped in damp: moisture, un-shed tears. Heart-deficient people are cut off from their connexion to the world. But they have to find it for themselves, you can't do it for them; all you can do is open them up to change, to possibility. He works on, tracing the meridians with care. Gareth appears to be half-asleep. Soon even the roar of the surf begins to recede in his head until the line of Norfolk pines along the Corso throws lengthening shadows across the sand. Marita shivers. The blue of the Pacific no longer shimmers; is a dull, late afternoon glint of grey–green. He feels Gareth's *hara* and there has been some change, a little. Perhaps this is what is reflected in his droll abstracted gaze as he stands now and brushes the sand from his clothes.

'How was that?' asks Marita.

'Good,' he says. And gives a little laugh. 'Yes, quite good.'

'Gareth,' she begins, 'I was wondering if you'd mind if I talked to you for a little bit on tape?'

He looks puzzled, taken aback. 'Why? What about?'

'Just a general chat. I'm making a collection of tapes, of voices.'

He hesitates for a moment. 'Okay. Where?'

'We could do it just here, on the beach. Wouldn't take long.'

He looks slowly around. 'The wind's coming up a bit. What about over there?' He nods in the direction of the Blue Stag.

Stephen frowns at them both. 'Not the pub,' he says. Another drink, or several, and all his work on the body undone by words, by Marita and her selfish, pointless obsession. 'Why don't we do this another day?'

'No, let's get it over with now,' says Gareth, in his slow drawl, smiling, colluding with her against his own body. Compliant.

'I'll take Camille for a walk. C'mon, mate.' He takes her by the hand and turns coldly away from the other two.

Forty minutes later he stands at the door of the pub.

Gareth and Marita are intent in conversation, as if they could talk only in his absence. Watching them he feels a tight knot of anger rising in his chest. Talk, talk, talk. From the doorway he lets out a low street whistle and when Marita looks up he beckons her over in a peremptory gesture, pointing at his watch. She frowns at him: how dare he summon her like this? Beside him, Camille shivers. 'I'm cold,' she says. 'Let's go home.'

On the ferry home they say little to one another and stare out the window. Behind them Manly recedes like a picture postcard slowly bobbing out of focus. Ahead, black clouds loom over the water. Marita frowns up at the sky. 'It's going to rain,' she says.

THE BOOSTER SHOT

PETER GOLDSWORTHY

1

Years had passed – more years than Alison cared to count – but she recognised him immediately.

Her thoughts were elsewhere, he was the last thing on her mind, but the red flame of his hair singled him out across the crowded airport lobby, raised his face as if in haute-relief from a background frieze of faces.

He hadn't spotted *her*. He was pushing through the crowd, approximately in her direction, glancing back across his shoulder. A woman she had never seen before was at his side.

'Blue!' Alison called across the lobby.'Blue! Is that you?'

The man turned as she approached, and smiled, and opened his mouth to speak – but the woman at his side spoke first.

'You obviously haven't seen Philip for some years,' she said.

'I'm sorry?' Alison stopped in her tracks.

'No one calls him Blue any more.'

'I don't think you've met my wife,' Blue intervened. 'Suzi – Alison Tully. You must have heard me talk of Alison?'

The wife offered her hand, limply. It was thin: a smooth, fashionable claw, encrusted with various configurations of cold metal and precious stone.

'I don't think so,' she murmured, and smiled, although the smile was also something of a murmur.

Blue was not quite so thin: still red-haired – source of the nickname that had fallen out of favour – and pale-skinned, and with those clear, childlike eyes. But there was a new puffiness to his face and cheeks. Alison recalled a boyish tennis-player, a Finn or a Swede, pale and puffy-faced, she had watched recently on television who, at the time, had reminded her of Blue.

'And this,' Blue turned, 'is little Sebastian.'

For the first time Alison noticed the small child tacking a loaded luggage trolley awkwardly back and forth across the lobby behind his parents. Of course Blue would have children by now, but she was still shocked; and to some extent shocked that she was shocked. Part of her was obviously not yet ready to grant him permission to father children with anyone else.

Even after all these years.

She bent and examined the child: 'And how old are *you*, Sebastian?'

The child's lips remained pressed together, a tight purse.

'Sebastian is five,' Blue answered for him. 'Aren't you, Sebastian?'

Alison forced a smile. She wasn't comfortable with children; she found the conversations that took place in these circumstances inane. She tried to summon back some other noise from the standard adult-to-child repertoire.

'Have you come to Adelaide to visit your grandma?' she came out with.

'We've come to see both our grandmothers, haven't we?' Suzi informed her.

Alison felt her hackles rise, slightly. She suddenly remembered another Suzi she had known, years before: a school enemy who when she signed her name had always dotted her i's with a cute little circle. It was unfair, of course, but already she had lumped the two Suzis together.

'What are you doing here?' Blue asked.

'Seeing Brian off. To Sydney for a conference.'

'Brian?'

She paused, sensing that he too was a little shocked by the dislocation of an ancient world picture. He also remembered her as he had last seen her: frozen in that time, that place. There were still things in the air between them, she realised; a faint perfume of accusation, and guilt. There had been no clean break, after all; more a slow rending, a long, jagged tear.

'Brian is my hubby,' she said, using the ridiculous word for some reason she couldn't identify.

Blue smiled: 'Of course.'

'How long are you here for?' she asked. 'You must have a meal with us. Brian would love to meet you.'

Aware that she was addressing only Blue, she half turned to include his wife: 'Both of you.'

The woman spoke again: 'We're only staying the long weekend.'

'Then you'll miss Brian,' Alison said. 'But come anyway. You must come. Tomorrow night. Or the next, whichever suits.'

'Give us a call,' Blue said. 'We'd love to come. Wouldn't we Suzi?'

Suzi was preoccupied with removing the luggage trolley from the tight grasp of little Sebastian.

'Where are you staying?' Alison remembered to ask as they moved away from her into the crowd.

Blue turned: 'At Mum's. Still remember the number?'

If she did, she wasn't prepared to admit it publicly.

'It's in the book,' she said. 'I'll find it.'

2

The table, a big, carved mahogany bench, a family heir-loom, had always been too large for Alison's tiny dining room. The three of them sat clustered at one end, like the last descendants of a once-great family. Suzi had brought flowers: a clutch of daffodils that spilled upwards and out-wards from a vase on the far end of the table.

Sebastian was asleep on Alison's bed; the wine and reminiscences were flowing freely. Even Suzi, so remote and suspicious in the airport lobby, had loosened up.

Alison had deliberately worn no make-up, and dressed herself in what Brian liked to disparage as 'gardening' clothes: a shapeless jumpsuit. The tactic had worked. Suzi had obviously decided there was no threat from *this* former girlfriend, still childless, but already gone to frump.

'Everyone said that Alison and I were meant for each other,' Blue was telling his disbelieving wife, 'when we first met at university.'

She laughed: 'I couldn't imagine two people more different.'

She was beautiful in a dollyish sort of way, Alison conceded: big eyes, small, upturned nose, hair teased thickly as if to render the head proportionately larger and more childlike.

'No, really,' Blue was telling her. 'It was incredible. We might have been twins.'

'Separated Siamese twins, we liked to tell people,' Alison said, and laughed herself, glowing inside with a warmth that was only partly due to the wine.

She remembered the game they had often played when they first moved in together, guessing how close they must have come to meeting each other in their childhoods, trying to fix actual dates and places when they must have passed within inches of each other, unknowingly.

'I played Joseph in my kindergarten nativity,' Blue, increasingly garrulous, was telling his wife. 'Alison played Mary in hers, same day, same year, a single surburb away. She was head prefect of her girls' school, me of my high . . .'

They had sat in the same audiences for interschool

debates, in the same crowds at combined sporting events, and had never met. But fate had no need to resort to accidents, to chance collisions in the street. Their separate paths were always going to cross at university.

'Those were golden times,' he said, and seemed about to add something, but checked himself. *The best times of my life?* The words seemed implicit in his hesitation, or was it just wishful thinking on Alison's part: these were the words she wanted to hear? She poured out another wine, drowning, half tipsy, in nostalgia. She suddenly wished she had dressed up a bit, or performed a more careful cosmetic miracle – tried to remind him of what he had lost.

'So what went wrong?' Suzi said, half tipsy herself, impervious to any undercurrents.

Suddenly Alison had no idea what had gone wrong, or why it had ended. She felt Blue's foot gently pressing against hers beneath the table, and knew he was wondering the same thing.

'What went wrong, Blue?' she held his pale gaze a moment too long.

He increased the pressure of his leg: 'Nothing that I remember. I guess we should still be together.'

Suzi chortled, secure in her girl-charms: 'Don't let me stand in your way.'

'I'll get some coffee,' Alison rose from the table.

'I'll help you,' Blue offered immediately.

He picked up a couple of plates and followed her through the swing door into the kitchen, and immediately set down his plates and seized her from behind and pushed himself hard against her back.

'When can I see you?' he whispered, pressing his lips to her ear.

She half turned her head, rubbing her cheek against him: 'I'll be home all day tomorrow.'

Then he released her, and they carried out the coffee things and she was forced to sit with the width of the absurdly big mahogany table between them for the rest of the evening, allowed only the teasing pressure of that leg.

After he had left she groaned aloud with desire and impatience, her threshold of pleasure as low, she felt, as it had ever been: a hair-trigger. It was midnight, and she was drunk, but she rang Brian in his hotel room in Sydney, waking him and inveigling him into a conversation of obscene suggestions and longings: the thrill of long-distance vicarious sex tinged only slightly with guilt that she was using her husband for the first time ever as a surrogate.

3

'I've a bone to pick with you, Blue,' she said.

He watched her with his clear, Finnish eyes, surprised.

'Remember that book I gave you? On your nineteenth birthday?'

They were sitting each side of the big table again, just the two of them. The spontaneity of the night before was gone; he had kept his distance since arriving, having second thoughts perhaps. Had he made love to his doll that morning, she wondered? Worked his lust out of his system? She felt vaguely irritated – and remembered for the first time how irritated he had often made her in the past. His mood swings, his unpredictability.

She offered another clue: 'A book of poetry.'

Still there was no response. The sun poured through a northern window, unobstructed, weightless. Vapour from their two coffees eddied lightly and mingled where it entered the light.

'It had an inscription in it,' she added.

'I *think* I remember,' he answered cautiously, slowing his speech as if sensing some kind of conversational radar trap ahead.

'I found it after you left for Sydney,' she said. 'I was in a second-hand bookshop. And there it was.'

He groped for an excuse: 'They printed more than one.'

'Not with your name in it. In *my* handwriting.'

He screwed his eyes shut, and grimaced: 'Oh, shit.'

'I was *very* hurt, Blue.'

He made an attempt to explain: 'I had to leave town in a hurry. There was no time to pack. The company found me a place in Sydney, but it was too small. And they only paid part-relocation costs. I had to sell everything. Jesus. Ali – I didn't think.'

'I had to order that book from America, specially.'

She decided not to tell him the rest of the story. How she had gone home from the bookshop and angrily dug through her treasure drawer, removing everything of his. His photos and love-letters. The soap she had kept for years since their first love-making: the perfumed soap they had used, together, lovesick teenagers, in the motel bath afterwards.

He tried to regain some sort of initiative: 'I've a bone to pick with *you*,' he said. 'You never wrote to me.'

'*That's* why I never wrote to you,' she told him. 'Because of the book. I couldn't believe you would do such a thing.'

And instantly she felt safe from him – or from herself, from the drunken lust that had overwhelmed her the night before. The fire was dead, and could not be rekindled, not in the sober light of day. Other memories were coming back to her: the real memories, she suspected. A kind of morning-after immunisation was taking place.

She knew he felt the same, but suspected also that he would still go through the motions of desire, halfheartedly, out of habit. Or to save face. Especially now that she seemed reticent. He could never resist a challenge.

'What about last night?' he asked, and pressed her foot again beneath the table.

She removed her foot: 'What about it?'

'You felt something.'

'I felt drunk. It wasn't real.'

He seemed a little stung by this: 'Hubby is real?'

She was stung herself by the way he flung the strange word back at her, and even more by the fact that he had stored it up all night.

'Just as real as Suzi,' she answered, and then couldn't stop herself. 'Tell me – when she signs her name, does she dot the i with a cute little circle?'

She couldn't believe her luck when he hid his face in his coffee cup, saying nothing.

'She does!'

After some time he looked up to face her, and smiled: 'I'm sure Brian is a wonderful man. You seem very content. I wish I could have met him. And told him how lucky he is.'

He had always had this knack, she remembered, of finding the right thing to say: of spoiling her anger, turning it back on herself, ruined, altered, loaded with guilt.

'I'm sorry,' she apologised. 'I shouldn't have said that. About Suzi.'

'You haven't seen the real Suzi,' he went on. 'I guess she felt a bit threatened. I've talked so much about you since the airport.'

She tried to hide her pleasure in hearing this: 'Another coffee?'

He shook his head and rose from the table: 'I must be off.'

'Before you go,' she said, 'I've something for you.'

She rose herself, and reached behind her and took a slim book from a drawer in the sideboard.

'Here – I'll give it to you a second time.'

He opened the book to the flyleaf and read the inscription.

'I'm sorry I sold it,' he said. 'I can't tell you how much. That was wrong.'

Apologising also had never been a problem for him. If he was wrong, he accepted it easily. She had loved this at first: she had never seen it in other men. But later . . . well, he was so *often* wrong.

'I'll be checking all the second-hand bookshops,' she smiled, trying to make light of her mixed feelings.

They walked to the door arm in arm, and she opened it, and he stepped out and glanced up and down the street.

'How are you travelling?' she asked.

'I borrowed Mum's car.'

'Where is it?'

'Around the corner.'

His eyes slid away from hers, sheepishly, before he added: 'You can't be too careful.'

Hearing this, her heart, still a little wayward from the night before, finally aligned itself with her head: she could almost hear a click. None of his smooth flatteries or apologies could change the fact that it was over. There could be no second innocence, no forgetting, no unlearning.

Or none at least without alcohol.

She suddenly wished she had been more friendly to Suzi, less jealous, more sympathetic. She might even have warned her of the sweet-and-sour road ahead, warned her that life with a man who was well practised in parking his car around corners, out of sight, might not be all it seemed.

But then surely Suzi already knew.

He bent and tried awkwardly to kiss her on the mouth. 'Bye, Ali.'

'Goodbye, Philip,' she said, and offered only her cheek.

SAUSAGE SIZZLE

NICK EARLS

Second year starts as it was always likely to. Frank Green is pissed on crème de menthe again.

Which would be fine, if we hadn't volunteered for barbecue duty at the faculty orientation sausage sizzle. Fine, if his naughty-French-maid apron didn't keep flapping so close to the heat beads.

'It's how to meet 'em,' he said when he volunteered us for it weeks ago. 'Be the man with the tongs. Save the biggest snags for the spunks and offer them up with some witticism.'

And he was about to move right into the witticism, I could tell, so I held up my hand and said, 'Save a little magic for the day, Frank. It's got to sound fresh.'

'Sure,' he said, the magic already on his mind. 'Mate. First years.' Said like a carnivore talking about gazelle flank. 'First years.' Said as though he was telling me right then he'd be rooting himself stupid by sundown.

First years. I was far too scared when I started first year to think that sex might actually happen. But deciding to be a lot less scared lately hasn't made it any more likely, and that doesn't seem fair. Hanging around with Frank was, I thought, a bit of a plus. Now I'm not so sure.

'So how long's it been since you've been close to a root?' Frank says, eyeing off the herd of grazing first years, as though he's doing it on my behalf. While reading my mind, but maybe it's easily read.

'Dunno,' I tell him, which is a lie, since it's no problem to add nine months to my age and come up with something just over nineteen years.

Already I'm thinking today will not be the day that changes my luck. Already I'm thinking that maybe my best possible outcome would be that we both miss out. Then at least I won't have to get the phone call from Frank in the morning. The lurid sweaty detail. I just hate imagining Frank naked. I wish he didn't feel the need to call.

He takes a sip of his tall green drink and the ice cubes clink against the sides. He's famous for it now, his crème de menthe. And its strategic implications. 'Much quicker than beer,' he said regularly. 'You'd be a fool to try to get pissed on beer once you know the green drink.'

So we've swapped, in a way. I'm okay with beer now, a few beers, and totally over our first trip to a pub, when I froze at the crucial moment of ordering. And my brain said, 'Beer, Fourex, a pot', but my mouthparts turned against me and said, 'Crème de menthe'. It looked like a short journey to a grim social death from there, until

Frank tried it. And with the barbecue fired up and a few dozen sausages to turn, he's on to at least his third green glassful and I'm on my second light for the afternoon, alternating with water. Which reminds me. Today I was gone before I started, really.

My mother drove me here, never a good beginning to an event.

'But I'm heading that way, Philby,' she said.

And I said, 'No you aren't.'

And she half-pursed her lips and said, 'Get in the car.'

And I sat there in the traffic in the foul sun, every second talking myself closer to ruin. Sweating and wanting to stay home and wallow in the pool. And hating barbecues and preferring watermelon and feeling the mad fluttering of trouble let loose once again in my stomach as I thought about the next few hours.

And she talked on and on, in vague and offensively encouraging tones, but didn't quite say anything encouraging enough that I could go off at her about it. She's getting better at me being a loser, and the only thing worse than that is so am I.

'It's stinking hot today,' she said as I peeled myself from the passenger seat upholstery and climbed out of the car, trying not to hear her say things like 'tenner for a cab home' (though I took it, of course) and 'I'll make a bed up for Frank, shall I?'

And I just wanted her to go away, go away, let me sneak away from her privately, and I'd made it as far as the refec steps when I heard her shout, 'Be careful, Philby. Watch your fluids.'

And I ignored her utterly, but the world knew just whose mother she was, and I got several pieces of good advice about fluids over the next half-hour or so.

It's my confidence problem, and it just isn't going. And putting a name to it's only made it seem like some disease I've got, and helped me to anticipate everything it puts me through.

Any time I'm in the vicinity of a heterosexual female of approachable age, I get a bit edgy. I think I've been saving myself for a little too long without ever meaning to. I am comprehensively inexperienced. I am stuck at the stage just before the conversation stage, and I know enough to know that that's very stuck, and far removed from the main game.

And it's all down to attitude, I know that, and I've worked on it. I rehearse in my room, saying plenty of clever things quietly into my pillow, factoring in a range of possible girl responses and working out where I might take the conversation from there. And my mother thinks my sensitive side's a plus and my pillow thinks I'm a right charmer, but in the real world I'm like a pencil-drawn outline of my better self.

I go to the faculty functions. Frank makes me. I'm the man with the plan (he makes me say that, over and over), and soon enough, I'm as dynamic as paint in there. Silent and desperately 2-D up against the wall and wanting to try again some other night. Or never.

Looking around at the casual talk and the coupling and realising I'm so seriously behind in this faculty that I have to have some form about me first time up, and practice (verbal or otherwise) just isn't going to get me there.

I thought this'd get better. It's got so bad my mother even told me that she'd thought it'd get better. It's so bad she offered to buy me a book on it, and in that instant it got much worse.

I think the eighteenth century was good. Plenty of other centuries were probably good. I think you could write poems for girls then (or sometimes even just quote someone else's), and make them love you before you even met. At least, in some cases. I'd be up for that. I write the odd poem.

Frank doesn't. Well, occasional limericks, but only when he can find two rhymes for 'hornbag', and that's not the same thing. But it works for him. He keeps the limericks for the guys and gets the girl action he wants, better than thirty per cent of the time, and he never gets stuck in a relationship.

We work the barbecue and heat wells up from the beads and the sun flogs us from behind, through the spindly trees that grow out of the rockery. And there's not much enthusiasm today for meat.

Frank toys with a fat ten-inch sausage and says, 'This beast'd be mine,' any time a first year (female) comes up to the barbecue area, but it usually only costs him eye contact and doesn't get him far.

He's surprisingly resilient though, when it comes to things like this. He calls it 'the numbers', reckoning he's got nothing to lose, a two per cent chance of success each time and an awful lot of sausages to serve. Frank's more strategic than he looks. Frank knows intercourse never happens by chance, even though you have to make it look as though it does.

'Never had a root I didn't have to work two hours for,' he once told me, as though it was advice.

I ask him if he wants just a plain water next, and he says, 'Nuh.' Quaffs a mouthful of green. He points out possibles in the crowd, telling me, 'I'd go her. I'd go her in a flash. Sizzle, baby, sizzle,' he says, staring shamelessly, poking his now-favourite sausage with the tongs and giving a bit of a jiggle of his hips.

'Those three over there,' he says. 'Those three. Second-year physios, aren't they? I've seen them at a few of these things before. I'm giving them heaps of eye, mate. You can even have first pick and I'll take the other two. Can't say fairer than that.'

And he slurps crème de menthe, gives me a dirty man's wink. Frank Green is the only person I know who expects to both get drunk and have sex every time he leaves the house, and that ends up giving him a great outlook on life. Even though most of the time he only manages to get drunk.

But he's going to get lucky today. I can tell. He's got the confidence going, more than usual even, mainly because of the sausage. He doesn't often get to operate with the aid of such an overt symbol of his penis. People like confidence. Frank told me once, or several times, that someone had described him as 'fully self-actualised', and he's quite proud of that. Sometimes he even tells girls. Sometimes he explains it to them as meaning that he's 'pretty much a hundred per cent horn, baby'. On two occasions known to me, he has alleged that this claim has led to intercourse, reasonably quickly.

There are days when Frank Green's whole world scares me, even though I'm a part of it. Days when I know the maths is stacked against me, and I know that I'm only about twenty per cent self-actualised, and feeling no more than fifteen.

'So pick,' he says. 'Which one?'

'The one with the nose,' I tell him, but I know that I'm fucked.

I slip into a tail spin and sludge a few onions around on the hotplate. I like the smell of onions cooking. I like it when people don't talk to me or when they just go, 'Hey, great onions.' I like the idea of someone wanting you, in a nice way, wanting to be with you and things, and other things arising as a consequence. I like days that are not dominated by performance anxiety and fear of the unknown, and I have them sometimes. Most recently, there was a day two weeks ago just like that.

I serve more onions, to low-key acclaim.

Meanwhile Frank has spiked his massive sausage with a fork and is passing one end of it in and out of his mouth in order to attract attention.

So far, no attention.

Frank, again, has managed to be the first person at a faculty function to have far too much to drink. So his crème de menthe theory's holding up.

And I'm here, the loser onion boy in the rain shadow of Frank's dumb porn display, and it's more than possible that we could both be looking like idiots.

'Put it down,' I tell him. 'I'll never have sex in my whole life if you don't put that down.'

'Oh,' he says, a little surprised. 'Okay, sorry.'

And my outburst costs us a customer, but it had to be said.

Then for quite a while nothing happens. Frank stares at the same three physio students, continues to deliver them heaps of eye. They laugh and show him the finger and stay right where they are, squirting more cask red into their plastic cups and looking impressively unenticed.

'Jeez, we're not doing so well,' Frank says, swigging a mouthful of crème de menthe right from the bottle and swaying subtly to the left and then back again.

'I think people have enough meat for now. There'll be some back for seconds.'

'You know that's not what I mean.'

And the day's about to get easier. He's about to join me in the tail spin. His confidence has risen to foolish heights and he's about to do the Icarus thing. It's a semi-regular pattern, and I can pick when it's going to happen. From Greek mythology, Frank has learned nothing.

'I can't believe we could both leave here today without pulling some action,' he says, totally believing it. 'I don't know what's going on. What's going on?'

'The usual. The seventy per cent of the time for you, hundred per cent of the time for me usual, dickhead.'

'Might have to pick up a mag on the way home. Would you be up for that?'

'What, buying you another porn mag?'

'No. Go you halves. The usual.'

'Frank, this is very depressing. No one even wants our food any more.'

'What is this?' he says. 'It's still only the fucking afternoon. I can't believe we're gone already.'

'Yeah, but it's too hot. Too hot to eat this stuff.'

'I don't care if they eat it or not. We're not cooking it so people can eat it. Will you stop talking about the fucking food?'

I'm finding it easier to deal with in terms of the food, but all of a sudden Frank's finding nothing easy. A shitty kind of silence seems to descend upon us. The three women, now no longer being worked on by Frank's eye, seem to have noted the substantial semi-circle of space in front of us, and seem to be smirking. He tips a couple of steaks and another tray of sausages onto the barbecue, but half-heartedly and only so that he's got something to do.

And I actually like Frank better when he's depressed, but it's not as though I don't feel guilty about it.

Fat spits and the sausages sizzle and one of them sticks on the hot metal and rips and Frank mutters something that begins with, 'Can't even fuckin' . . .'

'It's okay,' I tell him. 'I quite like the crunchy bits. That one can be mine.'

At the edge of the crowd, one of the three women (the one with the nose) crushes their empty wine cask under her foot and starts to make her way over to the bar. And then the other two start heading our way. They must have seen Frank put the new stuff on. I give him a nudge, and his instincts have kicked in by the time they get to us.

'Can I tempt either of you ladies with my meat?' he

says, mustering his most seductive patter from somewhere and emphasising the word meat as much as possible.

'Not really,' one of them says and smirks again. 'Not our scene.'

'Can't believe you've come all this way for Philby's onions,' he says, and I could kill him for it, but it's already too late.

'No. Listen,' she says. 'We were just thinking. You guys, you're working hard, and you're not looking too cheery. Specially you.' Looking at me. Which is bad, since Frank's still looking pretty glum. 'We were thinking, you'd be due for a break round about now, wouldn't you?'

'For sure,' Frank says, as though all the eye work's paying off and the day's finally starting to make sense.

'Yeah. That's what we were thinking. And, well . . .' she pauses, looks at the one who hasn't spoken, and gets a nod. 'We were feeling like a bit of a break from this ourselves, hey Louise?'

'Yeah.'

And even Frank is gawking at them, at the possibilities of this, and how easy it's looking for both of us. Even Frank doesn't think he's this good with the eye, and knows it's the kind of scenario he normally only lies about when we're driving to uni, not something that actually happens. And even though, in the usual way, I don't expect I'll be able to speak for the next couple of hours, it might not be a problem, since I guess I'm with Louise, and she doesn't seem like much of a talker.

'So what have you got in mind?' Frank says, pretty sure of what they've got in mind.

Am I ready for this? No. No way. Can I stop it? Can I go home now? Could I please meet someone nice, and have some say in what happens to me? My hand pokes around with the tongs, and shakes. I imagine Louise without clothes, and me in the vicinity. The shake gets worse.

'Well, this is the interesting bit,' the non-Louise one says. 'You know that totally bullshit guy fantasy? The one about getting to watch two lesbians?'

And Frank says, 'Yeah,' just as I'm saying, 'What?'

And she looks at me and says, 'That fantasy. The one about watching two women doing it. Well, we just thought, we were feeling kind of sorry for you. And some-times we quite like to be watched.'

And she's saying this right at me, so I have to say some-thing back, but all I can say is, 'God. Are you serious? Isn't it kind of a private thing?'

She gives a shrug. 'All right. Just asking. Just thought it could be, you know, fun.'

'Um,' Frank says, to stop them going, as he makes a big deal of turning a steak that doesn't need it.

'Yeah?'

'You'd be thinking, like, now? Inside somewhere?'

'Yeah.'

He turns the steak again, two or three times.

'Oh, I could be up for it,' he says. 'It's getting hot out here. And I reckon we've fed everyone. Hey Phil?'

And now I remember a few times when we've bought the mags. And how we often, well, usually, end up with one featuring an alleged lesbian scenario. And that whenever Frank's made me chip in, the lesbian scenario always ends up in his half. There may be a pattern at work, and one not quite covered by Frank's usual explanation of, 'Hey Philby, twice the norks'.

'Um,' he says, in a way that makes it clear there's more to it than um. 'Any chance of one of you, you know, giving me a bit of a working over?'

'What do you mean?'

'Oh, you know, physically. Whatever. Nothing funny. Just, like, with something. Like a belt, or . . .'

'Aw, yuk. What do you think this is?'

'Hey, just asking.'

And Louise says, quietly but firmly, 'I think I could.'

'And could you, you know, talk and stuff?'

'Not much of a talker.'

'I'm not looking for anything fancy.'

'Maybe, then. But, you know, it's not totally sexual. To be honest, you really shitted me off all last year at any of the faculty things we had. So, you know, I'm up for it.'

'Look, if we're being honest, I don't mind if you hate me.' And he passes me his tongs and says, 'You'll be right?' And I nod and he says, 'Well. Girls. What are we waiting for?'

And he picks up his bottle of crème de menthe, and the three of them walk off into the crowd, like people on their way to a lecture, no hint of what they're planning.

And now that I think about it, all the leather and pain stuff tends to end up in Frank's half of the mag as well. Actually, it's possible that we've never bought a mag that hasn't had at least one alleged lesbian scenario and something to do with riding crops, but the whole pain thing makes me very uneasy, so I've never complained when Frank guts the raunchy bits and I end up with only the articles. Which, come to think of it, always seems to be the way.

And the third of the women, the one who went inside first, the one with the nose, is now out again with a jug of red wine, and she comes over to me.

'So they've gone have they?' she says.

'Yeah. Frank and your two . . . friends? Yeah.'

'Not your thing, hey?'

'Well, no, to be honest. I don't actually get it.'

'So what do you get?'

'God, not much really.'

And somehow it's easy to say this to her, so I tell her I've never had brilliant results with girls, much as I'd like to. It's almost like talking to a guy, talking about girls with a lesbian, and knowing there's nothing at stake. So I tell her, sort of as a joke, that I think it must have been easier in other centuries, and I run my poetry theory by her. And she laughs, but nicely. I've never told anyone my poetry theory before.

And I say to her, 'Maybe you can help me. I've got this thing. This thing where I can't get started. It's like, I can't even start a conversation with a girl, a straight girl, in case it doesn't work out. Frank says I should play the numbers, and not care if it doesn't work out, but I just don't think that's me because I do care. And I'd like to, you know, get to know them a bit. I can't start the conversation maybe partly because I like it. I like the talking. I like the idea that one thing leads to another when you're ready for it to, but I don't think that's how things work. It's a dumb idea.'

'Is this some line?' she says, and laughs.

And I laugh too, since we both know how useless a line would be. 'No. I'm not that dumb.'

And I ask her her name, realising I can't keep thinking about her as Lesbian Number Three, and it turns out it's Michelle.

It also turns out that I like her and, without the possibility of sexual tension, that's much easier to do than usual. In other circumstances, though clearly not these, I could find her attractive. But even as things are we could be friends, which wouldn't be so bad.

I can make her laugh, and she seems to like it. I certainly do.

She takes Frank's tongs and we cook the food together for the people who want seconds. She tells me a few things about girls, straight girls, and I don't mind listening, even if she is making them up.

Demand dies down again, and it's just the two of us, turning things.

'You're looking a bit sweaty there,' she says.

'Well, yeah. It's thirty-seven degrees and I'm stuck behind a barbecue.'

'You know what? I think it's somebody else's turn.'

'Probably.'

'A swim'd be good.'

'I've been thinking that all day.'

'Yeah, but I live in a flat a couple of streets away, and we've got a pool.'

'Oh, that'd be great. So are you going to round up a few people?'

'No, I hadn't really thought of it that way. I was thinking you and me. It's not a big pool, but it'd be nice. And no one ever uses it. And maybe we could have something to eat other than this shit,' she says, turning a steak I'm in the process of thoughtlessly charring.

'Oh yeah?'

'Yeah.'

She pours herself more red wine from the jug, takes a sip.

And I'm thinking, can you actually ask someone if they aren't a lesbian? Can you actually get someone to confirm right now that they're the lesbian you'd thought they were, so that you can relax again and get back to the conversation.

'Yeah. Just us,' she says. 'A jug of wine, a loaf of bread and thou,' in a voice that turns self-consciously Elizabethan at the end.

And she shuffles a few crispy onion bits.

'Oh right. Once more into the breach, dear friends,' I say in something like panic, then crash internally as I contemplate simultaneously the sudden strange obstetric overtones, and the fact that I think the next line has something to do with our English dead. 'Sorry. I . . .'

'It's fine. I like *Henry V*. It was a bit of a surprise, but . . .'

'Can I've another go?'

'Sure. Got anything less war-like?'

'That's the plan. Um . . . give me a sec.' Someone

wanders up and I dish out another couple of overdone sausages, thinking frantically, thinking till I'm in such a knot it almost hurts. But there's nothing, nothing that'll work. And, damn it, I've come so far. Tail spin. Nose dive. Warning. This woman may not be a lesbian. 'No,' I tell her, and then I hear myself continue, ignoring the loud internal voice that's shouting *Idiot, idiot, shut up you stupid dumb virgin*, 'I'm stuck. I've got one from Marlowe, but it's a bit much. For just having a swim.'

'That's okay.'

'Even with the wine and bread. And the thou. A bit much.'

'It's okay.'

Frank lurches out from behind the building, waving his empty bottle and stumbling down the stairs. He staggers over our way, lifts up his apron front and shows me welts.

Where his shirt's gone I don't know. And his shorts too, unfortunately. And did Louise get his underpants as part of the deal?

'Snug fit you've got down there, Frank,' I tell him, but he just says 'Woo woo, woo woo,' jerking his right hand up and down as though he's pulling on something round about shoulder level. 'Woo woo.' Like The Little Engine That Just Did. 'And they reckon rubber doesn't show,' he shouts. 'They should try the tubes on the Bunsen burners in Two Twelve.'

'They've practically perished. They're pretty grungy. They'd sting.'

'Oh, yeah. And she really fucking hated me. You too.'

'What?'

'I kept saying to her, it's Frank, it's Frank, but all she wanted to scream was All men are bastards.' He burps, in a dangerous kind of way, as though there's much more than gas at stake. 'Fuck,' he says, in a deep, spooky voice. 'I smell mint.'

And he scrambles for the rockery.

'The man's an idiot,' Michelle says, as we listen to him turning most of his internal organs inside out among the cacti. 'Why would anyone ... he's an idiot. Sorry, he's your friend, isn't he?'

'Yeah, but ... Let's go for that swim. Let's go now.'

CANDELO

GEORGIA BLAIN

The fact that his name had remained unmentioned for so long, the fact that none of us had seen him or spoken to him for all those years, did not mean I couldn't picture him. With my eyes closed, he was there.

Mitchell Jenkins.

His bag at his feet. The zip broken, a pair of under-pants, leopard print, sticking out of the opening. The dust coating his feet dirty grey.

I looked at him from the ground upwards.

Tall, thin and slightly bow-legged. Tight jeans, thongs and a checked shirt, sleeves rolled up to tanned forearms. Dark eyes looking at us, the three of us, through a fall of long blond hair. Looking at us and grinning.

This, Vi said, *is Mitchell,* and she turned to us. *This,* she said, *is Simon, Ursula and Evie.*

He held out his hand and the smile widened. Impossible in its breadth. Challenging the wariness that was, without doubt, evident in our faces.

Gidday, and he turned to each of us, one by one.

But it wasn't just his smile that I saw. It was his foot tapping, his mouth chewing gum, the fingers of his other hand clenched against his thigh; these small signs of nervousness beneath the bravado of that grin.

And I did not give an inch.

Simon, however, reached out to return the greeting, shy for a moment, awkward, as their grasp missed and then caught.

I just met his gaze. Without a word. And in the silence that followed, I watched as he kicked his feet in the dirt, as he scratched a hole with the toe of his thong, and as he kept on staring at me, seemingly unperturbed by my failure to acknowledge him, until, with a further widening of that grin, he finally turned to Evie.

It's not 'gidday', she told him, mimicking Vi's own words to us each time we lapsed into any semblance of lingo. *It's 'hello'.*

Vi glared at her.

That's what you say to us, and she crossed her arms obstinately.

All the time, I added, but under my breath.

And Simon kicked me, hard, on the shin.

Mitchell had been to four foster homes. He didn't tell us this. Nor did Vi. I read it in the letter from the placement program.

When I asked her why, I knew the answer I was going to get. A lecture about disadvantages. About abuse. About single mothers. About poverty. All punctuated by sharp, angry taps of her cigarette against the side of the ashtray.

What I wanted to know was whether he'd ever been in trouble, serious trouble.

Vi told me to stop being childish. *Mitchell's past is Mitchell's business,* and she turned back to her work. *Stop being difficult and give it a try.*

I looked offended. I told her that of course I would. Who did she think I was?

But I didn't. Not at first. I remember.

We were hot and cramped in the back seat. Simon, Evie and I pressed against each other, sticky skin on sticky skin, furnace blasts of air rushing in through the open window, while in the front, Mitchell stretched out and tapped his fingers on the dashboard in time to whatever tape he had put into the cassette player, singing out of tune to whatever song happened to be playing.

Reckon I've got a voice? he asked Vi in all seriousness, and I saw her looking at him, uncertain as to how to respond.

The white of his teeth was reflected in the rear-vision mirror as he caught my eye and smiled.

Pretty bad, hey? and his look was sheepish, but he did not stop. He just turned the volume up another notch and sang a little louder, grinning with embarrassment whenever his attempts to hit the note went blatantly wrong.

How come he's allowed to choose what we listen to? I asked Vi at the service station. *And how come we have to listen to that?* I added, referring to his singing.

It wasn't that I hated what he put on, in fact it was a

relief from the usual Joan Baez or Harry Belafonte that Vi always played, and I had to admit that his singing was amusing us all, it was the unfairness of it. Simon and I were never allowed to play our tapes in the car. We always brought them with us, but they stayed in the glove box.

Mitchell hadn't even asked. One push of the eject button and Joan Baez was back in her case, replaced by David Bowie.

I had looked at Simon. I had waited for Vi's response.

Nothing. Simon had just shrugged his shoulders and Vi hadn't seemed to notice.

You never let us play our tapes, I complained to Vi as we waited at the counter.

She pushed her sunglasses up into her hair and searched for her money in her purse. She was ignoring me. But I was not going to be stopped.

How come he can?

Do you want a drink? she asked.

No, I told her.

Just as well, she said, and she held out her hand for the change.

I looked at her.

Because I certainly wasn't going to buy you one, and she turned her back on me, leaving me standing by the cash register, still waiting for an answer to my question.

Back in the car, Simon and Mitchell had swapped seats. Leaning forward into the front, Mitchell talked constantly. Asking endless questions about where we were going, the places we drove through and what Simon liked to do. Music, skateboards and surfing. He wanted to know everything. Comparing bands they liked, food, movies. He barely stopped to catch air as he leapt from topic to topic.

But it was the surfing that fascinated him the most. He had never done it before.

You surf, Ursula? and Mitchell was looking at me, grinning again.

No, I said, defiant, determined not to give him an entry, although I could see the exclusion that was going to occur. Him and Simon. Me and Evie. It was stacking up.

So what do you do? he asked.

I told him that there were other things in the world besides surfing. That I couldn't believe the ignorance of his question.

He just kept smiling. *Reckon?* and as his dark-brown eyes focused on mine, I could feel myself beginning to smile in response, my mouth turning up at the sides. I could not help myself. But then I saw them, Vi staring at me in the rear-vision mirror, and Simon, sitting next to her and glaring, and I became all the more determined not to relent in my behaviour. Not in front of them.

When we stopped for an ice-cream, Simon told me I shouldn't be so rude. *Imagine how he feels,* and my brother's eyes were wide with compassion. *There's all of us and only him.*

He'll cope, I told him, irritated with the way he was always on the side of the underdog. Irritated with how well he and Mitchell seemed to be getting on.

And I rolled my eyes in disgust as I heard him, Mitchell, hamming it up, yet again.

Jeez, he said as Vi passed him a Cornetto, *never had such a classy ice-cream.*

Evie couldn't believe it. I looked at Simon, but he had turned away.

Reckon the last time I had an ice-cream was ... and he paused for effect, *four years ago.*

Really? Evie stared at him. Impressed. Completely and utterly.

True, he answered, solemn, pitiful, to an extreme.

Back in the car, Simon stayed in the front seat, Mitchell in the back. Evie was sandwiched between us. Separating us. But I could still see his long thin legs in his tight jeans. The left jiggling up and down. Up and down. The tapping of his hand on his knee.

Vi put her Joan Baez back into the cassette player. Simon did not even attempt to change it, but I wasn't prepared to let things rest, not even from the back seat. I asked Simon to put Pink Floyd on. He waited for Vi's response. I waited for Vi's response.

I think we'll have something a little more peaceful for a while, she said.

See, I told her.

She ignored me.

And on we went.

Eight hours south. Hugging the coast. Small seaside towns with winding main streets. A pub, a post office, and a milk bar. Slow traffic clogging up each entrance and then dispersing out on the highway. Holding my breath each time Vi overtook a truck, clutching the steering wheel, foot flat on the floor, swearing loudly as she willed the car to go faster, faster. Swinging around a bend and being flung to the other side of the seat, Mitchell's side, where I would have been pressed tight against him if it weren't for Evie separating us. Just. And as I pushed myself up again, I could not help but touch him. There was no space for me to do anything else. My hand was forced onto his leg.

He looked at me, at where my skirt had ridden up my legs.

And I looked at him, at where my palm had rested on his knee.

And he grinned, yet again, his dark eyes resting momentarily on mine.

We drove until it was dark, turning off the highway into the quiet of the country night, on to a narrow road that twisted and turned inland. It was too early for the stars, and the sky overhead was black, unbroken by lights. Nothing but the sound of the engine. Evie was asleep, Simon was asleep and Mitchell was asleep. Vi was hunched forward over the steering wheel, and in the reflection of the rear-view mirror, I could see how tired she was, the match flaring as she lit another cigarette, her face ghoulish in the momentary flame.

But it was not her I watched.

It was Mitchell.

His head rolled to one side so that all I could see was his profile, half hidden by the long blond hair. His eyelashes, dark and thick, twitching slightly as he dozed. His wide mouth, soft, his lips pale against his tan. His hands resting on his thighs. Square and brown, the nails bitten down, and on his index finger, a long jagged scar.

When Vi pulled over for the second time, it was clear that she did not know where we were.

We all woke up, all of us except Evie, who stayed where she was, her head tucked into Mitchell's side as he leant forward to take the map from Vi.

Jesus, and his mouth was wide open as he stared out the window, forgetting the map for one brief moment, as he gazed out across the black of the country to the sky, *look at them all.*

I leant across Evie so that I could see, out past the reflection of his eyes in the window, to the thousands of stars now spread across the sky.

That's what it's like away from the city, Vi told him.

No kidding, and he shook his head in amazement as he spread the map out and traced the line of where we had been with the tip of his finger. I watched him as he paused for a moment, still stunned by the beauty of what he had seen, before telling us we were on the right road. *Shouldn't be much further,* he said.

And he was right.

It wasn't.

Candelo. Right around the next bend.

THE SWIMMER

LIAM DAVISON

Three miles off shore there's an island. From the right angle the jetty looks as if it forms a bridge between it and the hotel beach, as if you could walk there and back safely above the water. Each day I set out to make the walk and stop at the end of the jetty where the water lingers below, humming its music up at me. Strange lights and shadows move beneath it. Coloured fish swim between the pylons.

Sometimes, on the end of the jetty, there's something which has been ripped from the water, yanked upwards and left to die – a striped fish with puffing lips or a squid staining the wood with its thick black ink. The sun and the air work against them, stealing their colours. I throw them back and watch them float on the surface of their world. The fish float sideways like crusts of bread, one lidless fish eye looking down where they have come from, the other staring upwards at the world of men. Then they sink slowly down.

A small Japanese man, also staying at the hotel, used to walk the jetty too and lower himself into the water among the coloured fish. They would shoot like sparks away from him to regroup on the other side of the jetty as if to watch the intruder. Although he was small, he had the solid shoulders of a swimmer which hunched in their sallowness around an almost non-existent neck. His hair was short and black, cut in a straight line across his forehead and looking as if it were always wet, even before he reached the end of the jetty. His name was Yukio. Yukio Nagatsama.

Yukio would stir the water with his feet to keep afloat and pull a pair of goggles over his head. They sank neatly into the sockets of his eyes. The goggles were white plastic and shaped like eggshells with small black holes to see through. They robbed Yukio's face of any expression it might have had, his bulging eyes more like those of an insect than a man, or of some fish from the bottom of the ocean where the sun's rays never reached. Sometimes he pulled the goggles over his eyes before he reached the end of the jetty, the elastic holding his small ears flat to the side of his head. Once the goggles were down, Yukio looked only straight ahead, not once turning his guarded eyes towards the shore. From behind the goggles he must have seen the straight line of the jetty reaching towards the island in the distance with all that water in between. He walked as if he knew where he was going and what he was leaving behind.

Once in the water, Yukio's body became more fluid and relaxed. His shoulders looked less heavy. The water placed no demands on him except that he swim to stay afloat. Yukio swam well. Each day he swam to the island and back. Then he turned round and swam to it again, slowly and steadily, back and forth, three or sometimes four times a day. Yukio was a swimmer.

His arm and shoulder rose from the water with the regularity of a windmill. Sometimes I could see him far out to sea, a black speck heading towards the island. I wondered what his goggled eyes could see, what colours and shadows came up from the bottom, what creatures lurked there watching him swim or touching him as he passed.

Yukio's wife, Masai, waited for him on the sand. Her skin was darker than his, less yellow. Her shoulders were fragile like a bird's. Masai rarely looked towards the island and when she did, it was a passing glance, not the searching look you might expect from a young bride watching for her husband in the sea. Mostly she read or turned her slender body in the sun. Occasionally she walked towards their hotel room leaving a red towel and a slight depression in the sand.

Her body moved easily up the beach. At first she returned quite quickly, carrying a drink or tube of suntan oil, later she stayed away longer. Towards the end she stayed in the room for close to an hour at a time, her empty towel a beacon to the boats, marking the place where she should be. When she returned she paddled her feet in the water, walking to her waist and splashing drops across her shoulders. I watched from the balcony of my room.

When Yukio returned from his swimming late in the afternoons, he watched her too. Sitting on the edge of the jetty where he'd dragged himself up from the water, he watched her reading or sleeping on the beach. Then, with goggles still bulging from his eyes, he'd walk along the beach to her and lie without a towel beside her. The eggshells looked, spaceman-like, towards her and sometimes, in a tentative show of affection, he'd reach out to stroke her arm. His hands must have felt the silkiness of her skin which I was later to feel in the underwater belly of the aquascope.

Yukio and Masai came to the hotel to be married. 'To save my family from the shame,' he'd told me one night in the dining room, with Masai serving his vegetables and never saying a word. 'We could not marry at home. The family is . . . too much. Yes? Not too much, ah, too strong is what you say. Yes. Too strong. The family is too strong.' His mouth was smallish and round, a small opening between fleshy cheeks. 'We could not afford the gifts.'

Masai waited for him to eat.

'Many young people come here because they can't afford the gifts,' he said. 'Their families tell them to come. It's better that way. It's better to come back married than to have a wedding where the guests receive poor gifts. It's better for the family.'

Yukio was right. There were six Japanese brides the day Masai was married, all tulle and taffeta like dolls on sticks. They stood in the hotel lobby waiting on cars then were blown like dandelion clocks out into the sun. After the wedding they danced. Yukio was awkward being publicly in love. He shambled after Masai unsure of how to touch the lace and unable to follow her fluid movements. She on the other hand felt confident in the centre. Her quick eyes caught the glances of the men around her, ignoring some and flirting girlishly with others. Yukio felt more comfortable with his heart concealed from the world.

Later that day I saw him at the jetty. His goggles were pushed up above his forehead as he lowered himself into the sea. He swam with easy strokes away from us following his regular course and leaving Masai behind him on the beach. Her body, stripped of its lace and taffeta, seemed somehow vulnerable in the sun. I watched him swim away.

Yukio must have often crossed paths with the Frenchman, who lived at the hotel and drove the aquascope. Each hour on the hour he'd walk to the end of the jetty and, if there were people there wanting a ride in the aquascope, he'd take their money and arrange to bring it close alongside the jetty. His name was Claude.

From the beach the aquascope looked like the upturned hull of a catamaran. Hinting at tragedy, it floated a hundred yards or so off shore, slowly rotating in the breeze. From the jetty it was the skull of a bird half floating in the water. The arches between the hulls became empty eye sockets while the centre shaft became the white remains of a beakish face. It curved smooth and white from the water. When Claude brought it to the jetty you could see it for what it was. The twin hulls were there for stability, like outriggers on native canoes, while most of the structure hung, a swollen belly, beneath the water. The centre shaft was where the entrance was. A small hatchway opened to a ladder which led down to the glass bowl hanging below. It held eight people. Cramped together on tiny stools, they peered out into the underwater world. The effect was of a fishbowl with the people looking out instead of in. Like Masai, I found it unpleasant to be in.

Every second hour or so Claude took the aquascope out to the reefs on the far side of the island. It disappeared for half an hour then came back round the other way to return silently to the jetty. Sometimes in the busy weeks, it turned immediately around and half-floated eerily back to the island, often making three or four trips in succession. It seemed to be always half way between the island and the shore, at the point where I felt certain it must cross Yukio's path. The aquascope made two slow trips to Yukio's one.

On his way to the jetty, Claude used to pass Masai. He would steal a quick glance at her body and nod to say hello. On his way back he stopped to talk, squatting beside her towel like a grasshopper on his haunches. His back arched above her. The sun was gold on his shoulders. Conversation came more easily each time he stopped between the jetty and his room.

'You should come in the aquascope,' he said. 'To see beneath the water.'

He spoke with his cheeks and jowls, trying to twist the English words into a French mouth. His lips pouted. 'From the other side the water is like the sky. And you hang there floating in a balloon.' Claude felt comfortable with the sea. He dived with scuba gear, spent hours beneath the surface. He spoke with confidence to Masai where before he'd been unsure of what to say.

'The sea, it is a different world. You are, er, unusual under there. There are more directions to go. But it is also a difficult world to understand. You can get lost – go down instead of up. Sometimes when you come up you feel too heavy, like you should be back in there floating inside the water. Like you belong in there.' He laughed. 'We catch things in the sea with our hooks but sometimes the sea can catch one of us. It, how do you say – seduces us away.'

Masai didn't go in the aquascope then. She only went when she had to. The white skull made its slow and silent journeys to the island and back while she lay on the sand. When it was still, moored to the jetty pylons, she walked towards her room, staying there till the skull moved away again. All the time, Yukio's arm moved up and down in time to the sea.

One day, when there was no one waiting for the aquascope, Claude came back to Masai. He led her to the jetty.

'Come for a swim with me. I'll teach you how to dive.' He took her easily by the hand, as if he were used to her touch. There was no apprehension in his actions, no fear that she might resist or shy away from his contact. Masai went with him, quite comfortably linking fingers.

'You might not need to teach me very much. Perhaps I can already dive.'

'Maybe so.'

'Maybe I am a better diver than you think. Maybe better than you.'

'Maybe.'

'Perhaps I will teach you how to dive,' she laughed, teasing him and moving away so that her delicate fingers just touched his. 'Maybe the sea will seduce me away.'

Claude smiled, recognising his own imperfect English and allowing her the fun of mocking it. 'That would be sad for your husband.'

'My husband. No, my husband is already in the sea.'

Half way along the jetty they stopped, above the watching water. Masai stepped to the edge, flexed her toes and pushed herself upward and outward in a perfect arc above the water. Her long hair streamed behind, tracing the same curve as her slender body. She broke the surface of the water cleanly and disappeared like a pearl diver below, leaving Claude to see what treasures she would bring to the surface.

'You see, I can already dive,' she called from the water. 'There is nothing for you to teach.'

Claude laughed, a crouching grasshopper again. 'This is not what I meant – to dive. I meant to dive with the flippers and the snorkel, or the aqualung. Under the water. You have cheated me.'

'Now show me how you dive and we'll see who is the better. Maybe I can teach you something.'

Claude dived well but without the tantalising elegance of Masai. His arc was not quite perfect. He surfaced next to her.

'You dive well.' Masai splashed water at his face and swam to where the water was dappled with shadows beneath the jetty. Claude swam after her with strong strokes and disappeared into the shade. I couldn't see them beneath the jetty but I could hear them laughing together, their voices mingling with the water sounds which come from under piers. And I could hear the long minutes of silence between the laughter when only the sad sound of water brushing against wooden pylons came to me. It was during one of these silences that I saw Yukio's arm rise from the water at the end of the jetty and start its regular rotation towards the island. I wondered how long he'd been there and what his goggled eyes had seen.

When Masai and Claude climbed the wooden ladder to the jetty, he was well on his way to the island. Masai went back to her waiting towel and Claude, all confidence and charm, led a group of people to the aquascope. They set out in search of whatever it was they saw beneath the water.

I watched for Yukio's return. The skull of the aquascope rounded the island and moved as if by magnetism back towards the jetty. Yukio was lost in the sparks which the sea threw back at the sun. Every now and then I looked to see if he had appeared, expecting the reassuring rise and fall of his arm to come into view, waiting for it because, like the tick of a clock, it should have been there.

Another cluster of people disappeared from the end of the jetty into the mouth of the aquascope and it was drawn back towards the island again. Masai and I both watched the sea as the skull disappeared and reappeared again around the island. Seagulls followed it like confetti. Fish bubbled up at the people and idled in with the tide. The water sparked at the sun. The empty jetty reached out like a bridge to the island.

As the aquascope moved closer to the shore, Masai sat forward on her towel mumbling to herself. 'Surely he must be back by now. They must have seen him from the aquascope.'

Small waves slapped at the beach. They slapped away the seconds. 'He must be back at the jetty. I couldn't see because of the sun.'

The aquascope nudged the end of the jetty, nosed blindly along to the pole where it was tied, and emptied itself of people. They bubbled to the surface, as if the bulb was being squeezed beneath the water, and filed along the jetty, blinking at the sudden change in their worlds. Claude was the last to emerge. He stood flexing his shoulders in the sun waiting to see if he had to make another trip before it got too late.

'Claude must have seen him. Perhaps he's on the other side of the aquascope looking for the ladder to the jetty.'

Masai left her towel at the same time that I left my chair to walk to the end of the jetty. I walked there every day to look at the fish the fishermen had left behind. This day wasn't any different. Besides, I wanted a closer look at the aquascope, to see how it worked. Perhaps I could look inside. Perhaps also I could catch a glimpse of Yukio's arm clawing towards the shore.

Masai reached the jetty first; she stumbled onto it, her flapping thongs threatening to trip her up. 'Did you see him in the water? Yukio. Yukio has not come back.'

Claude took her by the shoulders, not understanding what she said.

'My husband is in the water, we must look for him.'

'But he'll come back. He is swimming like he always does. He'll be alright. He is a swimmer.'

'No, it's been too long. You've been to the island twice and he's not come back.'

'But he is a swimmer.' Claude looked towards the island, expecting to see Yukio's arm rising and falling as always. 'He'll be alright.'

The end of the jetty was the same as other days except there were no fish, only a few dry scales stuck to the wood.

'Wait. He will come back. There is no other place to go, only the island which is empty.'

The sea changed colour while we waited, from silver to gold to blue. It breathed beneath the jetty. Masai left Claude and turned her attention to me. 'Have you seen my husband?'

Her question asked too much. I looked stupidly at her as if I didn't understand her English.

'My husband. You spoke at the table for dinner. Yukio. Have you seen him?'

I shrugged and lied, looking from him to her. 'No, I've not seen him today.'

She stumbled back to Claude, distraught.

'We must look for him. It's been too long. We must look.'

Claude was quiet, then turned to me. 'Monsieur, a man is missing. You will help?'

Inside the aquascope the two of us hunched close together peering through the glass. Once my hand brushed against her leg and I felt the silkiness of her skin. Claude closed the hatch and, from somewhere above, steered us away from the jetty. Around the pylons, coloured fish flapped like butterflies, while further down, moths nuzzled the shadows for somewhere to hide. The light from the water turned our hands a sickly green. Jellyfish blubbered past in underwater rivers, strange clouds leaning into the wind. All was silent.

Further out we passed through belts of fish which loomed larger than life through the glass and disappeared as we slid out into the empty water. Weeds waved up at us and starfish with spikes studded the floor like burrs. The glass brought them closer till they threatened to scratch and burst the bubble we were in. The light played tricks on us. The bottom disappeared altogether. More than once I thought I saw the black shape of Yukio's body floating above us and imagined his arms hanging uselessly down as if to catch something thrown up from below. Each time it was something else – the shadow of a cloud or a boat tugging its rope like a kite. Neither of us spoke. I thought of finding Yukio's body, taking him back to the jetty and dragging him up from the sea. Out of the water, his goggles would stare up at us, the black holes seeing all and nothing.

Yukio was not on the island. We called for him and saw the hotel lights come on along the beach.

'Maybe he's back already,' I offered, trying to give her some hope. 'He could have swum back a different way and be looking for you now, wondering where you are.'

'He always swims to the jetty.'

'I know, but something could have changed his mind. The wind or the tide. He could have gone further along the beach. Maybe he saw something he didn't want to see and swam the other way.'

'What would he see?'

'Anything, I don't know. I'm not a swimmer. Maybe the current carried him down around the headland to the other beach. He could be there. We shouldn't have come to the island.'

Claude called us back to the aquascope. The sea closed in around us, black and thick, threatening to fill up the bubble. Masai sat sobbing at the darkness.

Back at the jetty we realised our mistake. Yukio was waiting for us, dressed and ready for dinner. He helped his wife to the jetty and led her to their room.

'I swam to the headland,' he told me while Masai served the vegetables without saying a word. 'From the island to the headland, then I walked around the beach. It is better that way – how do you say, for a change. Instead of straight back to the jetty.'

Masai waited for him to eat then served herself.

'Tomorrow we leave,' he said.

'I thought you were staying longer.'

Masai looked down at her food, letting her husband speak.

'No, tomorrow. We came to be married – for the family. It is better that way. We are married now. It's better for the family. There is swimming in Japan,' he said.

RIVER PICNIC

KRISTIN WILLIAMSON

Summer 1954

Tom and Sarah are home from boarding school this weekend and we're all meeting at the Merlin River for a picnic lunch today. I love picnics, even though this one will be slightly embarrassing for me, having to face Uncle Martin for the first time after telling him that he was one of the most selfish people I'd ever met. I've decided to be pleasant and polite to him but nothing more. If he tries to jolly me up or uses his famous sarcasm, I'll just withdraw with dignity.

Mother is very excited this Sunday morning, hurling things into the picnic basket with gay abandon and singing a rather rollicking sea shanty, 'What Shall We Do with the Drunken Sailor?', which is not her usual style. I hope it doesn't mean she intends to drink too much wine. She almost never drinks but she's recently discovered some dusty bottles in the cellar which I think must be the ones left by Aunt Ingeborg and Aunt Hedda all those years ago. They should almost be very fine wines by now. I notice she's polished one up and put aside two crystal glasses. Not very practical for a picnic.

Even Charlotte has decided to grace us with her presence on this family occasion. She is pleased about the picnic because she gets on well with Uncle Martin and Aunt Ursula, although she thinks Tom's 'too wild' and Sarah is 'smutty'. I like Tom a lot and enjoy Sarah's company although she is far more knowledgeable about sexual matters than I am and sometimes, when she tells dirty jokes, I'm ashamed to say I don't get them.

We set off walking towards the river, pushing the cream wicker pram full of rugs and beach paraphernalia – buckets, spades, towels, umbrella and the picnic basket. Charlotte refused to walk with us, as she thinks the pram makes us look like a family of hobos. It's quite a nice pram and except for the huge dark-blue barrel of homemade ice-cream sticking up where the baby's head should be, you might believe we had a real baby in there. This ice-cream is Mother's 'great contribution' to all picnics. She makes it herself and it takes days to prepare. First you have to bash up ice and saltpetre in a hessian bag with a mallet. Then you mix the ice-cream from a secret blend of gelatin, cream, nutmeg, sugar and vanilla (once she added rose petals but they tasted so awful we've objected ever since). Then it has to set and the barrel is sealed. Once the barrel is opened you must eat the rich ice-cream immediately or it turns back into a glutinous mess. We often return from picnics feeling sick from having eaten too much of it but today Tom and Sarah will help us to get through it.

As we approached the river we began to smell tea-tree and honeysuckle. At this time of year a silvery-white clematis climbs the trees and covers the fallen logs. It smells of honey and makes great dress-ups. When I was younger I would tear off long strands of it and wind them round my head and body, pretending to be a wild nymph bride.

We pushed the pram along the river track until it got bogged in the mud and then we pulled it, Jonathan and I pretending to be horses in harness and Eliza running behind with a whip of clematis. Mother followed, looking elegant as usual, swishing her parasol at the flies. Charlotte was further back, gazing dreamily about her and stopping to trail her hands in the creek whenever our progress was so slow that she was in danger of catching up to us – not that there was anyone about to think she might belong to us.

We turned the bend in the river and there was the picnic party, already seated under the tea-tree and folding tables set for lunch. Their smart maroon Humber was parked in the shade. We waved and called out excitedly to our cousins, who waved back with less enthusiasm. Suddenly I felt cross. Our small expedition must have looked bedraggled and comical to them, and we were late. I could tell they'd been talking about that. We were hot and tired and our ice-cream was melting, and they were cool and rested, sipping their drinks under the trees. Why hadn't they offered to come and collect us in their big car?

It was only an extra three miles. We were the poor relations and they enjoyed seeing us pulling our pramload of
possessions through the black mud in the heat. I broad-
ened my smile and waved at them joyfully. I would show
them that if they pitied us we simply didn't care.

Polite hugs and kisses were exchanged and Aunt Ursula
bustled about unloading their lunch baskets from the boot
of the car. We stood about, looking and feeling awkward.
Uncle Martin and Mother were the only two who seemed
to be completely enjoying themselves. They threw back
their heads and laughed together at almost nothing. They
seemed delighted with each other's company and didn't
notice how ill at ease the rest of us were. Jonathan and
Eliza grabbed their buckets and spades and dashed off to
find crabs, and Tom began collecting wood for the fire
we'd light in the evening, tearing whole dead trees apart
with his bare hands. Sarah grasped my arm and hauled
me aside to tell me about her latest adventure with the boy
she is currently mad about, and Charlotte, rolling her eyes
at the infantile things that amused the rest of us, began
rather primly to help Aunt Ursula unpack their picnic
lunch. I watched apprehensively as their perfect picnic was
displayed and wondered what our Mother would have to
offer, apart from the melted ice-cream. Aunt Ursula had
corned beef and lettuce sandwiches neatly packaged in
greaseproof paper, a cold egg and bacon pie, a homemade
sponge cake, chocolate crackles, scones with cream and
jam, lemon cordial, a thermos of tea and mandarins. All
this was neatly laid out on two card tables on a green and
cream chequered tablecloth, with cutlery, paper napkins

and cardboard plates and cups. Our mother flung open her picnic basket to reveal her contribution – a loaf of wholemeal bread, a wedge of old cheese, several artistic-looking bunches of sour grapes, some flowers, a bottle of wine and two crystal glasses. I gasped.

Uncle Martin held the picnic basket aloft. 'A jug of wine, a loaf of bread and thou ... the perfect picnic!' He laughed loudly, then opened the wine with a flourish and poured some into the two crystal glasses, one for Mother and one for himself. He toasted her and avoided Aunt Ursula's gaze. She doesn't drink.

'Katharine, this wine is brilliant!' he said in surprise.

'Thank you,' said Mother and, peeping over the rim of her glass, she added demurely, 'unfortunately the grapes didn't come from our vines.'

Aunt Ursula turned to Mother and said with tight lips, 'Did you bring anything for the children to drink, Katharine?'

'Lord, I forgot!'

'Let them drink brine!' said Uncle Martin and they both burst out laughing. 'No, really. They have a choice. Wine. Or wine,' he said, like a character in some English comedy.

They laughed again. Then, still smiling but slightly irritated, he turned to Aunt Ursula. 'Give them some of our cordial.'

Mother, sensing the need for escape, stood up and said charmingly to Martin, 'Take me for a walk.'

He gave a mock bow, put on his white straw hat, offered his arm and they set off along the sand, Mother twirling her parasol. They made an elegant couple. When they had gone about twenty paces, Uncle Martin turned and gave Aunt Ursula a little apologetic wave. She stared after them with a bitter smile, then flung a large piece of cheesecloth over the lunch to protect it from flies and plopped down on a deckchair with the latest *McCalls* magazine.

Charlotte, who loves foreign magazines, peered at it longingly, which must have irritated Aunt Ursula, because after a minute or two she said, 'Charlotte dear, it's rude to read over other people's shoulders. If you wait until I've finished this, I'll lend it to you.'

'Oh, really? Thank you, Aunt Ursula!' Charlotte said with such gratitude that I felt sick. I suddenly remembered one of the most embarrassing moments of my life.

I was about six and had been staying the night with Sarah at their holiday house at Merlin Heads. Next morning, because Uncle Martin had the car, Aunt Ursula said she would take me the three miles home to Skinners Bluff on her bicycle. I sat on the little seat behind her. Aunt Ursula had been in a hurry to set off so I was still eating my breakfast, a large slice of toast covered in butter and thick blackberry jam. As we were crossing the Merlin Heads Bridge, we hit a headwind. Aunt Ursula stood up on the bike to push harder. I looked happily out at the waves, and rested my toast on Aunt Ursula's seat, which was padded with white lambswool. To my horror she suddenly sat down! What could I do? The damage was done. After a few minutes I thought I should confess. 'Aunt Ursula!' I yelled above the wind. 'You're sitting on my toast.'

'What's that dear? I can't hear. Tell me later.'

Later, there was no need to say a thing. Aunt Ursula's cream slacks were ruined and the lambswool padding on her seat had to be thrown away. I looked sadly at my poor crushed toast.

'Why didn't you tell me, Anna?' asked Aunt Ursula with the same tightly controlled irritation as she had just spoken to Charlotte.

As it seemed that lunch would be postponed until Uncle Martin and Mother returned, and Sarah had no more to tell me about the Grammar boy she had a crush on, I decided to take myself off for a walk along the sand. I could see Mother and Uncle Martin up ahead, still arm in arm, laughing and talking intimately. When they reached the little river path they turned up into the tea-tree to avoid the mud. I skulked along behind, trailing them. When they disappeared into the bush, I followed.

Now I could hear them reciting lines from Sheridan's *The Rivals*. An Irish play, of course. On the rare occasions when we're all together at family dinners these two love to perform little scenes from plays by Sheridan, Goldsmith or Wilde.

'Objection! Let him object if he dare! No, no, Mrs Malaprop, Jack knows that the least demur puts me in a frenzy directly,' said Uncle Martin, playing pompous Sir Anthony Absolute. 'My process has always been very simple – in their younger days, 'twas "Jack, do this"; – if he demur'd – I'd knock him down – and if he grumbled at that – I always sent him out of the room.'

'Aye, and the properest way, o' my conscience! –

nothing is so conciliatory to young people as severity . . .' said Mother, playing self-satisfied Mrs Malaprop. Then they both burst out laughing.

It occurred to me that they were very like the two characters they were playing and they couldn't have been happier if they'd been a pair of actors performing this wordy old farce on stage in London or Dublin a hundred years ago.

I hadn't planned to spy on them but there I was, hunched behind thick bushes watching as they sat all alone in a clearing. Now they had stopped play acting and Mother was perched on a low bough in the shade while Uncle Martin sat on the grass at her feet.

'I shouldn't, of course,' Mother said.

'Take it!'

'You always were a bad influence.' She was teasing, amused, a bit coquettish.

'Think of the parties.'

'At the house of a bedridden old lady who hates noise?' She laughed.

'You'll be free one day a week. I'll come and take you out. You'll be living in the middle of town. I'll take you to dinner at the club, to the Law Society Ball, the art gallery, concerts . . .'

'And what about Ursula? Will she come too?'

Uncle Martin seemed to be considering this. 'I don't think so. She'll be far too busy. Bottling quinces.' They both laughed. Then there was silence.

'She doesn't like me, your Ursula. She never has,' Mother said thoughtfully.

'Oh, come on, she doesn't mind you.'

'She thinks I'm . . . fickle. A flirt.'

'Well, you are,' Uncle Martin said affectionately. 'Look at that poor young parson. Hangs around you like a lap dog. What are you trying to do? Make him ride his Norton off the bluff?'

'I like him. We have the same interests.'

Uncle Martin snorted in disgust.

'Music, philanthropy, and Moral Sciences,' said Mother playfully. 'Nothing carnal. Not at all what you think.'

He turned to her, looking concerned. '*Don't* make him fall in love with you, Kate. If you take that job, I'll introduce you to men far more interesting than Reverend Marsden.'

Mother smiled, turned her head away and said dreamily, 'Perhaps it's too late.'

From my hiding place I beamed a look of pure hatred at Mother. Uncle Martin just gave her a look of exasperation.

'If I do take that job,' she said, glancing back towards the picnic group, 'I'll really miss them.'

'Naturally. You're their mother.'

She shrugged. 'Well, I'll miss the children too. But I meant the people. The people in our township. The halt, the maimed and the blind. Those who get bashed up by drunken spouses, the deserted young mothers with not a penny in the bank to feed the baby.' She paused, noticed that Uncle Martin was not sympathetic, so she added a touch of ridicule. 'The mental cripples crying out for

Schubert, the people who cut themselves trying to bite the top off a beer bottle and need someone to mop up the blood.'

'Katharine, for God's sake.' He waved her to silence. 'I know where it comes from, this Lady Bountiful stuff.'

'It's all right for you with your law firm and your amusing friends and your good wife at home to look after things,' she said defensively. 'But I'm bored cross-eyed! I have to do something. People admire me in this "seaside backwater" you so despise.'

'No more than they pretended to admire our mother,' he said like a flash. This hurt her as he had intended it to. 'Get out while you can, Kate. Accept the challenge. I'm offering you an escape.'

'Blast you!' She got up and stalked off, walking back towards the picnickers. He followed, smiling. Suddenly she turned to him as if appealing for help and said, 'Anna is becoming appalling.'

'I agree,' he said sympathetically.

'And the little ones need . . . some sort of father figure.' He nodded.

I caught my breath. *I* was appalling? I, who was doing my utmost to keep the family together and the house from being sold and my mother from being put away in a lunatic asylum? How could they see me as nothing more than a troublesome child? I felt cut to the quick.

THREE WAYS

GERARD LEE

December 1979

I climb the steps of the Greyhound and arrive self-
consciously at the front of the bus. A dozen elderly people
watch as I struggle to manoeuvre my pack along the aisle.
There's only one seat left, or more correctly, part of it's left.
The woman sitting beside it has spilled over into a good
portion. Spilled over into what is necessarily my half.

'Is anyone sitting here?' I ask and in answer to the
question, she somehow triggers the internal muscles of her
buttocks and pulls herself back over the half-way line, at
the same time passing a hand through her red Rod Stewart
hair. I unload the backpack and sit down, readying myself
for 1500 kilometres of pure hell across the top end of
Australia from The Isa to The Darwin.

'Hot, isn't it?' I say.

'I'm melting away, boxed in like this.' She shuffles uncomfortably in her crimpelenes, gives me an uncertain smile.

We sit for ten minutes, the bus engine rumbling, waiting, sweating like pigs. No one speaks. Her rump is beginning to subside back into my territory. The strain of holding it up must be colossal. Soon we'll have contact. When we do touch, it's more comforting than inconvenient.

Perhaps noticing my enjoyment, she hauls herself back against the window.

I offer her a piece of bubblegum. She refuses. 'I've got to stop eating. I only have one meal a day now.' I nod disinterestedly, like I don't even notice she needs to cut down. 'But I'm smoking again,' she adds, glumly. 'Instead of a meal, I puff on a cigarette. Can't win, can you? If it's not cardiac arrest, it'll be lung cancer.'

She takes out a packet of Benson and Hedges, handles them in her small hands like one unused to smoking and lights up.

'When only the best will do . . .' She laughs and looks out the window. I follow her line of sight. There on the footpath, in front of the shops, is a haggard, grey-haired man with two boys swinging off the ends of his arms. They're watching her and she's looking back through the tinted glass as if they're a boring program on TV. The boys are smiling at her and pointing.

'That your father and kids?'

'My husband,' she says.

I'm embarrassed but she doesn't seem to mind. She

keeps looking out, expressionless. She must think they can't see her face.

As the bus pulls out there's no goodbye. Maybe she's too shy to wave, but he looks back as if he'll never see her again.

'He was a rough rider,' she says, almost to herself.

We're passing beneath the slag heaps of the Isa Smelting Works, heading out into open country. The sun's beginning to set. The earth itself now has a glow to it – outback reds and oranges. There's a breeze coming through the windows.

The driver introduces himself. His name's Dave. He'll be taking us to Three Ways, the crossroads of the northwest. From there, it's east to the Queensland border and across the top to Darwin. He also explains that the toilet's blocked, then adds: 'One more thing, ladies and gentlemen. The rules of the bus are that alcoholic beverages and obscene language are forbidden. They're a no-no, alright? So, if you don't want to find yourself out in the middle of the Never Never with nothing but your luggage . . . don't get caught.' My companion giggles. 'Over to the left, you'll see the north-west telegraph line.' All heads turn. Out over the dry grass, about fifty metres off, a wire droops between slanting telegraph poles, leading off behind and ahead of us. 'And over to the right . . .' – all heads turn – 'you'll see absolutely nothing.' A short chuckle from the passengers but behind us a raspy voice pipes up: 'That's not nothing, mate,' and continues with a drunken slur, 'that's some of the best bloody grassland in the Southern Hemisphere.' I turn around to see the speaker. He's about four seats back, wearing a moth-eaten twenty-gallon hat and trying very hard to get me in focus.

'Yeah, I'm still here,' he says to me. 'Haven't gotten off yet.'

I turn back to the front again, embarrassed. My companion's looking at me.

'He's a real bushie, been down at the rodeo.'

From behind, more quietly, '. . . the best grassland any-fucken-where.'

'He'll end up like all the rest. They're all the same in the end. Once they give up the rodeo they don't care. He'll be like my old man . . . burnt out. Won't go anywhere, won't do anything. All they want to do is ride. I like to move around a bit. Sometimes I just have to get up and leave a place. I can't stand another minute of it. And my husband's good, he says OK . . . couldn't do anything else, I suppose. But if it was up to him we'd still be rotting away in Camooweal.'

'Where are you going this trip?'

'All the way to Katherine. I'm worried though. I've never left him alone before, with the kids.'

'He'll manage.'

'Tonight he'll be alright. I've left them steak and eggs, an easy tea. But it's not right. Him having to come home and cook a meal. It's not man's work.'

'Haven't you heard of Germaine Greer, or didn't feminism get out this far?'

She laughs. 'That's what they said about dollars and

cents. But they got out here. We've even got the wireless and the motorcar. Wonderful, isn't it?'

'How old are you?'

'None of your business.' She waves the question away, looks out the window and then back, assessing me. She's facing me directly for the first time. It's a pretty face, slightly angry and bright. The drunk rider from behind is staggering around trying to force his way into the toilet. He finally pulls the door open and a stinking whiff races down the bus. The bus driver announces again over the speaker that the toilet is blocked. In a moment he pulls over and offers the rough rider a chance to relieve himself outside.

While he's gone, Dave says, unofficially, not through the mike: 'This bloke's got no shame. The rest of you will have to wait till it's dark.'

Cackles.

'Where are you from?' she asks.

'Brisbane.'

'Yeah, thought so. Me too. I ran away when I was sixteen.'

'How long ago was that?'

'Not saying ... Do you remember in the paper, about a bloke who used to rob check-out girls?'

'No.'

'He'd always escape on a motorbike. They called him the Armed Bikie.'

'Aww yeah, I remember him.'

Her eyes light up: 'I was his girlfriend.'

'Really.'

'Ooo, yeah. He got caught on a Friday afternoon at Morningside Fair. It was going to be his last job. I left Brisbane the same night. Haven't been back since. The only thing I miss is the movies.'

'That means you're my age.'

'What does?'

'If you were sixteen when you ran away from Brisbane. That bikie thing was about ten years ago.'

'Could be.'

'What do you mean, could be? That's when it was. You're sixteen plus ten.'

Her brow wrinkles. 'Don't say it like that ... caught myself out there, didn't I?' She stubs out her cigarette and looks at me carefully. 'We don't look the same age though, do we?'

'I've had a sheltered life,' I say.

She smiles and looks away.

'Have you seen *Close Encounters of the Third Kind*?'

'Yeah, I have,' I say. 'Didn't think it'd get out this far.' She smiles.

'It arrived here about a light year after everyone else saw it. I really loved that picture. I believe it too. There's always sightings up here in the out-of-the-way places ... there's been too many of them not to be true.'

'Yeah, it could be.'

'The fellas that make those pictures must be real characters – we get that out here too.' She's indicating the *Playboy* I tried to conceal in the seat pocket. 'Good articles in there, mate.' She gives me a nudge. I try to act nonchalant.

Her thigh is resting easily against mine now. 'Talking about movies, you should stop at Camooweal for the night ... for the flicks. Everyone'll be there. The blacks with their kids and all the dogs, fighting in the aisles. They laugh at all the wrong places: like when someone gets shot in the guts, they crack up. And they love John Wayne. One of them even calls himself John Wayne. You should go.' Her eyes are twinkling with the good advice.

I see us both sitting back in the canvas chairs like a couple of kids. She's got three packets of Smith's and I've got one. We're having a great time, her large form rollicking in the light coming off the screen.

We're in open country now. Over to the right, the red sun is disappearing. The earth seems to be breathing again, rolling over, recovering from another day under the heat. You can hear it sighing with relief. I reach for the *Playboy* and open it casually hoping it's not going to be the centrefold. I miss the centrefold but hit something equally shameful – a sweet-faced blonde sitting astride a motorbike. No clothes. Only black stilettos. My companion leans across to take it in.

'What a lovely face.'

'Mmm.'

'I didn't think they had girls like that in these stick books.'

'Stick books! Who calls them that? What's it mean?'

'Not saying.' She's holding her mouth tight against a smirk. She's being naughty.

It's not quite dusk. The sun has disappeared below the horizon but streaks of yellow light are still coming across from the west. The ground is already in shadow; just above it, grass and small bushes are high enough to be caught in the last rays. Inside the coach a golden light is being reflected off the panels. In front of us the heads of an elderly couple are bobbing together, bathed in light.

She's playing around with the gadgets above our seat. Her reading light comes on.

'How do you get on with the blacks?' I ask.

'Shoot 'em.' She's watching me to see if I believe her. I smile.

'No, I get on well enough with them. Some stations round here though, they give you a gun as soon as you arrive. One place, they wouldn't hire anyone with Aboriginal blood. I'm glad they didn't ask me because I don't know what's in me. All I know is it was some American after the war.' She looks out the window.

'You mean your father's American?'

She nods, sneaks a look at me. In the light from her reading lamp I see her eyes are reddening. She realises I've noticed and casually reaches up and switches the lamp off.

'I'd like to know who he was ... I still write to my mother.'

She's facing out the window. I pat her on the arm not sure how far I should go. Still facing away, she reaches up and wipes one eye. I glance idly about the bus. Two women in the seat opposite are discussing butter and cheese and how to keep them fresh.

'My fridge has a built-in sealed compartment for butter and cheese.'

'So's mine,' says my companion, turning to me, smiling.

In Camooweal, where she used to live, there's nothing of note except the General Store. She points it out as we drive past – a corrugated iron shed with a Coke ad along one side.

'Worked in that damn place for two years and then it closed down.'

'What, rude to the customers?'

She grins and threatens me and we're already out of town.

'Some good swimming holes out that way.' She's pointing at arid, thirsty landscape, a pile of empty forty-four gallon drums near a dirt track. 'Kimmy and I went in nude one afternoon and we saw this old fella spying on us. We tried to run for our clothes but we couldn't get up the bank. Kept slipping in the mud.'

'I'd like to have seen that myself,' I said.

'Yeah, you would.'

Ten kilometres out of Camooweal she says: 'It's only now I'm beginning to enjoy the country. I've seen all around Camooweal before . . . this is new.'

What we're looking at now is what we were looking at before – dried grass with here and there, a spastic eucalypt or two.

Driver: 'Our next stop is Barry Caves. We'll be there for half an hour, arriving at Three Ways about eleven p.m. for an hour stop.'

'An hour stop!' she says. 'I just want to get on to Katherine to see Kimmy. What can you do for an hour in the middle of the night?'

'Plenty.'

She laughs and takes a drag. 'I could say somethin' but I won't.'

We travelled on. At two she was adopted out, at twelve she found out, at fourteen she left home, at fifteen she met her boyfriend, at sixteen she was in court, at seventeen she was in Camooweal.

'And that was like being in jail,' she says, summing it all up. 'Silly things you do sometimes . . . and keep doing.'

I nod.

'I've been yakking on, haven't I?'

'No.'

'I have. Now you tell me what you've done. You've been keeping that very quiet.'

'I'm doing Arts at uni.'

'I thought so. Something like that. You look like an artist.'

At about eight we stop at Barry Caves. The place is a non-event except for a cockatoo chained to a veranda railing, trying to sleep. When she strokes the back of its head, it wakes up and starts to yell at the top of its voice something that sounds like, 'June! June!'

'Aww shut up,' she says quietly, and turning to me, 'it's a mental case.'

The bus snails along comfortably, lights dim, passengers dozing. Outside, the Australian night is slipping away. We read. Carol's is Leon Uris, mine is *The Idiot*.

'That a book about you,' she says, noticing the cover. I nod. She shifts in the seat, trying to make herself more comfortable. Suddenly she crumples up in pain.

'O God, O God Almighty.' Her face is screwed up. She's holding her stomach. 'It's my knee ... O God, it hurts like crazy.' She's breathing hard, her eyes watering. She takes a quick glance at me and looks away, humiliated. I rub her uselessly on the back.

'I'm supposed to be in bed for six weeks. My doctor would kill me if he knew I was on this bus. My knee keeps collapsing under me. All this weight doesn't help either. He'd just kill me. He told me this would happen.'

She seems to be in less pain now. She rubs her eyes with her sleeve.

'But it's no good me staying home, the kids're all over me.'

'What about your husband, can't he look after them?'

'He's not too good himself.' She's looking down at the back of the seat. There's an almost imperceptible sob. She reaches up and switches off the reading lamp again. 'He had a buster off a bull he was riding out on one of the stations. We didn't know whether he was going to live or not ... God, I'm telling you everything now.'

She puts her hand up, but it's too small. Beyond it, her face is screwing up. Her whole body begins to shake.

She's asleep, resting against the window. I want to lay my

head on her shoulder but fear a rejection. She's no angel, sleeping away there with a piggy snore, but I want to cuddle up to her anyway. I look around to the rough rider. He seems to be asleep but he opens one eye.

'Bad manners to watch a man sleep.'

I glance back at her again, studying her face, the flabby cheeks and there, something I haven't noticed before; her ear, sweet, neat, completely fat-free. I look away. It's probably rude to watch a sleeping woman, too.

I take out the *Playboy* and flick through. These girls look very thin. They're so thin. I put it away and look back at the sleeping woman.

The bus is tearing along now, pushing smoothly through the black night, passengers wrapped in sleep like sandwiches in tissue paper.

At Three Ways there's the atmosphere of an Arab marketplace. The depot is nothing more than an acre of concrete set down in the middle of nowhere with a few buildings on it. There are buses here from everywhere, going everywhere – Sydney, Perth, Alice Springs, Darwin, Townsville. You can almost hear the bleating of camels in the background. People zombied by lack of sleep wander around beneath the harsh neons.

An effort has been made to help you feel at home as you travel through these nether regions. In the cafeteria you can buy all the products – Coke, Cadburys, take-away coffee, Cherry Ripes, even cotton buds. Carol and I are waiting at the counter among the sleepy customers. She's brushed her hair but her face is still crinkled.

'See, she's fat too.' She nods discreetly to the girl serving. 'Out here there's nothing else to do but eat.'

'I could say something but I won't,' I say.

'Get outta here.' She tries to stand on my foot.

She orders a ham sandwich and then looks across at other normal-sized people tucking into plates of steak, coleslaw and chips.

'Love a carton of chips.'

I buy a salad sandwich and a Cherry Ripe and stroll outside amongst the buses, thinking about Carol. I'm standing around eating when I see the rough rider and another man sitting together on two plastic chairs. I tune in to the conversation. The other fellow is English and he's just come back from the highlands of New Guinea.

'They run around with axes and spears up there, nothing on.'

'Mmm, mmm,' the rough rider says.

'No, I'm not kidden you, mate.'

'Mmm, mmm.'

'They do! I saw it myself.'

'Mmm, what else did you see up there?'

I turn and head back to some benches I've noticed.

There she is, sitting alone against a brick wall in her pant suit. She's eating a carton of chips unhappily. I sit down beside her. She offers me the carton, I shake my head and offer her the clean end of my Cherry Ripe. She shakes her head and throws the carton under the seat. She's holding her greasy fingers out to dry, her hands so small and dainty.

'Want to come for a walk?'

'Where?' She's dubious.

'Out there, through the grass, under the stars.' She looks at me with that little bright face.

'The grass, the stars, eh?'

'Yeah, the grass and the stars.'

She looks away, then back. I can't figure out what she's thinking. 'That grass you're talking about is spinifex. It's all spikes, pricks ya.'

'We could take a blanket.'

She studies me a long moment.

'You don't want me.' Then barely mumbles: '. . . too fat.'

For a moment I'm stymied but finally burst out with: 'I love your fat.'

There's a silence in which her blush grows deeper. But she keeps looking at me – her blue eyes. A bus starts up somewhere nearby.

'You don't,' she says at last and lifts herself off the seat. 'Think I better have a cup of tea.'

I walk out to the front of the depot and step off the concrete into the dark. I keep going, on up the road, the stars out on the horizon growing brighter as I go. I'm still chewing on the Cherry Ripe but too upset to enjoy it. I made her blush, an ex-juvenile bikie moll. How could I?

The smell of the grass blows across from the dark. I feel lonely in a big way.

Looking back to the depot I see a couple of people talking near one of the petrol bowsers. They seem miles away. I decide I can't go back to the bus. I'll sleep out here and take the next one in the morning.

I walk a few paces into the grass and start to feel an itchy sensation round my calves. It gets so bad after a few more steps I'm forced back to the road. I take my shoes and socks off and see little spearheads of grass sticking in them.

A bus pulls out of the depot and heads my way. I strain to read the destination as it approaches. It says 'Darwin' and my pack's still on board. I decide to let it go and collect it next day at the depot. I step back into the grass so as not to be caught in the headlights but the bus glides to a standstill nearby, like a thing from outer space. The door opens silently.

'I'm staying here, mate,' I say to the driver from my position several metres into the spinifex.

'Get on, son.' There's no argument possible.

As I walk down the aisle, the oldies are having a go at me.

'Trying to walk it?'

'In a hurry, boy!'

'He's got his shoes off.'

I glance up the bus and see two strangers in our seat. 'Pst,' she says from way up the back. She's pointing to a space beside her.

'I told the driver you were up here,' she says and watches as I place my shoes and socks on the floor. 'Don't like to say I told you so.'

'Well, don't.'

She laughs and then gets serious.

'Enjoy yourself out there?'

'Yeah, not bad.' I look into her eyes. 'You should have come too.'

'Aww yeah, what for?' She's playing with the seat pocket.

It must be two or three a.m. I've been asleep leaning against her shoulder. She's awake now, too. She looks across at me in the half-light. Her jowls are crushed and wrinkled but her eyes are still bright. As I rub the sleep from mine, the voices of the women opposite come to me. It's the middle of the night and they're still talking cheese and butter.

'Why don't you stop off at Katherine in the morning,' she says. 'Meet Kim. You'd like her. Come out to the Gorge with us.'

'I don't know.'

'Kimmy's taken the day off work and we're going swimming.'

'Just like in the old days eh . . . in the nude.'

'God, you never stop.'

'OK, I'll stop.'

'Don't stop on my account . . . but you'd love it out at Katherine. What are you going to Darwin for anyway?'

'I don't know.'

'See!'

She winks at me and puts her head back against the window. I think about her, her languid form, lying on the rocks at the edge of the water. I think about nights with her in a flat in Katherine, Kimmy in another room. I think about her husband.

I close my eyes and begin to fall asleep, in her direction. I snuggle comfortably into her shoulder but I'm sneaky

about it. If she wakes up I'll have the excuse of somnam-
bulism. I let my hand slip down onto her lap and wait for
a reaction. None. She takes a deep breath, a sigh perhaps.
I wonder if she's still conscious, if deep within that flesh
her heart is beating faster. Mine is. My hand's like a snake
on her lap, ready to strike. I want it to slide up underneath
her clothes and suckle its lips around her breast.

We speed on through the night, through the grasslands
and the wilderness, through the rutted creeks and rivers,
clinging together like a couple of drought-proof seeds,
nestled in the arms of the Northern Territory.

Her friend Kimmy was waiting in the red dust.

'Oh God, she's fat too,' Carol said when she caught
sight of her. They could have been twins.

'Are you coming?' she said.

'I don't know.'

'Darwin'll still be there in a few days. Most probably.'

I looked at her bright face, her tough red hair.

'Come on, gorgeous.'

At dusk that evening I sat on the cliffs at Darwin over-
looking the sea, imagining what she was doing at that
moment. I saw her, the sun coming golden through a
flywire window. Kimmy sitting on a couch somewhere
behind her, laughing. She was laughing too, cooking them
an 'easy tea'.

AT MEREWETHER BEACH

MARION HALLIGAN

The yellow of the time Ray's mother was alive turned to a kind of red after she died. A hot colour. It gave Ray a hollow feeling in his chest, like fear. Red was breaking into a house you weren't certain was empty. Red was swimming out through the surf and not turning back when you felt tired. Red said, Just a bit further. Another few yards. Keep going a bit longer. And then when you convinced it you had to stop and turn back red murmured, Maybe you've come too far, maybe you've left it too late. Safe back on the beach, red said, Your mother is drowned but you are okay. Sometimes it seemed like a bargain, that Ray would not drown because his mother had. Ray's long strong arms and short strong legs carried him out on those punishing swims and brought him safely home again.

Step was a good swimmer too. He was graceful and fast over short distances, whereas Ray was a slogger and stayer. Step did well in still-water events, shooting through the calm waters of the baths at record speeds; Ray's strength lay in rougher seas. Mr Swann took them to the Surf Club. He had been a champion when he was young, now he was the treasurer. They did their qualifying certificates and then became cadets and went in championship events. Ray won the NSW Cadet Surf Race Championship, Step the Australian Junior 400 Metres Freestyle Championship. Ray won the Junior Surf, Step the Junior Belt. They were a winning pair in Rescue and Resuscitation events, taking it in turns to be the swimmer in difficulties and the belt-man who saves him. They made the March Past team. They travelled to carnivals. Step's father had a Holden station wagon and they all piled into that for trips to the north coast and to various Sydney beaches. A mob from the club would go and afterwards there'd be a lot of beer drinking, but of course Ray and Step were too young. They didn't like beer much anyway – they'd rather have Coke, that was a treat, and hamburgers. Keeping their strength up.

Ivy has a photograph taken by the *Newcastle Morning Herald: Northern Districts Junior R and R Champions*, says the caption, and there are six lads in clinging one-piece costumes and striped caps tied under their chins, in a row behind the reel with the line and belt wound on it. A kind of trophy this wheel is, itself, with *March Past Champions* painted on it. Step is second from left, Ray on the far right, and at the end is the coach, Bill Beale, whose nickname is Eel from his young days when he was a champion swimmer and moved through the water as slippery as his namesake. When they march they are like knights with banners entering a tournament only they have the clinging swimsuits and caps instead of armour, but the pride and triumph is the same, and their stepping out is a challenge to the other team, it says, Look at us, we can beat you, we're the best.

By the time they are fifteen they are full members of the club and in that year named Joint Club Champions. There's not a whisker between them, says the club president, a man who's a legend himself, not just for the championships he's won but for the real rescues performed in dangerous seas; once a brother and sister washed out by a rip, when the belt broke, and they all came close to perishing, but he saved them against all these odds. And he was not the only bloke to have performed legendary rescues. You were in the presence of heroes when you went in the clubhouse. Men with glorious names, of whom stories were told. The immortals, was what old Mr Renfrey, who sat in a chair in the official enclosure on special occasions and nodded his head, called them, the immortals.

What does that mean? asked Step.

Never dying, said Ray.

But Mr Renfrey's son's dead, said Step, killed on that motorbike.

Yes, said Ray, well, it's not their bodies, it's what they did.

Not a whisker to choose between these lads, not a hair's-breadth, says the president.

Just as well, says Mr Swann, whose name is Ern, Ernest

Swann engraved on a number of silver tropies. Jeez, if one should beat the other! Not that either'll let it happen.

There have always been Swanns in the Surf Lifesaving Club, Ern and his brother Bert, and their father who was Ernest too – he'd been one of the founders, coming back after the war, the first one, from that other beach, Gallipoli, him and some other men having this idea of looking after people at the beach, making sure swimming was safe. Starting off without a boat, not even a belt and reel, just their own strong bodies. And now their names in gold letters, or on the trophies, engraved. And this already starting for Step and Ray; they know they are the next generation, it will be in their hands. There are things to live up to.

School they attend, mostly, but do little work, they are vague but amiable in class; their teachers expect nothing of them and waste little time on them, not over academic matters, not that this school has much in the way of expectations of any of the boys in this direction. It's all an exercise in marking time, the teachers say to one another in the staffroom, and make little effort themselves. Not like Eel, who has them training early and late and never lets up. Push yourselves, he says. Just a bit more each day. Looking back on it, that is part of the redness of this time too. A kind of jangle behind the eyes that is the body trying to say to the brain, This is too much, I can't, and the brain blocking it, blocking the message, not letting the limbs flag. In their own world they are famous, famous for their surfing skills, for their sportsmanship, their good nature. The teachers know all about it, it's written up in the newspapers, the boys walk round in their own little states of glory and bring honour to school sporting carnivals. But this doesn't mean their teachers expect them to have any brains, the reverse rather; they see harmless good-looking dumbos. Good-hearted. Nice boys. Not troublesome like certain elements. Helpful rather. In certain ways the teachers need them to be not very bright: all this and clever too would be a bit much.

They are old enough to leave school but think they might as well stay on and finish their Intermediate year. Ray has the idea that they can do a last-minute swot and pass. Step isn't so sure. Both are confident some sort of decent job will turn up, no point in worrying. It's the middle of the sixties, good jobs do turn up. In the meantime, they've got plenty on their plates. And their cups are running over.

The day of the Merewether Surf Carnival was fine in a busy kind of way. The sun was hot, and there was a sharp breeze from the south-west that roughened the sea and made all the little pointed flags crack like cap pistols. It snatched at hair and towels, fouled umbrellas, shredded words, blew the sand into tiny stinging bullets. It was tiring just sitting and watching, what with the eye-piercing glitter and glare of the sun on the water, the constant snapping of the bunting, and having to hang on to your hat and turn your head and close your eyes and mouth against the attack of the sand. There was irritation and even a kind of malice in all this racket of light and noise, but still the beach was crowded, inside the hessian fence where you had to pay and outside it on the slopes of the sandhills and anywhere people thought they could get a free look, quite easy really and not even much farther away. There was a brass band and stalls selling ice-creams and watermelon and toffee apples, children getting lost and sunburnt, yelling, picnics getting full of sand.

What do you do when you go to the beach and forget to take your lunch? asks Michael Swann, who can't wait to be old enough to be a junior. But everybody knows the answer. You eat the sand which is there.

Trust Merewether to put on a good sea. Nobody could remember when there'd been a calm and easy surf for a carnival at Merewether. The National year had been a bobby-dazzler, even for this part of the world. Seas like mountains, and these puny people trying to crawl their boats up them, or jump out of the way; at least a mountain stays in one place, doesn't rear up and fall on you. Quite a few surfboats wrecked that day. Turned into heaps of matchsticks. Good for nothing but firewood. This sea is kind, in comparison. A bit of sparkle and energy, enough to liven things up a bit, nothing difficult.

Step was swimming in the first heat of the surf race. Ray was in a later one so he was sitting on the sand watching. Ivy was on the beach too, and Step's mum, they always came and watched, and Janice who was a gawky child still and Michael and the next one, Linda. Step's dad was one of the organisers, he wore the official swimsuit and cap like the swimmers. The path of the race went out beyond the surf, round a buoy, along parallel with the beach and back round another buoy. Step was well into the parallel stretch, far ahead of the rest of the race, when he threw his hand up in the air and disappeared under the water. He bobbed up again and again threw his hand up. The crowd craned their necks. Why was Step making this signal of distress?

Then the surfboat out beyond the course of the race raised its oars.

Through all the racket on the windy beach came a hush, and then a murmur. A kind of sibilant groan. Ray raced down to the water, grabbed a surfboard and paddled out. A third time Step's arm appeared, waving, feeble now, and a dark stain spread in the water. Through it the flash of a long pale shape.

The alarm sounded and the left-behind racers faltered, trod water, then turned back. Behind the place where Step had disappeared a wave began its lift towards the shore and the watchers saw it rise in a trembling green crest and at that moment, that angle, the sun shone through it and silhouetted the body of Step in the mouth of a shark. The shark's long pale body, and Step's held in its jaws. Inside the wave tall and shimmering, translucent as a vast glass marble. For a second the shape of them looked like a hammerhead, people might have persuaded themselves for a moment that it was a hammerhead and the boy nowhere to be seen, free of it, escaped. But even as they hoped, they knew it wasn't true. The boy and the shark hung there in the luminous green water for another moment, then the wave turned and they disappeared from view.

Ray on the surfboard reached Step and leant down into the water to pull him on it but the shark was still there hanging on to him. Step's arms were trying to grip the board and Ray was pulling him, the surfboard heaved and was tipping over. He couldn't get a hold of Step, the resistance was too great. He tumbled into the water beside him. Two other boards arrived, churning with their paddles, clustering and steadying, and suddenly the shark seemed to let go and Ray could get Step on to the board. Himself scrambling up behind him. Step's leg was gone, Ray could see the white bone of the knee. The flesh was shredded and blood poured out. He pulled off his cap, in his haste not managing to undo the strings so they knotted and he had to rip them, but still he managed to wind the cap round Step's thigh and tie it tight.

Step was still alive when they got to the shore but he died on the way to hospital. Shock, said the doctor later. Massive loss of blood. As well as his leg bitten off there were deep teeth gashes on his back and chest. Next time, said the doctor, don't wrap the victim in a blanket. The warmth doesn't help. Better to keep him cool. Let the body shut down. That way you minimise the loss of blood. And the trauma.

Statistically, said the newspaper, after its detailed account of the 'Carnival Shark Attack Tragedy', *statistically it might seem odd that a shark should attack on a sparkling sunny day, given their supposed predilection for overcast skies and sluggish waters. But it seems that carnivals, regattas or surf races attract sharks like dogs to a circus. And not all attend to watch the races.*

Nevertheless, the article went on, *it should be pointed out that more people are struck by lightning than die from shark attack. More people are killed by spiders. More die on the roads in one month than in 200 years at the teeth of sharks. You've got better odds of winning first prize in one of the 130 lotteries in the country than to suffer death by shark.*

Ivy folded this newspaper and hid it under the cushion of her chair but Ray sat in it and heard the crackle and pulled the paper out and read it. He sat at the table and tore it into morsels, smaller and smaller, until each scrap was as tiny as he could make it. Then he put the fragments in the fireplace and burnt them.

Sometimes it seemed to Ray that the green, transparent, looming wave had turned into a crystal in his brain, a solid, glassy shape, forever poised in that moment when the light shone through it, illuminating the body of Step in the mouth of the shark. A tiger shark, it was, twelve feet long, the striped markings faint on its back. He supposed that Ivy would have this crystal in her brain too, and the Swanns, and all those people on the beach who had seen it and could never unsee it.

Shut down. Keep cool. Minimise trauma. It was as if Ray had taken the doctor's advice. He stopped going to school. He mooched around the house. Sometimes he got a job and then gave it up and after a while got another. In the bloom mill at BHP. On the coal loader. Whitewashing the baths when the council emptied them in the winter. Digging up tramlines. Heavy jobs, tiring. He was in the nineteenth birthday ballot for Vietnam but his number didn't come up; Daryl Vickers wasn't so lucky. If it was luck not to go; sometimes Ray wished that he had been called up, it would have been something to do. Margaret Cole's brother Edwin got conscripted the next year and was killed before he'd been there a week. His mother cried in the supermarket. Daryl came back eventually, and shortly after got married, but didn't settle to any job – he was as much a wanderer as Ray.

When Ray went to the library and brought home books to read Ivy looked at them and worried, thinking of his grandfather. She could see that they weren't books to learn things from, useful books; Ray didn't look much like his grandfather but the bloodline was there, and he was clever too, maybe it was that going bad. Waste, it was all waste. Ivy could be thrifty in daily housekeeping but people's lives, you couldn't save those. But if words could have done it hers would have.

He'd stopped going to the Surf Club, though Ern Swann urged him to keep it up for Step's sake. He'd watched while his son was killed, all the cheerful holiday spectators watching the heroes perform, the danger of the sea important but supposed to be all so thoroughly under control, and suddenly it becomes real, they are watching the death of their son, friend, champion. You've got to snap out of it sooner or later, son, he said, you can't go on with your grief forever. Think what Step would have wanted. Ern was grey, gaunter, leaner, but he was still treasurer of the Surf Club. We need you, son, champions aren't that thick on the ground. But Ray wouldn't go back, though he kept on swimming, far out to sea until his lungs squeezed and his muscles ached, not the redness urging him on any further, the time he was living in had changed from red to something more like that dark stain in the transparent green water, a murky muddy purple, and it coloured the years from then on, a lot of years, until he was not far from thirty and got to go to art school.

THE SEA BREEZE

LARRY BUTTROSE

I was brushing my teeth when a pale, freckle-faced woman knocked on my compartment door. I recognised her, having seen her in a restaurant back in Mysore some nights before. Then she had been radiant in a lacy see-through blouse, her long red curls down, yieldingly soft and enigmatic, a high hippie queen and her court a cabal of chillum-smoking-velvet-vested-bare-chested Frenchmen in their later middle years. But now she looked fragile, her eyes puffy and pink. Her curls were worried, squashed down beneath a black beret.

'Hi. Do you have any Vitamin C tablets to spare? My sponge bag got ripped off with my passport back in Goa.' Her voice was soft and submissive, the sentence endings upturned. The accent was immediately Antipodean.

'I do actually,' I said. 'Please, come in.'

With a tired sigh, she entered and sat down on the vinyl

bench-seat. She introduced herself as Caetlin. Up close I saw a forty-ish face beneath the beret and curls, a pretty face, but losing out quickly to the South Indian sun.

'I also have some good sun blockout.'

'Do you?' She looked about distractedly. 'I've actually got some but I haven't had the mental space to use it. It's all been taken up avoiding a man.'

'Anyone in particular?'

'Oh, this Italian guy,' she said. 'You're Australian too aren't you?' I nodded. 'I met him in Goa.' She coughed harshly, her chest heaving. 'Sorry, my cold. And now I can't get rid of him.'

'You've been travelling together?'

'Travelling, smoking, fucking, driving each other crazy. I mean, he's really wonderful, Alfredo. But he's just too much, you know? Never sleeps. Never. Hyperactive. Manic depressive. Fucked up basically. Maybe *he* stole my Vitamin Cs.'

'Why should he do that?'

'They were with my dope and passport.'

'He stole them too?'

'Oh, I don't care. I only want him to stay away from me. Mind you, I wouldn't mind my passport back. Doesn't the bureaucracy here suck?'

We were getting close to Cochin now, and the train was travelling very quickly, as trains seem wont to do as the pull of the destination gets stronger. It was foggy and rainy outside, a blur of shabby grey–green. Schoolboys with black wet slicked-down hair waited impatiently on bicycles at barred rail crossings.

'But he'll come after me,' Caetlin went on. 'I know he will, bastard.' She glanced around quickly, as if posing for an unseen eye. 'You from Sydney?'

I nodded. 'And you?'

'Uh-huh.' She yawned. 'Nice of you to offer me the vitamins.'

'They must be here somewhere,' I replied to the prompt. I pulled my medical kit from my bag and opened it.

'I haven't been myself, haven't been taking care of myself. PMT, break-up, ripped off, period, flu,' she snuffled. 'I've just come from Poona. The Rajneesh place, you know. It's like a fucking concentration camp that place. They tell you what colour clothes to wear, when to eat, how to wipe your bum, everything. They censor the bloody mail. You have to have an AIDS test when you get there. When I first arrived I had to piss in the Non AIDS-Tested toilet. The place is run by these Germans. For Italians and Japanese really. Like a war reunion or something. There's no Australians there. They couldn't hack it. I had to wear a pair of maroon bathers or they wouldn't let me swim in the pool. I spent so much fucking money and I don't even know why I was there. No, yes I do. I was there to get a salad. You can eat the salad there, tomatoes and lettuce, washed in filtered water and made up by people with these plastic gloves on. That's what Rajneesh is good for, the only safe salad in all of India. But you know what? I still got sick there anyway. Vomiting. Shitting. It's where I met Alfredo.'

'Didn't you say you met him in Goa?'

'That was the second time I met him. First time it was in Poona. Then in Goa. I see him all the time. He's everywhere. Probably on this train.'

I laughed, but she lowered her voice.

'No, I mean it. He's near. I know he is. I can feel his presence. The countryside is lousy with him.'

I handed her the vitamin bottle, and she spilled out a handful of tablets and pocketed them.

'My real problem is I broke up with this guy just before I left home,' she said. 'We'd been having a really good relationship, just really nice. I was taking him through the whole process. Full initiation. Kundalini energy, Tantric sex, the lot. And then he goes up to Cairns and just fucks this fucking Brazilian woman there. Totally blows it.'

'How long were you seeing each other?'

'Weeks, months,' she shrugged. 'We were just so compatible. That's the really, like, galling thing about it. I was so pissed off that he fucked it up. So now I'm just cruising, just enjoying being in India. Slowing right down.'

The train also seemed to be slowing, entering a big town of some sort. 'I think we might be coming into Cochin.'

'Ernakulam,' Caetlin said. 'Not Cochin. They're twin towns. The station's in Ernakulam.' She drew a quick breath. 'Did I tell you I saw The Mother last week?'

'I thought she was dead.'

'No, no, that's the *Pondicherry* Mother. The French one. This is the *Indian* Mother. You really should meet her. She lives right here, in Cochin. You'd like her. There isn't anything she can't give you. She told me my new show's going to be a success. She says to me, The Mother, just complete it and it'll be a big success. All I have to do is just keep painting. Her ashram, it's vibrating with this awesome God Consciousness. Before I got to talk with her I was sitting outside her little, like, hut. And I was thinking she doesn't love me any more because of this guy back home, you know the one who fucked things up with the Mexican bitch in Cairns . . .'

'Didn't you say she was Brazilian?' I heard myself quibble again.

'. . . and I was thinking how he'd, you know, filled me up with all this darkness? But, The Mother, she *knows* everything that's going on in my head . . . and she *knew* I was still carrying it all around inside me, all this fucked up darkness, and she told me my problem was lack of awareness, right? Over the initiation I did with the guy? That I shouldn't have done that? That I shouldn't have gone through with it because it was wrong for me to do that initiation, because I'm not a guru? Which is fair enough – I'm not. I'm an artist. But because of all this I was thinking she didn't love me any more, right? So I was deeply depressed. Then, you know what? She called me right back in, she just smiled at me, and gave me a *lot* of attention. You see, she *knew* what I was going through. And I asked her if I should go with her on this, like, pilgrimage she goes on up to Calicut? And she said yes I should go with her if I want to. So that's why I'm here. And I should be really happy but I'm actually really fucking tense because I don't want to run into that cunt Alfredo again. And now I have this cold. And I really appreciate you giving me your Vitamin Cs by the way . . .'

She stopped. 'Oh shit, there, you see, I've done it again.'

'What?'

'Spent ten straight minutes just talking about me all the time. What about you?'

'What about me?'

'What are you doing in India?'

'Just travelling.'

'Alone?'

'Yes.'

'By choice?'

'Not entirely.'

She nodded. 'Uh-huh.'

With a sudden harsh braking we were pulling into Ernakulam Station, and with a gasp that she had to rush back to her compartment and collect her bags, Caetlin was gone as quickly as she had come.

I was intrigued to see Kerala, touted as it was as an ideal coconut state, a happy and bizarre collision of Hinduism, Islam, Christianity and Marxism. As the taxi rolled out over a series of bridges across natural and man-made islands towards Fort Cochin, an Indian Venice of sorts revealed itself. The hammer and sickle symbol was all about, on signs, banners and bunting, stencilled on roads, the walls of houses, but just as common too were temples, mosques and churches. The driver continually honked, just avoiding a column of oncoming trucks garlanded with flowers and emblazoned with signs declaring allegiance to some movie star, to the Virgin Mary or Joseph Stalin.

Cochin Harbour was deep and handsomely wide, most of its scattered green islands inhabited, but some apparently not. The tropical waters shaded down to cobalt-blue, and as the taxi pulled up on the foreshore out at the old Fort I saw a tall white ocean liner, a single tug in its train, making stately progress down the narrows of the main channel towards the green enclosing folds of the harbour.

I took a room in an alley near the Church of Saint Francis, and made a sortie to see da Gama's tomb before returning to sleep an hour or two that became three. Thus it was mid-afternoon before I found my way to the Sea Breeze, a restaurant on a headland with views up and down the shipping channel where scrubby ferries plied and high-prowed fishing smacks traipsed. As I entered, I could not help but notice Caetlin, in a long and billowing scarlet silk shirt, alone at a table writing with fierce attack into an antique leather-backed journal. She happened to glance up, and saw me.

'Oh, look, sorry, do you mind if we don't sit together right now? I can't really talk. I've just *got* to get these ideas down for my next solo exhibition, and you know what it's like when people interrupt and want to talk? I'm sure you understand. You do, don't you?' She looked about. 'Oh, fucking Alfredo's going to find me here, I just know he will. Bastard.'

After a few more minutes, I managed to extricate myself and sat at a table on the other side of the room. A waiter came and I ordered a *thali* – the South Indian staple of assorted vegetarian dishes and *dhal* served in little pots on a platter with rice and *chapatti*. Next to me a group of Germans joked across a table cluttered with empty Kingfisher beer bottles, while directly opposite me an obese Englishman, a fiftysomething cetacean in sandals, toyed with a bright-eyed Indian boy who had somehow strayed into his clutch.

The Englishman was loud in mid-complaint to the waiting staff, that he had not received the four eggs he had ordered for his breakfast, one entire meal back. He threatened to deduct these lost eggs 'orf' his lunch bill if they were not immediately 'supplied'. This little sideshow went on for some time, the words 'four eggs', 'deduct' and 'ets just the prenciple of the metter' loudly repeated by him at regular intervals and overheard by the other patrons, none of whom tried to hide their amusement. The Englishman finally got his way, received a compensatory deduction from his bill of a few rupees, and promptly ordered a celebratory tumbler of milk for himself and an ice-cream for the boy. As he toddled off later, arm draped proprietorially about the child, I wondered whether the kitchen staff hadn't spat into his milk.

My *thali* arrived. I ate slowly, sipped a cold Kingfisher. The lunch crowd thinned out until there were only a few other patrons left. One was a pink–blonde German woman who sat alone and lonely, forlornly drunk. Well on her way to sixty and obviously once quite beautiful, she was now very much a wilting bloom, if not actually dropping the petals. She had bailed up one of the waiters, an attentive, sparrow-like old man, and held him in her captive orbit while she recounted the woes of the world.

'I am not a happy person. I am wealthy, yes. But not

happy.' Her worn grey eyes looked up at him, demanded a response.

'I am sorry to hear that madam.'

'I will never be happy, not in this lifetime.' She drained her glass. 'Four or five lifetimes, then maybe I am happy.'

She watched a dirty little freighter chug down the channel while she forcibly retained the old man's attention. 'You do believe in reincarnation don't you?'

'Pardon madam?'

'Pasht lives.'

'Yes madam.'

Her lips twisted in a smile, and a claw clutched his arm. 'You don't want me to die, and be re-born as a dried-out camel in the desert do you?'

'No madam.'

'Then get me another drink. I'm thirsty.'

He turned to go, and the woman chanced to make eye contact with me. I watched her a half-moment. To be fifty-seven years old, drunk and alone at 3.30 p.m. in a tourist café, I thought, age holds such appalling potential.

She looked about blearily and spoke up loudly, not to me but to Caetlin in her blazing red silk on the far side of the café, still scratching frenziedly into her journal.

'And what is a young woman like you doing alone here in India, eh? What is wrong with all the men these days?' Her sideways glance alluded to me. Caetlin looked up, forced a smile, returned to her page. The German woman went on. 'I tell you. I tell you what's wrong with them. What has always been wrong with them. They are more interested in each other than us, and that is the truth.'

Her fresh drink arrived on the waiter's tray. She grabbed it, stood and turned sharply to me. 'And what do you think of that, young man? Do you think they are more interested in each other nowadays, the men?' She laughed harshly before I could speak, and raised her glass with a flourish. 'So here's to you men!' As she downed her drink, I saw a big tear glisten down her powdered cheek. Then a low howl erupted from her, and she doubled over in pain.

'Madam has had enough now I think,' the old waiter said, extending his arm round her quivering frame.

She did not protest as he helped her up. Caetlin glanced over and watched for a half-instant as the old man shepherded her out the door.

'Sad,' I said.

'Uh-huh,' she agreed. 'Such low consciousness.'

As I rose to leave, I glimpsed a male face she was sketching in violent, staccato thrusts into her journal.

'Oh, and thanks again for the Vitamin Cs,' she said, not looking up.

'I hope they did the trick.'

She nodded.

'So what did you think about what she said . . . about how men aren't really interested in women any more?'

'They're not, if you're like her.'

'You don't feel any pity for her?'

She looked up. 'Why should I?'

'But . . . isn't that what all this searching is meant to lead you to? Some kind of compassion?'

She shrugged. 'Look, I'm really sorry, but I've just

gotta keep working here. You understand don't you?'

The waiter came back in. 'The lady is alright now,' he said. 'She is sleeping.'

'You know her?' I asked.

'Oh yes, sir. She comes in every day. I think she stays nearby. It is a pity she must drink so much.'

'I'd like another coffee,' Caetlin said. And with a final worried scan around the room, went back to sketching her lost but ubiquitous Alfredo, his lean shadowed face like a gunslinger in a Wanted poster.

A moon a sliver short of full crowned the sky as I strolled the deserted alleys of the old fort town that night. I passed down twisting lanes between houses, two or three storeyed, sandy coloured for the most part, dogs asleep out front, goats and cats scouting the gutters. From the upper window of a hippie dosshouse came the closing chords to 'The Dark Side of The Moon'. A candle flickered up there. In a dormitory sack somebody, perhaps it was Caetlin, would be reading *The Celestine Prophecy*. A lazy cyclist passing a fraction too close by me whispered, 'Opium?'

DUST SLAPPED

NIKKI GEMMELL

Snip wakes from a fat sleep to the noise of a scrum of dogs tearing another apart. There's a protracted squeal amid a flurry of barks that rises to a sharp crescendo and then bluntly nothing.

Snip is in a room eight hours' drive from Alice Springs, a room with bulletproof glass in the windows and door. Outside is a post. YOU BIG RED HOLE is textaed strongly upon it. Snip rolls on her back and stretches and puts her hand between her legs.

Heat banks up at the windows, pressing at them, wanting inside. Snip puts out her hand to No Food, lying, at last, quiet by her side. His stomach heaves still, rattling with the pain. She wills his paw pads to stop weeping and grow back, she wills the skin on his raw haunch to close over. There's no change over the days. Just this lying.

And the light gone from his eyes.

Snip is slapped and streaked by red dust in this place, the tips of her fingers are valleyed as if all fluid has been drained from them, her long hair is weighted with smoke and dirt and wind, there are compacted crescents of dust under her nails, vivid accumulations between her fingers and toes, and in the palm of each hand a river map of ochre lines.

She's stinky in this place, sweaty and smoky. She's manless and motherless in this place. She's been ordered to come here.

The land where the light hurts is beyond the bullet-proof glass and beyond the bulletproof glass, touching lightly the earth of the Tanami Desert, is a scattering of houses and humpies. Four hundred or so Aboriginal people from the Walpiri tribe live on mattresses and blankets and bedframes around those houses. Thirty or so non-Aboriginal people live firmly within them, within barbed wire and mesh and bulletproof glass.

'Within the walls of a house you cannot see far,' says Queenie Nungala Mosquito, a person of this place. It's six hundred and fifty kilometres from Alice Springs. The only way to it is along a highway of sand.

The land where the light hurts is pushing changes upon Snip's body. Over the days the hairs in her nose are growing longer and fine furrows are coming upon the skin of her hands. A hide is thickening on the underside of her feet, a hide sliced with deep chasms on the side. Her walk is dropping to a slowness, there's a bowleggedness as if there's a rock between her legs. Her feet are leading, her back is following. It's stopping energy, she's been told, it's the Yapa way – the Aboriginal way – that way.

And in the oven-baked light, her eyes are narrowing thin to a line.

No Food's stomach still heaves. He barely raises his head from the floor for a feed, barely eats, barely licks Snip now. She rubs meat on his gums and feels his hot, sour breath on her hands. His paws are scabbing over but still he won't stand. People of this place tell her he'd be better off dead, that it's not right for a dog to survive like that.

Snip has been here six days or maybe eight or maybe twelve, she doesn't really know. It's just like the teenage Yapa kids of the community when they're asked their age – they say fourteen or maybe sixteen or seventeen, they don't really know.

And in the times before falling into sleep Snip takes out the memory of Dave like a box of chocolates hidden under her bed. She unwraps the clothes from his body. She curls her torso around the warmth of his sleeping back. She imagines taking his earlobe between her lips and sucking again at the softness, her tongue playful with his loop of gold. He's under her skin and he won't let her go. In failed love, her mother had whispered to her once, lie the seeds of madness. It's in her journal, ten years back, the whispered warning. If she could run a razor along her veins and pour Dave out of her, Snip would. He whispers and sings and calls through her blood.

And it was only four days, and she doesn't know why, and she doesn't recognise the pull. She can't paint with the mind-clot of Dave. And the anger over his gift of the dog. And her helplessness. She can't fix No Food, she can't seek revenge, she can't go back to that roadhouse place. Because she knows that's what those three men are waiting for.

Snip feels damaged in this place.

'You take me hunting, Napaljarri? In your big car?'

Snip's called Napaljarri and she's a woman of value in this place, because she's a woman with a bush-bashing car.

'Napaljarri?'

The sharp shout skids across the dust of the street.

'Yehwah, I take you hunting.'

Snip yells back to the humpy. 'Later later.'

Later this afternoon or tomorrow or the next one again, it's the Yapa way that way. Just like later later she'll see Bud because that's why she's back in this place. Later later is the rhythm of this place.

The last time Snip was in the community, a year ago, she was frozen out. She took some Yapa ladies out hunting a long way with Kate. The minibus they were driving in got bogged. Snip and Kate and the Yapa women got out and the Yapa women looked at the white women and nothing was said.

Snip got down on her knees by a tyre.

Kate grabbed at the shovel, viciously, in a huff.

The two of them started digging, cross that it was the white women, once again, doing the work.

They dug the bus out.

As they all drove back a silence that was deeply wrong

settled on the white women, thick. They got back into the community and the Yapa women didn't smile as they said goodbye to them, they averted their eyes. It was three days before Kate and Snip were told the reason they weren't helped: because the white women were digging into the surface, they were breaking the soil, of another tribe's land.

Kate's mortification was so swamping she's never been back to this place. 'I'll never understand,' she said. 'Their lives and their beliefs are too complex and secret for me, I'm sick of crashing like a bull into all that. I don't mean to, but I do.'

Snip has returned to hunt Bud down. She's returned to a gentle, warm welcome from the women of this place.

'Napaljarri, my daughter,' said Queenie Nungala Mosquito in welcome, hitting Snip on the cheek with the softness of a whisper on the day she came back. And as always, Snip is astonished at the generosity and the capacity for forgiveness in the people of this place.

No Food is to stay firmly indoors in the place that Snip is houseminding. She doesn't risk him among the dogs and the heat and the dust of outside. On his blanket by the door his stomach strains and his tongue lolls still. Snip refuses the rifle proffered her by Kevin, a keen-eyed neighbour.

'He'll come to. I just know it.'

Ferociously willing it.

When Snip wakes early in the mornings, to get away from No Food's listless paws and rasp, she goes outside and walks by mattress huddles and blankets and sleeping people and watching dogs. She walks by bush-bashed Falcons and utes. By the boarded-up community hall with the sign 'Hard Rock Cafe' skewed across its mouth. The missionary house, skull-hole gapped where windows and doors should be. By a car-crammed mechanic's compound with petrol pumps out the front, snug in their coats of mesh. The art centre that is hand-stamped and paint-dotted to head height. The health clinic, windowless, the store, windowless, the church, windowless. She walks by wrong trees planted by missionaries and as the desert laps at the edges of people she walks by flaccid silver bellies of cask wine, bleached-to-silver beer cans, a gutted television, and a graveyard of cars that has somewhere in there the Valiant Regal that first brought her to this place twenty-three years ago and then stopped.

Snip walks beyond all that to a place where she knows there's nothing but bush sapped of colour, stretching ahead of her to the sky.

She pulls off her pants and squats and pisses strong and hot like a horse. Foamy rivulets run in unruly streams from beneath her and she widens the gap between her feet and widens the gap again. The smell of wet hitting dirt replicates in a tiny way the storm smell of the roadtrip and plunges her back to the nag of Dave. To his earlobe and his loop of gold and his crooked nose and his sifter's hands and the softness of his neck as she held her face to it.

The fizz of piss splashes Snip's boots in the thick of the thinking and she curses the sky with a very loud 'Fuck'. Works her feet into the sand, wiggles her boots clean as she furiously thinks. Maybe he's with her so much because he was the one who did the leaving. She's not used to that.

A thin blade of a leaf is Snip's toilet paper. She flicks herself dry and tickles her clit. She stands and drops her skirt and plumes dust over the spreading damp as ants rush to worry the rim. She walks to a river gum and runs her hand across its shiny skin that's broad as a person's back and slides into a sit with her own back leaning against it and stares for a very long time at the great stretch of blue arching above and around her, at the shin-bone beauty of a lone ghost gum against a reddened hill, and she lets the spreading slow push through her, she lets stop wash over her like a cool bath after a sticky-hot day, she lets stop like a tonic flood through her. She's come to this place not only to find Bud but to lose roads paved with bitumen and skies of thick cloud and now, after six days or maybe eight or maybe twelve, they're nearly gone. The last swag stop and job interview and order pad are almost wiped out.

In readiness for Bud Snip's head has to be rested and clear. She rolls the instructions in her head like wine in her mouth – *hunt him down*. The words hold a fury or a playfulness and she doesn't know which. Their meaning she cannot dissect.

She's here to find out.

Snip closes her eyes and the shapes of gum-leaves murmuring above her glow yellow and red in her lids, and for now Bud can wait. He's out of town, in Alice or Darwin or the Kimberley she's been told, and it's not known why or when he'll be back. Snip knows it won't be serene when she finally gets to him. Under the sky and the tree the stopping seeps through her and it has the sweet coolness of soft mud and she lets it stay, for a long time, because she knows it's a rareness to be savoured.

THE IMMOLATING NUN

RAIMONDO CORTESE

To His Most Christian Holiness Pope Sigismondo Malatesta:

It first happened almost imperceptibly and, what was most surprising of all, it happened when one would have least suspected it, during that infinitely pious occasion: morning mass. Myself, along with all the other nuns, had assembled in the aisle for the rite of processional thurification when Sister Carmella from the Order of Our Lady of Perpetual Solicitude and Grace diverted her eyes from the clay feet of the Blessed Jesus and, like a tentative butterfly, settled them briefly on the face of Father Roberto.

Now I should mention at this point, though I have no desire to tarnish the exemplary character of Father Roberto, nor to petition Your Holiness for segregation of the sexes, that the priest had been glancing more than curiously in young Carmella's direction throughout the

174

ceremony. No sooner had her vision alighted on him than her pale and pretty cheeks veritably blossomed with violet.

We had never seen our devout Sister afflicted like this before and the spectacle came as a shock to us all. Her reaction may seem a trifle oversensitive to Your Holiness, but one has to appreciate that poor Carmellina was born into an impoverished peasant family, which lived and worked on Duke Bentivoglio's large estate, near the village of Ascoli Piceno. As Your Holiness is aware, this quaint though otherwise unremarkable village has derived some degree of notoriety through the painting by the Venetian master Tiziano Vecellio which depicts the brutal vanquishment of its ancestral women (I refer of course to the Sabines) by Roman soldiers all those years ago. This cruel violation of innocent flesh has left a certain mark of reserve in women from this area to this very day, a mark that was acutely pronounced in Sister Carmella.

She possessed an unsurpassed chastity, even by convent standards! Imagine it, Your Holiness! Carmellina was completely ignorant of the baby-making mystery that occurs between married men and women. Sister Cruda took it upon herself to enlighten Carmellina with a basic understanding of this 'delicate' procedure, to insure against her falling prey to the evil designs of male lust – made so plausible in that story by Boccaccio, where the man deceives a poor girl into believing that his devil will be the bane of all goodness unless he forces it back into her Hell. Most girls are thankfully familiar with this story, and are suitably wary of such a deception. But not our dearest Sister.

'I simply don't believe it!' Carmellina said. 'How can you even suggest they have such a thing? Where on earth could they keep it? Surely I would notice! Anyway, I've already been warned all about it. The miracle of conception happens when a man whispers certain words into a woman's ear.'

'But Carmellina dearest,' replied Sister Cruda, 'no man ever made me pregnant in this fashion, and may God never will it so!'

'That's because our habits block our ears!' Carmellina said. 'Why do you think we wear them at all times?' After that she would countenance no further conversation on the subject.

Carmellina suspected that all men were innately guilty of lewd intentions. To avoid what she called 'aural procreation' she deigned never to go near a man if she could help it. Not even Bishop Bruno, the reverent old Dominican from Faoli, was permitted to give her communion without first passing the Eucharist to another nun, who then placed it on Carmella's tongue. I often observed that whenever a priest, and on one occasion a boy of fourteen, chanced to walk by, Carmella would quickly avert her eyes until the man was safely in the distance.

This typical reaction cannot be dismissed as hysteria. If the truth be told, our darling Sister was not only innocent, she was also beautiful beyond earthly belief. No priest, bar the blind, could ignore her exquisite beauty if he chanced to see her, a beauty that was all the more intensified by her innocence.

So one must never lay blame at the foot of Father

Roberto. He was a novice at our Church of Saint Beatrice, and quite obviously stunned at seeing Carmella for the first time. I'm certain that he was only glancing at her in disbelief. I happened to be standing next to her and saw for myself the startled expression on his face.

But Carmella's fiery blush was the first sign of what was to come.

The next sign appeared one Saturday afternoon at bathing time. We usually availed ourselves of the bath house in groups of five to save firewood, but Carmella was far too modest for that. Nobody had seen her naked, except of course her mother, but only before Carmella was three. She was so shy she worried that the saints might be able to see through her undergarments.

'Naturally, it is all right for God to do so. He is incapable of sin,' she politely bade us remember. 'But the saints were all too human once.'

'But Carmellina,' I protested, 'they are in paradise. Surely up there they only have good thoughts?'

'Then how do you explain how Lucifer fell from heaven?'

'He became envious of God's love, by all accounts.'

'But he was an angel, was he not? The saints must be fallible also, Sister Bernada, and temptations of the flesh are the hardest to resist.'

Carmella bathed alone in a nearby river. I was returning with a group of nuns from Saturday afternoon horseriding lessons when we came across her drying herself in the sun and wind. This may seem slightly anomalous to Your Holiness, but our caring Sister believed, as we all do, that natural things are made by God and are therefore pure, while cloth is made by men's hands and is therefore impure. And so she chose instead to use the evaporating influence of the elements.

When she saw us approach, she instantly stood up in dismay. I noticed a discharge of what I assumed was steam rising from her lovely black hair. But as the horse drew closer – the beast couldn't resist and pulled on the reins – I realised beyond a doubt that the steam was in fact smoke.

After that Carmella began to smoke regularly. Knowing how sensitive she was, and not wishing to aggravate the situation, I pretended not to notice when smoke billowed from the top of her head.

It was around this time that she also began to set fire to some of the things she touched. Nothing terribly important, Your Holiness. Just a few odds and ends. Napkins, letters, rosary beads, prayer books, unconsecrated hosts, and candles had the habit of igniting whenever her sleeve brushed past. Carmella became increasingly distressed and kept to herself. I often heard the poor darling crying as I passed her door at night.

We decided to clear her room of anything flammable: all the furniture, the drapery, her vestments, her ecclesiastical texts, even the poor girl's bed linen. Her existence became even more ascetic. She slept at night under a rough leather blanket, and was provided with a special diet of nuts and carrots which her mouth still managed to burn to a cinder.

What could we do! All the Sisters were at a loss on how to proceed.

'Perhaps you should consult a physician,' we suggested.

'No, absolutely not! I'm atoning for my sins and that's all there is to it!'

'Really Carmellina, sweet child, what sort of sins could you possibly be talking about?'

But there was nothing we could do to persuade her. We decided it was best to drop the subject for good and hope instead that her condition would vanish of its own accord. Many nights were exhausted praying on her behalf.

Still Carmella grew anxious that she was becoming a bit of a nuisance. Against the wishes of the Mother Superior, she confined herself to her room, interrupting her voluntary incarceration only to fulfil certain appointed tasks as dutifully as before: picking the grapes, washing all the dishes, participating in the liturgies, the sabbatical rites of penance and flagellation, the venerable custom of painting the tree-trunks yellow, a duty she performed with particular relish.

She also continued to play the many leisurely games of which nuns are fond. Cards, hopscotch, hoop races, animal imitations, that sort of thing. It was possible to trace her precise movements throughout the convent by the trail she left of tiny footprints composed of fine white ash.

The gravest problem arose from the interminable smouldering of her leather garments. Whenever she entered the House of Our Lord, as inconspicuously as possible, mind, the priests persisted in turning around. Some actually whispered to one another. Her beauty was enhanced by the melliferous odour, not dissimilar to frank-incense, that enveloped her being. It must have been a miracle (strictly a colloquialism, Your Holiness, I would never wish to overstep my jurisdiction by suggesting such a phenomenon) that her skin and hair remained intact.

The priests uniformly swooned as she passed, so irre-sistible was the virginity of her scent. Their indiscretion, however, always precipitated a further exodus of smoke. Enormous clouds burst forth, causing everyone to splutter and flee the church for want of air. On one occasion she also set fire to a pew and scorched several nuns who rushed to her assistance.

It soon became impossible for Carmella to comply with her ordinances. She completely withdrew into solitary con-finement, and received raw carrots, potatoes, nuts and freshly mixed dough under the portal. She abstained from wine, unless for communion which she admitted daily. To this end, myself and Bishop Bruno devised a simple strat-egy. He blessed the host and passed it to me, whereupon I would call out to Carmella. The sweet girl would then poke her tongue through the spyhole. As soon as she felt the miracle of Jesus touch her flesh, she snapped it up before it roasted to nothing.

Unfortunately, and it makes me angry to even think about it, some of the altar boys who accompanied our reverend Bishop were at that age when nature transforms them dramatically and they obviously fancied themselves satyrs. Whenever my back was turned, they began to leer at her nakedness through the spyhole.

'I've heard them, Bernada. They stand there breathing

coarsely and make brutish noises,' Carmellina confided to me one morning.

A few days later, all this proved too much for our Reverend Sister. She screamed and simultaneously exhaled a tremendous flame, which completely destroyed the east wing of the convent, but through divine providence caused no loss of life.

The accident created a very awkward position. Nobody wanted to see Sister Carmella leave but she was placing us in danger. By now she was living outdoors, in a secret part of the convent gardens. She had no alternative but to roam about naked. Anything that touched her skin burst into flames, including armour and clay. Only a select few entrusted with her care were permitted access to this enclave.

Some difficult decisions were called for. One of the elderly Sisters proposed the brilliant solution of housing her in a special iron shed by the river, to be constructed well away from the vineyards. That way she could keep cool in summer and douse her flames in water whenever necessary.

Life for once seemed to be quite tolerable for the sweet girl. She made merry with rabbits, trying all the while to resist patting them, chatted to butterflies and beetles, prayed to the Holy Trinity and the Virgin Mary on her special rock, and sang in accompaniment to the wind. Her lifestyle must have been similar to Christ in the wilderness (though I gasp at drawing such a comparison), or Eve before she got obsessed by that apple. Each day a nun was assigned to provide her with food. We also took it in turns to maintain a constant guard, and frequently intercepted intruders who desired to follow her little white footprints.

Carmella ceased to be a drain on our resources. In many ways she was very helpful. Whenever she bathed in the river, no doubt to remove the ash and mud smeared over her body, a number of fish were boiled, and one of the nuns would gather them for supper. She also spent several hours a day, Your Holiness, praying for our sins and wishing good upon the Earth.

The Terrible Thing happened when, in our folly, we permitted the annual liqueur and cheese seminar to convene at the convent. Eighty or so tipsy priests from the local diocese poured into the garden during their lunch-break. A minority of them devilishly conspired to hunt out Carmella's hut. I must have sensed danger, for I ran out to see what was happening. It was too late. They had stumbled across Carmella praying, her body naked as the tree that loomed above her. The priests encircled her, urged on by their lust.

Poor Carmella turned around and immediately stood up, not knowing that certain parts of her body were more shameful than others. She revealed all to the priests. Her skin turned crimson and sweated smoke. Tears steamed from her eyes. The priests (and I must confess I was equally affected) became as beings possessed and moved closer towards her.

Flames began to pour from all sides of her body. Suddenly she erupted with a blinding radiance. Five seconds later nothing was left. Her presence in this world was reduced to a burnt patch on the ground, which still persists to this day. As you are aware, Your Holiness, this place has already been consecrated with a stone. Her departure for Heaven has been engraved as 8 August 1532.

On behalf of the Sisters of the Order of Our Lady of Perpetual Solicitude and Grace and the Church of Saint Beatrice, I submit and implore Your Most Christian Holiness to preside over Sister Carmella's official canonisation and to declare that the eighth day of the eighth month be set aside for festivities and prayer.

Your humble and obedient servant,
Sister Bernada D'Appugli

ANZAC DAY

MATT DRAY

Sebastian Capilano loitered in the empty quadrangle with five sets of keys jangling in his breast pocket. His eyes scanned the area for any vehicle that matched one of them.

He was trying his best not to look conspicuous but that was a difficult task as the college was still basically deserted. Most of the boarders would not be returning from vacation for several hours at least.

He checked his watch. It was a quarter past eleven. They were behind schedule already and he still hadn't found a car. Dumasis, Miller and Daley were waiting for him just outside the main gate. He'd told them he'd only be five minutes but it was now close to thirty.

He saw Miller standing in the shadows of the tenth grade classroom block, frantically waving at him. Sebastian resisted the temptation to jog straight over and kept walking in his original direction until he reached the seclusion of the junior dorms. He changed tack and raced over to Miller, who had the look of a man with things to do, people to meet, all packed up and raring to go.

'What's goin' on, Flea?' asked Miller.

'There's no cars around, Danny.'

'What about the Mazda near the library?'

'Crowley just parked it there a minute ago. He'll know it's gone.'

'Fuckin' hell!' Miller stood and thought for a second. 'Right. Don't worry about it. Go out to the gate and tell those other two to wait.'

The Flea walked to the main gate, slightly chagrined. He spied Brad and Luke nearby, looking decidedly edgy.

'What's the crack, Flea?' Daley asked, doing his best to sound casual. He couldn't believe he'd let Miller talk him into this scheme in the first place and was quietly relieved to see Capilano turning up empty-handed.

'I don't think we can get a car. They're all taken.'

Daley breathed easier. Perhaps they'd all see sense now and just take a bus into town to see a movie.

'Where's Danny?' asked Dumasis.

'Dunno. I think he's still looking.'

'Well, if he's not here in two minutes, I'm going into town. Bugger this for a game of soldiers,' announced Daley.

'Steady on,' said Dumasis.

'Hey! You've only known him two months. I've had to put up with him for four years. He's all talk.'

'Fair enough,' replied Luke. 'If you want to go, go.'

'Don't worry, I will. He's got ninety seconds. How about you, Flea?'

'Ohhh. Geez, Brad,' implored The Flea. 'Give him a chance.'

'You blokes are kidding,' said Daley. 'There's no way we'll pull this off.'

A horn tooted behind them and they turned to see Miller sitting behind the wheel of the school mini-bus. Daley swore under his breath and climbed into the back with Dumasis. Miller moved into the passenger seat and let The Flea take the wheel.

'Get onto Gympie Road, Flea, and then take the Bruce Highway to Pomona,' instructed Miller. He adjusted his sunglasses and put a U2 cassette in the tape deck.

'Pomona? Where's that?' asked Daley, not really wanting to know the answer.

'Ohhh, about a hundred and fifty clicks away.'

'*What*?? You're bullshitting me, aren't ya?'

'Hey! Hear me out. There's an RSL there that just goes off on Anzac Day. Everyone goes there and they hold the biggest two-up game you've ever seen out the back.'

'I've never been to a two-up game,' argued Daley.

'Well, you'll love this then.'

'Bloody hell, Danny. We'll stick out like a greyhound with three nuts in this rig. You're just asking for trouble. We're stealing a bus. Don't you realise that?'

'Listen!' said Miller, turning around to face Daley. 'If I knew you were going to turn into *Jiminy fuckin' Cricket* the moment we got out the gate, I would've left you behind. Now short of crying tears of *blood*, I have done

everything in my power to get this little venture off the
ground and I *DON'T* wanna hear about all the bad things
that just *might* happen. There's a good chance we just
might enjoy ourselves. Think about it.'

'We should've brought Crusty along,' said Dumasis,
referring to Mick Warner, an old retired Brother who
rarely went out much.

'Listen to this, Flea,' said Miller, his patience wearing
thin. 'We've got Mahatma Gandhi riding with us. Bugger
me dead, Dumasis. You think Crusty didn't get up to this
sort of thing when he was our age? Stop thinking about
everyone else for once. If you want to worry about someone,
worry about me. You think my life's a bed of fucking roses?'

'Actually I do.'

'Ohhh leave me alone. What would you know? Just
once I'd like to soar like an eagle. Can't you turkeys appreciate that?'

'Do you want me to pull in for petrol?' asked The Flea.
'We've only got a third of a tank.'

'She takes diesel, Flea, and no, I don't wanna pull in.
We're late already. We'll fill up on the way home.'

'Have you got enough money?' asked Daley.

'Don't worry yourself, Jiminy. I've covered every emergency. You all owe the kitty ten bucks. And that's another
thing. When we get to this joint, don't start drinking like
there's no tomorrow. We've all had sheltered lives, it's
nothing to be ashamed of, so don't start getting pissed to
prove yourselves. A few beers and that's it. Agreed?'

'Yes Dad,' they answered.

The Returned Services League in the heart of the small town of Pomona was a rustic old building that rarely saw more than a dozen patrons at its bar at any one time. Except on its one day of the year when ex-servicemen came from all over the south-eastern corner of Queensland to remember those who hadn't made it home and drink and laugh and bet with the ones who had.

The crowd that swarmed around the front and back bars was ninety-nine per cent male. As well as ex-diggers, there were others there from all walks of life. Bikies wearing their colours rubbed shoulders with cattlemen and farmers who'd come in for the day. Football players from a local club slowly made their way through the crush selling tickets in a meat raffle and the next raffle to go off was to be run by the surf lifesavers.

Cigarette smoke hung in a thick haze above the heads of the mob, the ceiling fans making no impression on it what-soever, and although no music was being played, everyone had to raise their voice to be heard when they spoke.

Miller sidled up to Dumasis and gave him a mischie-vous grin. 'Well you can . . .' he threw four pelvic thrusts into Daley's backside '. . . me if I'm not havin' a good time. What about you, big fella?'

'Yeah, Dan, you've done well,' said Dumasis, not wanting to burst Miller's bubble. He wasn't enjoying it as much as Danny obviously was.

'I'll get the next shout,' announced Miller. 'The two-up's about to start.'

'Hey Danny. Be careful,' warned The Flea. 'The barmaids are asking for identification.'

'I don't need ID while I've got a tongue in my head,' replied Miller as he pushed his way through the throng. He bumped into a nineteen-stone bikie who was completely bald, causing him to spill his beer. 'Sorry, Kojak.'

Dumasis prodded Daley in the small of his back. 'Has he been drinking the same stuff as us?'

Daley turned to face him. His eyes were like road maps. 'Yeah. I think so. I should never have let him have that smoke with me.'

'Well, how do you feel?'

'I'm good,' answered Daley calmly. 'Glad I came.'

Shelley Brease worked as a casual barmaid at the Pomona Hotel and occasionally, like today, came over to give the RSL a hand. Shelley was thirty-eight years old and her bust size matched her age. Although nearing the mutton-done-up-as-lamb stage, she still turned her fair share of heads and most blokes wouldn't have minded doing a few steps of horizontal folk dancing with her.

She saw a young boy come up to the bar with a dimpled smile and a look about him as if he owned the place. If he asked for anything more than a glass of water, he was going to get thrown out on his ass. She went over and served him.

'What would you like, honey?'

'You with your clothes off for a start, sweetheart.'

The head barman raised an eyebrow. 'Nah. Just jokin'. My dad wants four beers.'

'Where is he?'

'He's over in the corner. He's only got one leg.'

Shelley studied the face.

'And I'll have a sarsaparilla for myself, thanks,' added Miller.

She began pouring the beers. 'Do you want a tray to carry them with?' she asked.

'That'd be great. You're not only a good sort but you're a lady as well.' Miller took the tray holding the drinks back to the boys. Luke drank the soft drink. The Flea drank Luke's beer.

The two-up ring chalked on the floor behind the back bar was surrounded by a five-deep circle of punters. An eighty-seven-year-old veteran of both World Wars flicked two pennies, marked with white crosses on the tails' side, with a short flat stick high into the air. The noise level rose and fell in time with the coins and then exploded aloud again as they landed on the concrete floor, both showing heads.

The Flea and Miller both squatted next to each other at the edge of the ring with almost two hundred dollars in a square marked with an H in front of them.

'Whaddya think, Flea? Beats jumping out of a trench and charging a machine-gun nest.'

'What?'

'This is why fifty thousand blokes bit the dust. So we could enjoy ourselves on days like this.'

'What'd you say?'

'Never mind.'

'Are we backing heads again?'

'Whatever you want mate. I'm just happy bein' here.'

Daley went to the bar and bought the fourth round of beers. He'd bought the third as well but Dumasis couldn't get served. The barmaid had seemed extra-friendly and he was looking forward to another opportunity of talking with her. He didn't take his eyes off her cleavage once while she served him and Shelley didn't mind that one bit.

'There you go, handsome.'

'Thanks Shelley,' replied Daley, handing the money over, a big grin spreading over his face. He hoped no one would notice the lump in his pants as he walked back to the two-up ring. Dumasis walked past him and was being chased by Miller.

'Mate! What's wrong? Where're you goin'?' asked Miller incredulously, grabbing Luke by the arm as he walked out the door.

'Nothin'. I'm just getting some fresh air.'

'You're sure you're having a good time? 'Cause we'll all leave if you're not.'

Dumasis looked at Miller and smiled. He knew the offer was an empty one, at least Miller would be hoping it was.

'No mate. This is great. I'm just gunna take it easy. Remember what you said about going easy on the piss?'

'Ohhh. Yeah. Fair enough mate. We'll only be another half-hour anyway. It's getting close to five o'clock.'

'I'll wait outside then.'

'Okay big fella. I better get out the back. The Flea's braining 'em.'

Dumasis walked out of the door. Miller returned to the two-up to resume the story he'd been telling a group of drinkers about how his father had been killed flying choppers in Vietnam, fourteen years ago.

Dumasis went down the street, feeling a little melancholy, and then sat on a park bench. Although it was autumn, the sun was still warm and he felt comfortable in the boardshorts and singlet he wore. He thought about the real reason he'd left. The barman had told him to go home and wait until all his pimples had dried up before coming back without any identification. He'd wanted to try buying a round, seeing as the other three had done so without any drama and now he had to swallow another helping of humble pie for his troubles. It was a petty little' incident, one that he knew he should just throw off, and the fact that he couldn't made him even more annoyed with himself.

He sat forward, resting his elbows on his knees and watched life pass him by. A car cruised slowly past and Luke saw the profile of a young girl in the back seat. She couldn't have been any older than nine or ten but she still struck him as breathtaking. As he watched, she turned around and looked back at him. His eyes followed the car as it travelled down the street then turned off and went out of sight. He suddenly felt very lonely.

The Flea stood in the middle of the two-up ring and pushed his glasses back onto his nose with trembling fingers. He'd thrown heads twice and he and Miller stood to win close to three thousand dollars if he could repeat the feat once more. He looked on in an almost dreamlike state as the rouseabout placed the two coins onto the small paddle and handed it to him. The noise reverberating in the huge room from well over two hundred revellers was almost deafening but he could still hear Miller shouting at him from the edge of the ring.

'Flea! Flea! Gold Coast! Escort girls! *You* are a champion! *You* can do this!'

The Flea shivered and tried to wipe the grin off his face but it wouldn't budge. He flicked the pennies and the crowd noise rose again as they twirled in the air and then hit the ground. The first coin hit the floor and showed heads. The other bounced across the ring and then rolled on its edge. It made a wide circuit and fell over. A white cross faced upwards. A re-throw would be needed, all bets froze.

'That's okay, Flea. You can do it maaaate,' encouraged Miller.

The Flea wiped his palms on his shirt as he waited for the stick to be loaded and given back to him. He looked over to his right and could just see Daley at the bar talking to the barmaid. The rouseabout handed him the stick and The Flea threw the pennies. Daley couldn't see what had happened from where he stood and didn't very much care. Miller watched as the coins bounced briefly and came to a stop in front of him. He and The Flea hadn't lost all day but two white crosses were staring up at him now.

Miller screwed his face up and spat out a couple of four-letter words. But he wasn't too upset. They'd drawn well over their quota of luck getting this far and not just with regards to the gambling. The Flea looked absolutely gutted.

'Don't worry about it,' consoled Miller. 'We've had a good time. What more could you want?'

'A dirty weekend at the Gold Coast,' answered The Flea.

'There'll be other days. Come on. We've gotta get home.'

They squirmed their way through the crush. 'C'mon Brad, we're goin',' said The Flea.

'Hey?' asked Daley. 'Hang on. I'm doin' all right here.'

'Please yourself but we're leaving now.'

Shit, thought Daley. He watched them leave.

'Hey Shelley,' he said as she walked past. 'Do you work on weekends?'

'Sometimes.'

'I might see you round then.'

'You might,' she smiled.

Too right I might, thought Daley. He left the bar and walked to the door. Pomona hadn't seen the last of him. 'Oi! You two!' he called as he stepped out into the street.

Dumasis was eating a bacon and egg burger on the step of the bus when they arrived. 'Are you up to driving, Flea? You look like the Knight Rider after his car's been stolen,' observed Miller. The Flea did not reply.

'I'll drive,' offered Daley.

'Yeah. Okay. Thanks Brad,' said The Flea vaguely. Five minutes ago he'd been on top of the world. Now the world was a terrible place. He had the head spins and his mouth was filling up with saliva.

'Can I have a bite?' said Miller.

Luke offered up his burger. 'You want to buy a few more for the trip?' he asked as Miller crammed as much of it into his mouth as he could before biting.

'I'm broke,' said Daley. 'How much money have you got, Danny?'

Miller was incapable of speech. He raised his palms outwards to indicate he had nothing.

'Flea?' asked Daley. The Flea was on his hands and knees throwing up round the back of the bus. He looked up and shook his head.

'What about you?'

'Twenty cents,' replied Dumasis.

'Well we'll just have to go hungry then,' said Miller as he swallowed the last of his mouthful.

Daley drove the bus down a couple of streets before reaching the highway. He checked the fuel gauge. It was just above empty.

'Have you still got money for petrol?'

'Diesel, Bradley. Diesel.'

'Okay then. Diesel. You've still got money for diesel?'

There was a long pause as Miller searched for the nicest possible answer. 'Not exactly.'

'What's that supposed to mean?'

'It means no, I guess.'

'Ohhh fuckin' hell, Danny. Geez you give me the shits at times.'

'Hey! Don't get up me. We could've hired a plane home if The Flea had thrown heads, the useless bastard.'

'Leave The Flea out of it. You said you'd set aside some money. Where is it?'

'Don't worry yourself. I've got a plan. Just keep driving.'

Miller's plan involved his grandmother, Ruby. She lived

on the outskirts of Nambour and he hadn't seen her in five years. He hoped she remembered what he looked like.

Daley parked the bus about a hundred yards down the street from her house and the three of them watched as Miller entered the front yard and knocked on the door. They saw him give them the thumbs-up just before he went inside.

'We'll be flat out getting home in time,' said Daley. 'He'd better not be long.'

'Fuck it. I should've thrown heads,' said The Flea.

It was almost an hour before Miller rejoined them.

'What've you been doing?' demanded Daley. 'It's half-past six.'

'Having a cup of tea.'

'Did you get any money?'

'No.'

'*What*!? What the fuck have you been doing in there then?'

'Ohhh mate. It was her wedding anniversary yesterday. I haven't seen her in years and she thought I'd remembered,' explained Miller. 'I couldn't ask her for money.'

'Get fucked Danny. You go back and ask her or I will.'

'Ohhh mate I can't.'

'You bloody can.'

'Take it easy, Brad,' said Luke. 'He can't do that.'

'Hey?' replied Daley. 'What's wrong with you pair? Don't you realise the trouble we'll be in?'

'Think of her. He's made her day. Don't spoil it.'

'Ohhh turn it up, Dumasis. We're in deep shit here. Surely you can see that.'

'Something'll come up mate. Don't worry about it,' soothed Luke. 'Just drive.'

'Yeah Bradster,' echoed Miller, gently touching Daley's arm. 'Something'll come up.'

'Don't touch me! Don't you ever fuckin' touch me again,' seethed Daley. He started the bus and drove off.

The service station looked about as decrepit as any building could possibly be without actually being abandoned. The windows that were still intact were opaque with dust and cobwebs, and the bowsers looked as ancient as the little old man seated in the canvas chair under the awning, quietly dozing. No lights were on and the occupants of the bus had a sneaking feeling that trading was finished for the day.

Daley brought the bus to a halt next to the diesel bowser, which was padlocked, and drummed his fingers on the wheel.

'That bloke looks like Danny DeVito,' said Miller, pointing at the person in the chair.

'Except he's got more hair,' said Dumasis.

'And he's a bit fatter,' added The Flea.

Daley climbed out of the bus and slammed the door violently. He couldn't think with those three morons going on about the similarities between two people they'd never met. He was obviously the only one who appreciated the graveness of the whole situation.

He walked over to the snoozing figure and tried to look and act as charming as possible. He was going to have to ask a complete stranger if they could fill their tank and then give him his word that they'd pay him back as soon as possible. He didn't like his chances.

'Gee. Brad's a bit upset,' observed Miller.

'He was feeling good a while back,' said Luke as they watched Daley and the old man, who must've been the owner, enter the building and continue talking.

'We should've been back at school five minutes ago,' pointed out The Flea.

'Ahhh. They won't mind if we're a bit late,' dismissed Miller. 'We're only an hour's drive away.'

They waited in silence as Daley kept talking. The look on his face when he returned didn't seem very uplifting.

'What's the crack, Brad?' asked Luke as Daley slumped into the driver's seat.

'Yeah Bradster. What's he gunna do?'

Daley breathed out slowly and looked down in his lap before looking at Miller and turning around to face the other two. 'Well, for a start, it's not a he, it's a she.'

'You're kiddin',' replied Miller before getting an attack of the giggles. It was infectious. The other two joined in. Daley did not. When he thought he had their attention again, he continued.

'She doesn't speak much English but from what I can gather, she understands our predicament and is willing to help us if we help her.'

'Hey?' said Miller.

'Well, Danny, she's a very lonely woman.'

Daley let it sink in and was glad to hear the giggling dry up.

'You're kidding,' said Miller, no longer smiling.

'I wish I was,' replied Daley.

'Bullshit.'

'Mate. She wants someone to go upstairs with her.'

'Gee whizz,' said Dumasis.

'Don't look at me,' said Miller. 'I'm not doing it.'

'Me neither,' cut in The Flea.

Dumasis said nothing but shook his head when Daley looked at him.

'I knew this'd happen,' said Daley. 'There's only one thing for it. We draw matches.'

The others looked around in disbelief. They made some noises but no one thought of a better idea.

'Yeah.'

'Okay.'

'Fair enough.'

Daley pulled a box of matches out of his pocket. He was extremely pissed off with Miller. If anyone had to volunteer it should have been him.

'I can't believe we're doing this,' said Miller, starting to cackle again. He thought it was funny already. Daley held four matches between his thumb and forefinger with only the heads showing. He offered them to Miller. 'The longest match has to do the deed.'

As Miller hummed and hahed over his choice, Daley gave Dumasis and The Flea a look. Miller pulled out his match. The Flea followed, then Dumasis, leaving Daley with only one. Miller was looking at his match the way a poker player studies his cards. Daley leaned back and snapped his match with his right hand behind his seat so Dumasis could see what he was doing. Luke followed suit and motioned to The Flea to do the same.

'Right. This is it,' announced Daley. 'Fair dinkum. No muckin' around or backing out. Whoever it is, gets in and does it. Okay?'

'Yeah.'

'Okay.'

'Right.'

They all compared matches and Miller couldn't believe what he was seeing.

'SHIT!'

'Tough luck, Dan,' said Luke.

'Yeah mate,' added The Flea.

'I wasn't ready,' spluttered Miller. 'That wasn't the match I wanted.'

'Of course it wasn't,' said Daley. 'No one wanted it.'

'No! I mean that wasn't the one I meant to pick. You rushed me.'

'No way, Danny. You said we all had to go along with it. Don't start your bullshit with me.'

'Ohhh. C'mon Bradster. Re-draw. I honestly wasn't ready. Honest.'

Daley sat and reflected for a minute. 'All right. But this is it,' he said, looking back at the other two sternly, as well as Miller. 'This one's for real.'

The other two grudgingly agreed on a re-draw. The Flea pointed out that the odds were now stacked in Miller's favour, the chances of him drawing the long match again being mathematically smaller.

'It's not fair on us.'

'Life isn't fair, Flea,' answered Miller as he chose

again. They picked their matches and compared a second time.

'FUCK IT!!' Miller threw his match on the floor in disgust. 'I can't believe this. What're the odds of that?'

'Don't worry about the odds,' said Daley. 'You're the man with the wheelbarrow. It's all in front of you.'

'One more time. Come on.'

'No way, Danny. That's it. You've gotta do it.'

'Come on, Danny. It won't be that bad,' added The Flea.

'Get fucked Flea! Come on, Brad. Please?' pleaded Miller with more than a hint of desperation in his voice. 'I can't do it.'

'You have to.'

Miller sat glumly in silence for a brief period. He was going to use his last get-out-of-jail-free card, no matter what embarrassment or shame it might cause him.

'Bradster. I'm a virgin.'

Daley began laughing. Miller's eyes were like a baby seal's about to be clubbed to death.

'I know you're a virgin,' he answered.

'Whaddya mean?'

'Ohhh fair suck, Danny. If you expect me to believe you popped your cherry in the first-class cabin of a jumbo jet with a six-foot blonde stewardess on a flight to Hong Kong, you must think I'm as thick as a post.'

'It could've happened.'

'Pig's ass.'

'Okay. Fair enough,' said Miller. 'But can you see where I'm coming from? The first time should be special.'

'Well I can't think of a more special time than now.'

'But I want it to be with someone nice.'

'She seems pretty nice to me,' said The Flea.

'Well *you* fuck her then. Anyway it's a mortal sin to have pre-marital sex.' It looked like a Mexican stand-off was going to develop. Miller was prepared to argue his case all night if he had to.

Luke spoke up. 'Listen Dan. I'd hate to do it if it was me but someone's got to. Now I don't wanna pull rank or anything but you drew the match. Be a man and face the music.'

'But – '

'Just do it!'

Miller slowly opened the door and got out of the bus. He walked into the service station like a man going to the electric chair.

'Geez, Luke,' said The Flea. 'I can't believe you made him do it.'

'Neither can I,' added Daley. 'What do we do now?'

'We wait,' said Dumasis.

They waited.

Dumasis was stretched out on the back seat of the bus. The Flea lay on the floor. Daley checked his watch and cursed. 'Hey Luke!' he shouted. 'What's he doing in there?'

'How should I know? What's the time?'

'Half-past eight.'

'Bloody hell. He's been in there over an hour.'

'Maybe he can't get it up,' suggested The Flea.

'Maybe they're still onto foreplay,' replied Daley. They all shuddered.

'Maybe he's shot through,' said Dumasis.

'Ohhh. He wouldn't have. Would he?' asked The Flea in a scared voice.

'Ohh no!' said Daley. 'That's it all right. The little bastard has shot out the back door. He's probably thumbed a lift down the road. I bet he's back at school already.'

'Ohhhhh shit. What'll we do?' wailed The Flea.

'Bugger it!' spat Daley hitting the steering wheel with his fist. 'I'll screw her. But make no mistake. When we get back, that little arsehole will pay for this. It's his fault we're in this mess and he's just left us high and dry. He's nothing but a yellow-bellied, green-eyed low-down little prick.'

'Hang on,' said Luke. 'Here he comes.'

'Ohh,' said Daley. 'Forget everything I just said.'

Miller approached them carrying a brown paper bag. He opened the door and slumped into the passenger seat.

'How'd you go?' asked Daley.

'Fill 'er up,' replied Miller, producing a key.

'You little *beauty*,' whooped Daley.

'Good on ya, Danny,' cheered The Flea.

'Yeah. Well done little man,' added Luke.

The three of them laughed as the bowser light came on. Daley undid the padlock and filled the tank. They left the key on top of the bowser. Daley climbed back in and started the bus.

'What's in the bag?' asked The Flea.

'She thought youse might be hungry so she made some sandwiches,' replied Miller wearily.

'You're a champion,' exulted Daley. 'I'm starving.'

'Give us one,' said Dumasis.

'They're all right,' said The Flea, devouring his. 'What about you, Danny?'

'I'm not hungry thanks.'

'You must've put in a decent effort to get these,' said Daley, reaching for another. 'What's on them?'

'I dunno. Some sort of canned meat.'

'You're a legend,' said Daley, turning out onto the highway.

'Yeah. Well ... You reap what you sow.'

Danny sat quietly in his seat. He'd made the sandwiches himself from the cat food he'd found sitting in a bowl, festooned with cockroaches. A chopped onion and lashings of tomato sauce made them edible.

'How was she?' asked Luke, swallowing the last of his sandwich and grabbing for another.

'She was no Brooke Shields.'

'How did you go?' asked The Flea.

'All right I guess.'

'Come on,' said Daley. 'Give us a blow by blow description.'

'Go to hell.'

'Maate.'

'Get fucked.'

'Just one word then. How was it?'

'TRAGIC,' said Miller. 'This has been the most tragic day of my life.'

'Did she get on top?' asked The Flea.

'Ohhhh. Please.'

'Is she on the pill?'

'What? Ohhh you're sick, Daley.'

'Hey! I'm just saying we could turn up at that servo again in a few years time and a little tragedy could be running around the bowsers.'

'She might even have twins,' said Luke.

'Hey you lot! That's enough. You bastards owe me. Remember that when I come to collect.'

'I can't drive,' said Daley. 'I think I'm gunna wet myself.'

'Ahhh what?' growled Miller. 'You want me to drive the friggin' bus as well? That'd be right.'

'It was your destiny,' said The Flea.

THE LAST DAYS OF SUMMER

PENNY FLANAGAN

In the dark of the living room, Margaret could see the green lights of the stereo glowing and blinking like a control deck. Adrian buried his face in her neck and held her firmly against him, swaying gently from foot to foot. If she tried to wriggle away he pulled her back, lifted his mouth to her ear and sang softly.

> *You will surely love again,*
> *You will sureleeeeeh love again,*
> *You're just waiting on a friend,*
> *To come and take you for a ride.*

When he came, Adrian thrashed around like a fish. Afterwards he curled himself around her, spooning his body against the curve of her back, fitting his knees into the bends of her legs, an arm across and around to cup one small breast with his hand as he fell asleep. Margaret drifted all night long through warm, restless sleep, dreaming lightly but always aware of him, locked into her shape behind, always knowing when he was asleep and when he was awake.

Sometimes he stirred and said, 'Kiss?' and she would turn her head and kiss him on the lips.

Sometimes he flipped over and said, 'Your turn,' and she would curl up behind him like a spoon. When she put her arm across he took her hand and kissed her knuckles before falling again into a heavy, rhythmic sleep. Once, when it was his turn to be behind, he said, 'Here's your little seat.' And when she bent herself into the shape of him she realised it was like sitting on a chair.

In the morning she didn't expect him to stay. When he got out of bed and then leant down to kiss her, she assumed he was making his exit. She thought about getting the Sunday papers, making herself a pot of Earl Grey tea and sitting in the sunny corner of the kitchen.

But he said, 'Will you sing for me now?' pulling his jeans on without undies.

'Don't be stupid.' Margaret rolled over with her naked back to him.

'Why won't you sing for me?' He struck a match, and the fresh burn of a cigarette cut through the slept-in air of the room to her nostrils.

'I'm not your monkey!'

'What's that s'posed to mean?' He laughed, climbed onto the bed on his hands and knees and caged her in. He blew a stream of smoke up to the ceiling and then arced the cigarette away, his arm stretched right back behind him, as though that would make it more acceptable.

'You can't just grind your organ and make me dance,' she said.

'I don't want you to dance, d'ling,' he said very precisely. 'I want you to sing.'

'Hey!' She pushed him away. 'No smoking inside!'

'Ooo – snaky!' He climbed off her, went over to the window and proceeded to smoke awkwardly from there, half leaning out, dropping grey ash onto the sill every few puffs and blowing white streams of smoke through the two-inch opening.

'And what does the day hold for you, my d'ling?' he asked as he carefully balanced the spent brown butt on its end, a little tower of grey ash still smoking just outside the window. He left it out on the sill like that and then persisted with the futile gesture of waving the last of the smoke out the window before sliding it shut.

'Not much,' Margaret tried for nonchalance. She didn't want him to feel obliged and had her mind set on spending the morning alone anyway.

'Have you got time for brekkie?'

'Yeah.' She smiled.

'Yay!'

It was the end of February and they spent the last days of summer chasing the sun round the rock platforms of Wylie's Baths. Each day they edged their towels forward, out of the growing shadow, so that by late afternoon there was nowhere else to go but the hot sundecks high above the pool. The decks caught the heat of the day and trapped it there in their wooden surfaces for hours, even long after the sun had disappeared behind the dress sheds. They would sit resting their backs against the timber walls, closing their eyes to the hot afternoon sun, or lying on the deck, peering through the gaps to the big green sea pool below.

Or lazy sun-soaked days lying side by side on the beach with the light hairs on their forearms just touching, diving into the cool turquoise ocean and then stumbling back to their towels, where they collapsed face down and let the sun dry a thin layer of salt across their skins. Adrian liked to stay baking in the sun for hours, and was determined to brown himself beyond the limits of his Caucasian genealogy.

After two hours Margaret, feeling the backs of her legs beginning to tingle, would say, 'Come on, let's go.'

'No ... please.' Adrian inspected the colour on his arms. 'Just ten more minutes.'

Margaret looked at him lying there. He was nut brown all over.

'Adrian, how brown do you want to be?' she said.

He sat up, looked around the beach and said, 'As brown as him,' pointing to a dark Puerto Rican man lying face down on the sand, his smooth Spanish skin the colour of a roasted coffee bean.

Margaret hadn't spent so much time under the summer sun since childhood when, blissfully ignorant of the growing hole in the ozone layer overhead, she and her sister would pass the entire school holidays lying by the side of the swimming pool, turning their soft girlhood skin from tender pale flesh to robust golden hides. In those days it was common for children to miss a day of school due to sunstroke, a feverish state caused by spending entire days unprotected from a native sunlight too harsh for pale colonial skin. Mainly it was caused by not wearing a hat: Margaret remembered the thin strip of scalp where her hair parted turning bright hot pink, and so much heat emanating from her skull that she had to stick her head under a cold shower to feel any kind of relief. And the peeling on her back and shoulders. The familiar itching sensation, then the bubbling skin before the top layer dried and flaked, peeling off in large sheets, to reveal brand-new pink skin like a baby's underneath.

When the spectre of skin cancer began to reveal itself, Margaret's mother was the first to slap large hats on her girls, slathering them all over with fifteen-plus sunscreen and trying to keep them indoors during the hottest part of the day. As a result of her mother's paranoia, Margaret hadn't lain out on a wide, hot stretch of beach, smack-bang in the middle of the day when the sun was directly overhead, since childhood. Mostly she went late in the afternoon, when the sun was pale and soft, and cool shadows had formed in the dents of the sand. Even then, she sat with her towel cloaked around her body and a wide-brimmed hat shading her face. But Adrian was reckless, and he dragged Margaret out of her room and into the bright sunshine day after day after day. He said to her, 'You worry too much,' and offered himself up to the Australian sun, as fearless as a child in the 1970s.

THE BOY,
SUMMER 1961

NICHOLAS JOSE

At fifteen Penny Tregenza was sent away to school. She didn't argue at the rupture. As a changeling child she never presumed to challenge her circumstances, accommodating herself to a world that proved to be home: Uncle Jack, the southern peninsula, the squat square house and the fat paddocks, the land's end and the little grey shack over-looking the bay; the faces old and young watching her sidelong, remembering, all her days; the weatherboard school where she was content to do well (without exertion), the girls who discussed boys incessantly, boys who never lifted a finger for the girls.

Because he had a wider view, Jack sent his girl to a ladies' boarding school in Adelaide where she would study for her Leaving Certificate. As the major influence on her life, he was aware of his own inadequacies. There were things only women could teach. Jack had overcompensated with love, and never knew that Penny prof-ited richer than rubies.

He chose the ladies' college as a cloister from the worst of what the city offered. He was wrong. The school's unexpressed purpose was to initiate girls to the dainty, perfumed rough-and-tumble of a lady's life. Snobbery, money, keeping up, grooming and deportment, the fear of plainness or oddness, sighting a prospect, chasing, clawing: such were the lessons learned.

Penny was not taken in. However, she could not read about life without becoming aware of danger as part of its stake. She discovered heroes and heroines – Cleopatra, Jeanne d'Arc, Napoleon, E. B. Browning – to be emulated in a girl's afterlife, in Adelaide, on a property, on the boul-evards of Paris or in the squares of London, for these were now places on her map.

The broadest horizon was still the bay. She got a prize for improvement at the speech day and afterwards Jack drove her home. The black road shimmered in the December heat, low eucalypts pressed towards her and golden paddocks of full-headed grain swam in her eyes. Soon she smelled the salt and saw the sandhills between road and shore. The track rose straight between long fences over a high sown hill, and at the top was the sweep of the bay with its contours of virgin blue and darker blue, a running fringe of white, and trawlers at rest in the jetty's lee. After being away she had points of comparison, words and images for a gentle shore that was paradise before paradise was ever heard of. Any visitor who did not feel the same had not grown up there from first breath, was not returning from an epic year in the crowded places of the world. Penny was half sophisticated now, bursting with the warm pulsation of air and cloud, paddock and mottled wave.

Jack had been lonely while she was away. He did not recognize the sluggish unhappiness that coiled around him that year. A kind of pining, unaware of its object, made him snap uncustomarily, like a dull drizzle that sets in for winter. At night he would use any groaning roof or whistling fence as an excuse for getting up and walking about in his pyjamas to frighten off the prowlers from his mind. To writhing in bed he preferred the quietened night world of stars or cloud; in the daytime he looked haggard to those who could see. That was when Jack Tregenza started to be old, wrestling at night with the angel of emptiness in his arms.

For Penny's return he repainted the woodwork in her room and put his best African violet by her bed. When she threw open her case, he wondered if he would have to make extra shelving for the books, magazines, clothes and cosmetics that came tumbling out. There was an atomizer that she tested in the air for his benefit. There were pictures to tape on the wall.

'That's pretty jazzy,' he said, when a carton revealed a hard bright plastic record-player.

'A present from Vera for doing so well.'

'Did she send it?'

'She took me out to lunch. She took me to the Bohemian Restaurant on North Terrace and bought me stockings that I hate and nail polish.' She made a comic face. 'You should've seen her.'

'No thanks.'

Her presence recovered his purpose.

After work he would put on old clothes and they would go about the garden, Penny talking. Next year, next year ... She was definitely going back for Leaving Honours. She had been assistant stage manager for the school play and would be stage manager next year. Their hockey team was second in the tournament and her best friend would be captain next year. After next year she would go to the university to study law. There was no reason why a woman shouldn't be a barrister. She could see herself in court, like Portia. All hail to the modern world! Those who died for freedom had not died in vain if the young could inherit a world of such scope. Next year ... It was easier to contemplate the summer that intervened.

The sun baked the flesh and the garden responded to their touch. That Christmas the hibiscus were the finest ever: masses of little papery trumpets, flame coloured, salmon, brick and blush coloured, creamy white and bloody crimson, single and double, Jack's pride and joy. He had overcome his distaste for the slimy stench as they rotted, the whiff of bodies in decay. Now they were sweet flowers he managed to grow with difficulty in his limey garden.

At dusk, Penny and Jack would go inside and drink a beer in the kitchen while she prepared the food – steak or fish and salad, and the local fresh bread, ice-cream, tinned pears and chocolate sauce – nothing fancy. She had made him get a television set for his solitary evenings. A huge aerial was erected to pick up the transmission from Adelaide. But Jack seldom settled to stare at world events through the black-and-white snow. Penny wanted to discuss politics. From her school debating, she was full of the communist threat – a new worry for Jack Tregenza. She introduced instant coffee after dinner and he allowed himself a nightcap of port. Occasionally he declared that science was the way of the future. He slept like a baby in those days, in the cocoon of knowing that Penny was in her room, playing rock-and-roll records till all hours, and would still be there in the morning.

For Christmas Eve they moved across to the shack and kept vigil on the verandah, in darkness so as not to attract insects. The night was star bright and they could see with insect eyes. Black *wok-wok* beetles soldiered over the cement towards them. Further along the beach they could see holidaymakers' bonfires. They could see lamps on the water where waders were looking for flounder, or moving faster where boats were out dabbing for garfish, and the southern stars brighter than all the lights, thicker than swarming bees.

'You know, it's so calm,' said Jack, 'you could be forgiven for believing it's been like this from time immemorial. Not so. One Christmas Eve she blew up like the worst storm you'd ever get in winter. Worse because it was so completely out of season that no one was prepared. No one could give credence. You couldn't open the front door against the wind. Six-foot-high waves in the bay coming right up against the cliff. A real freak. Peter and I were out in the boat with Dad. Nineteen thirty-four it was. I'd have been about ten, I reckon. Dad had taken the trawler round to Parawurlie Bay with us boys to get some cray for the festive season. She was flat enough when we set out, but not right, a weird milky calm like something was fuming there. We remembered afterwards. She started blowing up when we were just out of Parawurlie, but you couldn't believe it would be anything. You'd have been daft to go back. In those days even if someone had a vehicle you had a rough job getting out from Parawurlie overland. Dad reckoned it would be easier round Point Light – slow going alright – and once we got past the lighthouse the sea got worse. The big trawler was a toy, and the spray was *hot* – that was the strange thing – hot water coming down drenching us from over our heads. Still, the boat kept going thank the Lord, and Peter and I hung on for dear life. I remember grabbing his ankle one time so he wouldn't be swept off, and another time he grabbed on to mine. Dad yelled out that us boys had to fend for ourselves because he needed all his wits to bring the boat in. We were truly rocking and rolling then.

'We just kept going somehow. The old man had a sixth sense when it came to direction. Somehow he pointed her right. Suddenly Peesey Point was there to starboard and we were crashing towards the jetty. That was a close shave. The whole place was out shouting and carrying on. Once we made the lee we threw out the anchor and jumped into the dinghy to scramble on shore. We were washed side- ways, but what did it matter? Your Granny Irene was there with the old Vauxhall. She'd spent half the day and all the night worried sick. At three-thirty in the morning, Dad came wading out of the sea carrying the sack of crays he promised to get. Irene scolded him before she said a word of welcome. She grabbed Peter and me by the scruff of our ratty necks, whisked us to the car, pulled off our sodden clothes and wrapped blankets round us. Then she slipped Dad a hipflask of scotch. She was crying, I remember, as wet as the weather. She had given us up for dead, all three. "The best Christmas present I've ever had, Willie Tregenza," she said, biting her lip, "and never again!"'

'I can remember Irene biting her lip,' said Penny, 'not letting you see that something was wrong, then smiling wonderfully.'

'It's funny,' said Jack. 'Peter and I were sitting in the car while Dad conferred with the grown-ups on the beach about what to do with the boat, because it wasn't properly moored, and in that short space of time the light came up. The wind dropped just like that. The sea died down. It happened instantly, as if ordered to stop. By six o'clock the sun was shining, the sky was blue, the sea was back to its usual mild chop, only all churned up. The beach was a mess, trees uprooted, weed, bushes, shags, cuttlefish, all strewn together. But already it was like a hot summer's day. No one would believe it who wasn't there. The Wooka pub opened at seven o'clock that Christmas morning. The whole mob arrived for a few grogs before church. Peter and me got a bottle of stout to drink 'cause we were the heroes. We had mountains of beautiful crayfish to eat that day.'

Their own Christmas was different. Jack slept heavily in the little back room away from the sea. Penny woke early in the front bed when the sun flooded in making the bed too hot. In bare feet and cotton nightie she crept across the floor and put the kettle on. Waiting for the water to boil, she stared through the screen door at the opal sleepy sea and hugged herself. The movement of the globe, and of history, made this dawn particular.

She took two mugs of tea to Jack's shadowy room and shook his shoulder where he lay on his side on the iron-frame bed, breathing deeply. His body gave off heat.

'Happy Christmas, Uncle Jack,' she said eagerly.

He twisted round to face her through his sleep, rubbing his screwed-up eyes. 'Happy Christmas,' he smiled, putting his big arm round her neck to pull her down for a kiss.

'Wait,' she said. Quickly she fetched her present and settled comfortably against him while he opened it. She nestled into his chest as she had done as a child. He folded back the paper and shook out what was inside, a thick brown jumper that she had been knitting for months.

'Try it on.'

'It's too hot!'

'Go on,' she said excitedly. 'I'm terrified it won't fit. I copied one of your old ones, but I think you've got fatter.'

He sat up and pulled the jumper over his head. Then he rolled out of bed, tightened his pyjama cord, and modelled for her.

'Fits perfectly, eh? You're very clever, darling.'

'I am clever,' she said smugly, drinking her tea.

'Well if you're so clever, miss, see if you can find what I've got for *you*.' He propped himself against the wall with his arms crossed. 'It's somewhere in this room.'

Penny pulled a long face. 'That's not *giving*.'

There was next to nothing in the room. Under the bed-frame with its thin mattress was nothing but an empty suitcase. A small chest; a single wardrobe like a broom cupboard, piled full of old magazines, with a mirror on the door. Over the window was a sun-bleached yellow curtain printed with faded red-and-blue yachts that had been there since Jack was a boy. On the wall was a chart of deep-sea fish in descending sizes. Nowhere to hide a present.

'Steady on,' cried Jack as Penny started to toss the socks and handkerchieves about in the drawer.

'Hmph! I'm not giving up.'

'You're getting warm,' he said as she picked up her mug from the bedside chair.

'It's not on your person, I hope?'

'Not exactly.'

'I'll tickle you to make you tell me. I'll torture you!' she squealed, lunging at her uncle.

He held her by the elbows as her fists beat against his chest.

'Think hard,' he instructed with a toothy smile. 'Where was the Saint Christopher hidden? You know the story.'

Jack had a wide-brimmed straw sunhat, a coolie's hat, sitting on top of the wardrobe.

'Errh,' growled Penny. 'That's not fair because I can't see that high.'

'You need the chair.'

Climbing up, she lifted the hat and found the parcel. 'It's not very big.'

She sat with Jack on the bed as she unwrapped it.

'Now that you're a serious student,' he said, 'with a future. Do you like it?'

It was a gold fountain pen on which her initials were engraved. She buried her face against Uncle Jack's neck, suddenly went coy and pulled away. She drew her legs up and clasped her knees, and her hair covered her eyes. To be given an adult present was wonderful!

Jack stretched, and his bare toes touched hers. He hardly dared move. He had played with her all his life, and she was full of intensities he could scarcely guess at.

'Drink your tea,' he said, looking at his watch. 'Church time.'

'The weather's too nice for church,' Penny complained. 'I'd rather have a swim.' She didn't want to announce that she had started to disbelieve.

'For old times' sake,' he said. He wasn't pleading, nor would he resort to the blackmail of love. 'If we don't put in an appearance, they'll think we've gone bush.'

'Who cares?'

Church was a simple affair. The people were comfortable in themselves, as in their pews, and there was no embarrassment about the free drop of wine and the wafer. Conscience-searching in Wooka was confined to neighbours' scrutiny, with eyes practised at sizing up stock. Afterwards they stood about under the noble line of gums on the hill that marked the church. A group of young 'uns appraised Penny in silence. Decently she stayed by her uncle. 'Doesn't she look gorgeous,' said Kath Hocking to

Jack, insisting that they come home for Christmas dinner. 'I've got food for an army – eh, Les?'

But Jack spread his arm across Penny's shoulder to claim her, ignoring the shadow of her reluctance. Once they were back at the shack, in the blazing heat of the still morning, with the lustrous sea and the chook spitting in the pan, cold beer on the card table on the verandah, they were glad to be the elect of light and air.

In the afternoon, figures began to appear on the beach, free for their holidays. Family groups settled under awnings. Old people strolled along the shore in pairs. Children tried out their Christmas clobber. Teenagers drove out from Wooka to release themselves off the rocks into the clear deep water.

While her uncle dozed, Penny went to swim with kids she had known since childhood. They welcomed her warily, since she had been away. To swim underwater was easier, with eyes open to observe zebra fish and clay-coloured mullet paler than their shadows on the white sea floor. She was out far when a black goggled head with a snorkel aimed at her. Suddenly the head went under. She didn't believe anyone could hold their breath so long, or travel so far, beneath the surface.

Only a little space away the exultant harpoon speared into the air with a flapping trophy of fish. The boy came after, pulled up his goggles, shook his head and swore. 'A blasted tiddler. They're much bigger underwater. S'pose I should throw it back,' he called out, mocking. She laughed. 'The big fish will eat it if it's bleeding, but. Too bad. Least give the thing a chance.'

Deftly he prised out the prongs. The fish was stunned, then wriggled drunkenly.

'It's fantastic to get one at all,' consoled Penny.

'I s'pose,' he snorted. 'Bloody things sit on the bottom like sitting ducks. It's not that hard to pick 'em off. Some get up to three or four pounders.'

He was not used to talking to strangers, or girls or anyone at all really. He heard himself say, 'You stopping down here?'

'Up there,' she pointed.

He nodded. His dark crew cut was a wet spiky fur of little spines. He had dark eyes, tufty eyebrows, and a long, swarthy, serious face. He was sixteen and a half.

The boy signalled a provisional farewell and swam away. Penny sidestroked to the beach, pleased with the encounter as she picked her way round rocks and rock-pools to the sand in front of the shack. She acknowledged him later when he walked past. He was shy. He didn't know what to do with himself. Lanky, muscly, he was a brown stick in the distance.

That evening she sat mooning on the verandah while Jack also dreamed, sentimental given the chance.

'I'll be hitting the sack early,' he said.

'Me too.'

She gave a little yawn.

The boy was Rob Stewart. He was at the beach next morning when she came down the steps with her uncle. He called out 'G'day'. He was playing a ball game in the water with his cousins, the most loutish of whom threw the ball at Penny. Jack intercepted and tossed it back with boyish glee. But Penny swam in the opposite direction, not wanting to join in.

She was face down on her towel when Rob came up and started putting questions. What was she doing? Did she want to go for a walk?

'Will you be here this afternoon?' he asked, slouching.

'Yeah, this afternoon.'

'Hey Rob!' yelled his cousins from the water. When he rejoined them, there was a burst of laughter. When she thought about boys, Penny decided that Rob was an exception – he was chivalrous and decent.

In the subsequent days they walked and swam and went out in the boat. One night he came round to listen to records and they sat on the bed talking and talking until Penny was worried that Uncle Jack would be kept awake and hear. But Jack did a good job of snoring audibly.

They played the same records and said the same things until at midnight, as at a signal, Rob took hold of Penny's hand, leaned across and flatly kissed her lips. Gently she pushed him away. Even the brush of his mouth was a shock. She indicated her uncle behind the partition. Rob kissed her again. Neither quite understood how their short, pure courtship had been leading to this.

'No,' mouthed Penny, 'you better go.' It was loud enough for Jack to hear.

'Yeah,' Rob mumbled, straightening himself.

'Gee the tide's out far,' he said, when they were outside. She followed him down and they sauntered across the wide cold sand to the silvery water's edge. Standing against her, Rob put his hands on her shoulders, gripped her in his hard arms and kissed her until she felt dizzy. He was delicious. He kissed her neck and ears, and squeezed her until she would break. She was in love with him, and couldn't let go of his hand when at last he pulled away.

'Tomorrow.'

Head bowed, he was vanishing in the starlight. She heard the low rumble of stones and, after an interval, his whistling. She curled her toes in the sweetest dream.

Next morning he banged on the door at ten o'clock.

'I'm afraid she's still asleep, Rob. Come in.'

The boy was not prepared for that. He had come under a compulsion. Nor was Jack Tregenza prepared for Penny's first beau, and was excessively affable. He was surprised too when Penny emerged sleepy-headed to tell Rob to wait five minutes, and in less than five minutes was ready without a protest.

So quick! Jack had had no chance for love as a youth. The war had come before all that fiddle, stealing his passion. Afterwards he had not let himself. Then there were Irene's salty lectures – 'Watch out, my boy. Keep yourself to yourself' – and Peter's experience, getting caught. Jack laughed about the women who wanted to rescue him – he was always too much of a duffer to say yes. Until now he did not consider what he had been denied. Besides, there was Penny.

Penny and tongue-tied Rob were in a diving-bell of their own. To find out what they were doing, Jack had to knock on glass. She would promise to be back at a certain time, definitely in time for a meal; then she would cut it fine, or her watch would have stopped, or she would come at the end of the day to ask if Rob could stay for tea. The boy giggled as Penny reverently served his plate, touching his shoulder like a parody of a mother. And when he wasn't around, she spent hours doing herself up for him. It was life with a mooncalf – yet Jack was thankful.

Towards the end of the holiday, the stock and station agency reopened. The summer was at its most splendid, so Penny stayed on at the shack, and Jack came out at the end of each day. Though he was glad to be back at work, the problems piled on his desk made him grumpy. The first evening he came home to a scrap of paper from Penny on the kitchen table, saying she'd gone to a barbecue with Rob. He poured himself a beer and wondered whether he could be bothered to cook a meal for one. He ate a lump of bread and butter and poured another beer, opening another bottle before he made up his mind. It was ridiculous to be so miserable. All the year she had been away and he had coped. But he had grown used to her being in his life again, and now that she was absent, taken, the raging hurt of his loss made him realise his joy in her. Jack's emotion got quicky out of control. He could not think back or imagine forward to any consoling perspective. She was only fifteen. What if something happened to her? You could trust Rob up to a certain point, but these young lads didn't have much sense, not if he was showing off, not if he'd had a bit of booze. He would force himself on her like a tireless puppy. God knows what sort of mess they would get into: she was so gone on the boy. Jack poured himself another beer, worried sick, and decided the best thing was to drive to the place where Rob was staying and calmly have a word with whoever was in charge. He wouldn't embarrass her, he'd just call in casually . . .

Through the open door of the shack down the road, Jack saw Old Man Stewart and his wife playing cards with the boy's aunt and uncle. They were suspicious people of few words. Ignoring Jack's evident anxiety, they offered him a sociable chair and said that the kids had gone off in one of the cars for a barbecue tea on the beach. 'Your Penny,' said Old Man. Jack was pale and furious, keeping his composure. He said it was nothing important – to tell Penny to come on home if they saw her – and gave a brisk cheerio and left. He would have squashed any rabbit that hopped into his headlights on the way home. Little Penny, his charge, his darling, gone without counsel, God knows where.

As he lay on his bare bed in the darkness of the shack, his nightmares came to the surface of his mind, all the fears dammed up behind his responsibility for the gift of Penny. He was almost in a frenzy when in the small hours of the morning there was the languorous melody of her voice at the door saying goodnight to Rob. In her muffled tones he heard the summer magic of youthful love, their lips touching, the rustle of goodbye. In the surge of his relief, Jack forgave them everything.

'That you, Pen?' he called when she came inside.

'Yes,' she whispered. 'Sorry I'm late, Uncle Jack. Talk to you in the morning. I've got to sleep.'

All that night Jack stared at the ceiling, frightened by the depth he had uncovered in his feelings for Penny. Thank God he was given a chance to learn.

No one ever knew that through the hottest weeks of that summer Jack Tregenza loved his niece with a fervour that he thought would consume him. He never said a word or made a sign as day after day, night after agonizing night, Penny went off with young Rob Stewart. She wasn't his to keep. Nor did he allow himself curiosity, when even the most innocent questions came out wrong –

'Where are you going tonight? What do you and Rob find to talk about all the time?'

She was sensitive enough to say, 'I promise I'll spend tomorrow night at home,' but come tomorrow she would say, 'Rob might drop around after tea. That's alright, isn't it? We'll just watch the television.' And they would sit awkwardly in the living room until Jack had the grace to go to bed.

Only once there might have been a scene, a drowsy, humming Sunday afternoon when Penny and Rob had gone off to play tennis and Jack went to the shack for a swim. When he returned towards teatime, the young ones were already back, their drained cups and tea things on the kitchen table. Wondering where they were, Jack determined not to go looking and ambled to his study instead. He found Penny and Rob bent over his desk there. The study was a room where Penny would not normally go. A drawer was open. When Jack's eyes fell on the tiny Saint Christopher medallion glinting between the boy's fingers, he went prickly all over. He blurted, before Penny had a chance to speak,

'You're not giving him the Saint Christopher!'

Penny started, and stared. It was Rob who spoke.

'She's just showing me, Mr Tregenza.'

They were nervous and uncertain, as if there were guilt. 'You were out, Uncle Jack. I was telling Rob about the Saint Christopher and wanted to show him. I'm sorry for going into your study without permission.'

Rob's face was long and angry. He touched Penny's arm. 'I better be going.'

After she saw him off, Penny slumped down opposite Jack in the living room.

'I can't always keep it a secret,' she said. 'Sometimes I have to tell. But how could you imagine I would just give it away like that? Anyway, if I did want to give it away, I would. I would know what I was doing, Uncle Jack. I would be free to give someone the most precious thing if it was right.'

'You're only fifteen.'

'What's that got to do with it?'

'You're so thick with the boy anything could happen. I hope you know what you're doing, that's all. People get fired up and rue the consequences. Think of Vera and poor Peter.'

'My parents.'

She gulped, turned and ran to her bedroom. He heard the door slam. He had spoken to wound. He was still shaking from seeing the Saint Christopher, the size of a pea, catching the light between the boy's nails. In a moment's carelessness it might fall to the ground and roll out of sight where no one would ever find it again even if the whole room was turned upside-down.

Penny couldn't grasp how Jack suffered. She understood

only that he who wanted her happiness considered the romance to be wrong. Time would prove its rightness. But she had no way of knowing what else time might do to her burning feelings. She was starting anew. That's what made her sing. There was nothing to remember except what dated from the day she met Rob, from the beginning of the new life she had not found at school up in town. With Rob a new world came within reach, as in their lovemaking – timid, exploratory, unconsumated – they danced into tomorrow, not hankering after the past.

Penny already had a woman's shrewdness. She understood her uncle's fears, and had her own plans too, for next year, and Leaving Honours, and beyond. Now there was a deeper plan. She wanted her love for Rob to reach maturity. She wanted to enjoy its evolution, its changes, its shaping of her world. That meant waiting.

From February Rob started to work long days on his father's property. Penny got her schoolbooks out and put them by her case. They didn't discuss the matter. One Saturday, a cloudy day that anticipated autumn, they were meandering among the rock pools in front of the shack – purposeless, motionless lovers, putting their fingers in anemones, plucking out crabs or white round pebbles – when Rob, whose thoughts were expressed crabwise, led up to the suggestion that Penny should not go back to school but should stay in the district, get engaged, wait for a year and then marry him.

His desire to be a man, his will for ownership (she knew) made him speak his plans, when she was still a virgin. He assumed things too easily, yet a pulse of warm satisfaction ran along her nerves.

'It's not that,' she said. 'You don't understand. I *want* to study. I *want* to become a lawyer. That's what I want to be. Not just a farmer's wife, even if the farmer is you.'

Rob stuck out his lip. He took her message obliquely. 'Is it anything to do with your uncle?' He clenched his fist.

'No, it's *me*. It's nothing to do with anyone else, it's just me. Please see that, Rob, or if you can't see, accept it anyway, that it's me, how I want my life to be. It doesn't get in the way of how I feel about you.'

'Bullshit. You'll be up in town. Out of reach. What am I supposed to do? Aren't you afraid I won't stick around?'

'If you don't, it will only be to spite me. If you don't stay around, good riddance.'

He hung his head, seeing that she was striking a bargain.

'Rob –' She touched him, 'I know it's a hard test, but it's better for both of us.'

'I can't wait like that, not all the time. Without a promise. With no guarantee. It's not natural. It's not bloody fair.'

'Do what you like. If we do come back together, then it will be real.'

'It's the end then. Is that what you're saying? You want to be free to go off with other people. Hell, I only asked you to marry me! Sorry I ever spoke.'

She stopped her stepping round pools and looked him in the face frankly and earnestly. Because she loved him, she would risk losing him.

'Wait,' she said, 'only wait. Wait.'

He had nothing to reply. He took her hand, squeezing it as a baby squeezes its mother's finger. On the cliff top the door banged as Jack Tregenza came out, shading his eyes to look for them. Penny saw and waved. Rob, squeezing her hand, made her turn seawards. That empty, tranquil, rippling space was where he would lose her, because he had no rope long enough to tie her to him across the distance she wanted to go.

'There's nothing out there, Pen. Nothing.'

He had hurt in his voice. She smiled, victoriously. It was the test. He had to let her go.

They crossed the sand to the base of the steps and climbed up together to where Uncle Jack stood planted on the verandah, watching, his arms firmly crossed. A week later Penny Tregenza put on her school uniform and caught the bus to Adelaide.

Later, pulling the plough, Rob Stewart began to wonder if he shouldn't go back to technical college.

Jack Tregenza ate his solitary meal and was pleased when, periodically, Rob called in as a matter of loyalty and asked for news of the girl.

POSTCARDS FROM SURFERS

HELEN GARNER

One night I dreamed that I did not love,
and that night, released from all bonds,
I lay as though in a kind of soothing death.
COLETTE

We are driving north from Coolangatta airport. Beside the
road the ocean heaves and heaves into waves which do
not break. The swells are dotted with boardriders in black
wet-suits, grim as sharks.

'Look at those idiots,' says my father.

'They must be freezing,' says my mother.

'But what about the principle of the wet-suit?' I say.
'Isn't there a thin layer of water between your skin and
the suit, and your body heat . . .'

'Could be,' says my father.

The road takes a sudden swing round a rocky outcrop.

232

Miles ahead of us, blurred in the milky air, I see a dream city: its cream, its silver, its turquoise towers thrust in a cluster from a distant spit.

'What – is that Brisbane?'

'No,' says my mother. 'That's Surfers.'

My father's car has a built-in computer. If he exceeds the speed limit, the dashboard emits a discreet but insistent pinging. Lights flash, and the pressure of his right foot lessens. He controls the windows from a panel between the two front seats. We cruise past a Valiant parked by the highway with a FOR SALE sign propped in its back window.

'Look at that,' says my mother. 'A WA number-plate. Probably thrashed it across the Nullarbor and now they reckon they'll flog it.'

'Pro'ly stolen,' says my father. 'See the sticker? ALL YOU VIRGINS, THANKS FOR NOTHING. You can just see what sort of a pin'ead he'd be. Brain the size of a pea.'

Close up, many of the turquoise towers are not yet sold. 'Every conceivable feature,' the signs say. They have names like Capricornia, Biarritz, The Breakers, Acapulco, Rio.

I had a Brazilian friend when I lived in Paris. He showed me a postcard, once, of Rio where he was born and brought up. The card bore an aerial shot of a splendid, curved tropical beach, fringed with palms, its sand pure as snow.

'Why don't you live in Brazil,' I said, 'if it's as beautiful as this?'

'Because,' said my friend, 'right behind that beach there is a huge military base.'

In my turn I showed him a postcard of my country. It was a reproduction of that Streeton painting called *The Land of the Golden Fleece* which in my homesickness I kept standing on the heater in my bedroom. He studied it carefully. At last he turned his currant-coloured eyes to me and said, '*Les arbres sont rouges?*' Are the trees red?

Several years later, six months ago, I was rummaging through a box of old postcards in a junk shop in Rath-downe Street. Among the photos of damp cottages in Galway, of Raj hotels crumbling in bicycle-thronged Colombo, of glassy Canadian lakes flawed by the wake of a single canoe, I found two cards that I bought for a dollar each. One was a picture of downtown Rio, in black and white. The other, crudely tinted, showed Geelong, the town where I was born. The photographer must have stood on the high grassy bank that overlooks the Eastern Beach. He lined up his shot through the never-flowing fountain with its quartet of concrete wading birds (storks? cranes? I never asked my father: they have long orange beaks and each bird holds one leg bent, as if about to take a step); through the fountain and out over the curving wooden promenade, from which we dived all summer, unsupervised, into the flat water; and across the bay to the You Yangs, the double-humped, low, volcanic cones, the only disturbance in the great basalt plains that lie between Geelong and Melbourne. These two cards in the same box! And I find them! Imagine! '*Cher Rubens,*' I wrote. '*Je t'envoie ces deux cartes postales, de nos deux villes natales . . .*'

Auntie Lorna has gone for a walk on the beach. My

mother unlocks the door and slides open the flywire screen. She goes out into the bright air to tell her friend of my arrival. The ocean is right in front of the unit, only a hundred and fifty yards away. How can people be so sure of the boundary between land and sea that they have the confidence to build houses on it? The white doorsteps of the ocean travel and travel.

'Twelve o'clock,' says my father.

'Getting on for lunchtime,' I say.

'Getting towards it. Specially with that nice cold corned beef sitting there, and fresh brown bread. Think I'll have to try some of that choko relish. Ever eaten a choko?'

'I wouldn't know a choko if I fell over it.'

'Nor would I.'

He selects a serrated knife from the magnetised holder on the kitchen wall and quickly and skilfully, at the bench, makes himself a thick sandwich. He works with powerful concentration: when the meat flaps off the slice of bread, he rounds it up with a large, dramatic scooping movement and a sympathetic grimace of the lower lip. He picks up the sandwich in two hands, raises it to his mouth and takes a large bite. While he chews he breathes heavily through his nose.

'Want to make yourself something?' he says with his mouth full.

I stand up. He pushes the loaf of bread towards me with the back of his hand. He puts the other half of his sandwich on a green bread and butter plate and carries it to the table. He sits with his elbows on the pine wood, his knees wide apart, his belly relaxing on to his thighs, his high-arched, long-boned feet planted on the tiled floor. He eats, and gazes out to sea. The noise of his eating fills the room.

My mother and Auntie Lorna come up from the beach. I stand inside the wall of glass and watch them stop at the tap to hose the sand off their feet before they cross the grass to the door. They are two old women: they have to keep one hand on the tap in order to balance on the left foot and wash the right. I see that they are two old women, and yet they are neither young nor old. They are my mother and Auntie Lorna, two institutions. They slide back the wire door, smiling.

'Don't tramp sand everywhere,' says my father from the table.

They take no notice. Auntie Lorna kisses me, and holds me at arms' length with her head on one side. My mother prepares food and we eat, looking out at the water.

'You've missed the coronary brigade,' says my father. 'They get out on the beach about nine in the morning. You can pick 'em. They swing their arms up really high when they walk.' He laughs, looking down.

'Do you go for a walk every day too?' I ask.

'Six point six kilometres,' says my father.

'Got a pedometer, have you?'

'I just nutted it out,' says my father. 'We walk as far as a big white building, down that way, then we turn round and come back. Six point six altogether, there and back.'

'I might come with you.'

'You can if you like,' he says. He picks up his plate

and carries it to the sink. 'We go after breakfast. You've missed today's.'

He goes to the couch and opens the newspaper on the low coffee table. He reads with his glasses down his nose and his hands loosely linked between his spread knees. The women wash up.

'Is there a shop nearby?' I ask my mother. 'I have to get some tampons.'

'Caught short, are you?' she says. 'I think they sell them at the shopping centre, along Sunbrite Avenue there near the bowling club. Want me to come with you?'

'I can find it.'

'I never could use those things,' says my mother, lowering her voice and glancing across the room at my father. 'Hazel told me about a terrible thing that happened to her. For days she kept noticing this revolting smell that was ... emanating from her. She washed and washed, and couldn't get rid of it. Finally she was about to go to the doctor, but first she got down and had a look with the mirror. She saw this bit of thread and pulled it. The thing was *green*. She must've forgotten to take it out – it'd been there for days and days and *days*.'

We laugh with the tea towels up to our mouths. My father, on the other side of the room, looks up from the paper with the bent smile of someone not sure what the others are laughing at. I am always surprised when my mother comes out with a word like 'emanating'. At home I have a book called *An Outline of English Verse* which my mother used in her matriculation year. In the margins of *The Rape of the Lock* she has made notations: 'bathos;

reminiscent of Virgil; parody of Homer'. Her handwriting in these pencilled jottings, made forty-five years ago, is exactly as it is today: this makes me suspect, when I am not with her, that she is a closet intellectual.

Once or twice, on my way from the unit to the shopping centre, I think to see roses along a fence and run to look, but I find them to be some scentless, fleshy flower. I fall back. Beside a patch of yellow grass, pretty trees in a row are bearing and dropping white blossom-like flowers, but they look wrong to me, I do not recognise them: the blossoms too large, the branches too flat. I am dizzy from the flight. In Melbourne it is still winter, everything is bare.

I buy the tampons and look for the postcards. There they are, displayed in a tall revolving rack. There is a great deal of blue. Closer, I find colour photos of white beaches, duneless, palmless, on which half-naked people lie on their backs with their knees raised. The frequency of this posture, at random through the crowd, makes me feel like laughing. Most of the cards have GREETINGS FROM THE GOLD COAST or BROADBEACH or SURFERS PARADISE embossed in gold in one corner: I search for pictures without words. Another card, in several slightly differing versions, shows a graceful, big-breasted young girl lying in a seductive pose against some rocks: she is wearing a bikini and her whole head is covered by one of those latex masks that are sold in trick shops, the ones you pull on as a bandit pulls on a stocking. The mask represents the hideous, raddled, grinning face of an old woman, a witch. I stare at this photo for a long time. Is it simple, or does it hide some more mysterious signs and symbols?

I buy twelve GREETINGS FROM cards with views, some aerial, some from the ground. They cost twenty-five cents each.

'Want the envelopes?' says the girl. She is dressed in a flowered garment which is drawn up between her thighs like a nappy.

'Yes please.' The envelopes are so covered with coloured maps, logos and drawings of Australian fauna that there is barely room to write an address, but something about them attracts me. I buy a packet of Licorice Chews and eat them all on the way home: I stuff them in two at a time: my mouth floods with saliva. There are no rubbish bins so I put the papers in my pocket. Now that I have spent money here, now that I have rubbish to dispose of, I am no longer a stranger. In Paris there used to be signs in the streets that said, '*Le commerce, c'est la vie de la ville.*' Any traveller knows this to be the truth.

The women are knitting. They murmur and murmur. What they say never requires an answer. My father sharpens a pencil stub with his pocket knife, and folds the paper into a pad one-eighth the size of a broadsheet page.

'Five down, spicy meat jelly. ASPIC. Three across, counterfeit. BOGUS! Howzat.'

'You're in good nick,' I say. 'I would've had to rack my brains for BOGUS. Why don't you do harder ones?'

'Oh, I can't do those other ones, the cryptic.'

'You have to know Shakespeare and the Bible off by heart to do those,' I say.

'Yairs. Course, if you got hold of the answer and filled

it out looking at that, with a lot of practice you could come round to their way of thinking. They used to have good ones in the *Weekly Times*. But I s'pose they had so many complaints from cockies who couldn't do 'em that they had to ease off.'

I do not feel comfortable yet about writing the postcards. It would seem graceless. I flip through my mother's pattern book.

'There's some nice ones there,' she says. 'What about the one with the floppy collar?'

'Want to buy some wool?' says my father. He tosses the finished crossword on to the coffee table and stands up with a vast yawn. 'Oh – ee – oh – ooh. Come on, Miss. I'll drive you over to Pacific Fair.'

I choose the wool and count out the number of balls specified by the pattern. My father rears back to look at it: this movement struck terror into me when I was a teen-ager but I now recognise it as long-sightedness.

'Pure wool, is it?' he says. As soon as he touches it he will know. He fingers it, and looks at me.

'No,' I say. 'Got a bit of synthetic in it. It's what the pattern says to use.'

'Why don't you –' He stops. Once he would have tried to prevent me from buying it. His big blunt hands used to fling out the fleeces, still warm, on to the greasy table. His hands looked as if they had no feeling in them but they teased out the wool, judged it, classed it, assigned it a fineness and a destination: Italy, Switzerland, Japan. He came home with thorns embedded deep in the flesh of his palms. He stood patiently while my mother gouged away at them with a needle. He drove away at shearing time in a yellow car with running boards, up to the big sheds in the country; we rode on the running boards as far as the corner of our street, then skipped home. He went to the Melbourne Show for work, not pleasure, and once he brought me home a plastic trumpet. 'Fordie,' he called me, and took me to the wharves and said, 'See that rope? It's not a rope. It's a hawser.' 'Hawser,' I repeated, wanting him to think I was a serious person. We walked along Strachan Avenue, Manifold Heights, hand in hand. 'Listen,' he said. 'Listen to the wind in the wires.' I must have been very little then, for the wires were so high I can't remember seeing them.

He turns away from the fluffy pink balls and waits with his hands in his pockets for me to pay.

'What do you do all day, up here?' I say on the way home.

'Oh ... play bowls. Follow the real estate. I ring up the firms that advertise these flash units and I ask 'em questions. I let 'em lower and lower their price. See how low they'll go. How many more discounts they can dream up.' He drives like a farmer in a ute, leaning forward with his arms curved round the wheel, always about to squint up through the windscreen at the sky, checking the weather.

'Don't they ask your name?'

'Yep.'

'What do you call yourself?'

'Oh, Jackson or anything.' He flicks a glance at me. We begin to laugh, looking away from each other.

'It's bloody crook up here,' he says. 'Jerry-built. Sad. "Every conceivable luxury"! They can't get rid of it. They're desperate. Come on. We'll go up and you can have a look.'

The lift in Biarritz is lined with mushroom-coloured carpet. We brace our backs against its wall and it rushes us upwards. The salesman in the display unit has a moustache, several gold bracelets, a beige suit, and a clipboard against his chest. He is engaged with an elderly couple and we are able to slip past him into the living room.

'Did you see that peanut?' hisses my father.

'A gilded youth,' I say. '"Their eyes are dull, their heads are flat, they have no brains at all."'

He looks impressed, as if he thinks I have made it up on the spot. *The Man from Ironbark*,' I add.

'I only remember *The Geebung Polo Club*,' he says. He mimes leaning off a horse and swinging a heavy implement. We snort with laughter. Just inside the living-room door stand five Ionic pillars in a half-moon curve. Beyond them, through the glass, are views of a river and some mountains. The river winds in a plain, the mountains are sudden, lumpy and crooked.

'From the other side you can see the sea,' says my father.

'Would you live up here?'

'Not on your life. Not with those flaming pillars.'

From the bedroom window he points out another high-rise building closer to the sea. Its name is Chelsea. It is battle-ship grey with a red trim. Its windows face away from the ocean. It is tall and narrow, of mean proportions, almost prison-like. 'I wouldn't mind living in that one,' he says. I look at it in silence. He has unerringly chosen the ugliest one. It is so ugly that I can find nothing to say.

It is Saturday afternoon. My father is waiting for the Victorian football to start on TV. He rereads the paper.

'Look at this,' he says. 'Mum, remember that seminar we went to about investment in diamonds?'

'Up here?' I say. 'A *seminar?*'

'S'posed to be an investment that would double its value in six days. We went along one afternoon. They were obviously con-men. Ooh, setting up a big con, you could tell. They had sherry and sandwiches.'

'That's all we went for, actually,' says my mother.

'What sort of people went?' I ask.

'Oh . . . people like ourselves,' says my father.

'Do you think anybody bought any?'

'Sure. Some idiots. Anyway, look at this in today's *Age*. "The Diamond Dreamtime. World diamond market plummets." Haw haw haw.'

He turns on the TV in time for the bounce. I cast on stitches as instructed by the pattern and begin to knit. My mother and Auntie Lorna, well advanced in complicated garments for my sister's teenage children, conduct their monologues which cross, coincide and run parallel. My father mumbles advice to the footballers and emits bursts of contemptuous laughter. 'Bloody idiot,' he says.

I go to the room I am to share with Auntie Lorna and come back with the packet of postcards. When I get out my pen and the stamps and set myself up at the table my father looks up and shouts to me over the roar of the crowd, 'Given up on the knitting?'

'No. Just knocking off a few postcards. People expect a postcard when you go to Queensland.'

'Have to keep up your correspondence, Father,' says my mother.

'I'll knit later,' I say.

'How much have you done?' asks my father.

'This much.' I separate thumb and forefinger.

'Dear Philip,' I write. I make my writing as thin and small as I can: the back of the postcard, not the front, is the art form. 'Look where I am. A big red setter wet from the surf shambles up the side way of the unit, looking lost and anxious as setters always do. My parents send it packing with curses in an inarticulate tongue. Go orn, get orf, gorn!'

'Dear Philip. THE IDENTIFICATION OF THE BIRDS AND FISHES. *My father*: "Look at those albatross. They must have eyes that can see for a hundred miles. As soon as one dives, they come from everywhere. Look at 'em dive! Bang! Down they go." *Me*: "What sort of fish would they be diving for?" *My father*: "Whiting. They only eat whiting." *Me*: "They do not!" *My father*: "How the hell would *I* know what sort of fish they are."'

'Dear Philip. My father says they are albatross, but my mother (in the bathroom, later) remarks to me that albatross have shorter, more hunched necks.'

'Dear Philip. I share a room with Auntie Lorna. She also is writing postcards and has just asked me how to spell TOO. I like her very much and *she likes me*. "I'll keep the stickybeaks in the Woomelang post office guessing," she says. "I won't put my name on the back of the envelope."'

'Dear Philip. OUTSIDE THE POST OFFICE. My father, Auntie Lorna and I wait in the car for my mother to go in and pick up the mail from the locked box. *My father*: "Gawd, amazing, isn't it, what people do. See that sign there, ENTER, with the arrow pointing upwards? What sort of a thing is that? Is it a joke, or just some no-hoper foolin' around? That woman's been in the phone box for half an hour, I bet. How'd you be, outside the public phone waiting for some silly coot to finish yackin' on about everything under the sun, while you had something important to say. That happened to us, once, up at – " My mother opens the door and gets in. "Three letters," she says. "All for me."'

Sometimes my little story overflows the available space and I have to run over on a second postcard. This means I must find a smaller, secondary tale, or some disconnected remark, to fill up card number two.

'*Me*: (opening cupboard) "Hey! Scrabble! We can have a game of Scrabble after tea!" *My father*: (with a scornful laugh) "I can't wait."'

'Dear Philip. I know you won't write back. I don't even know whether you are still at this address.'

'Dear Philip. One Saturday morning I went to Coles and bought a scarf. It cost four and sixpence and I was happy with my purchase. He whisked it out of my hand and looked at the label. "Made in China. Is it real silk? Let's test it." He flicked on his cigarette lighter. We all screamed and my mother said, "Don't *bite*! He's only teasing you."'

'Dear Philip. Once, when I was fourteen, I gave cheek to him at the dinner table. He hit me across the head with his open hand. There was silence. My little brother gave a high, hysterical giggle and I laughed too, in shock. He hit me again. After the washing up I was sent for. He was sitting in an armchair, looking down. "The reason why we don't get on any more," he said, "is because we're so much alike." This idea filled me with such revulsion that I turned my swollen face away. It was swollen from crying, not from the blows, whose force had been more symbolic than physical.'

'Dear Philip. Years later he read my mail. He found the contraceptive pills. He drove up to Melbourne and found me and made me come home. He told me I was letting men use my body. He told me I ought to see a psychiatrist. I was in the front seat and my mother was in the back. I thought, "If I open the door and jump out, I won't have to listen to this any more." My mother tried to stick up for me. He shouted at her. "It's your fault," he said. "You were too soft on her."'

'Dear Philip. I know you've heard all this before. I also know it's no worse than anyone else's story.'

'Dear Philip. And again years later he asked me a personal question. He was driving, I was in the suicide seat. "What went wrong," he said, "between you and Philip?" Again I turned my face away. "I don't want to talk about it," I said. There was silence. He never asked again. And years after *that*, in a café in Paris on my way to work, far enough away from him to be able to, I thought of that question and began to cry. Dear Philip. I forgive you for everything.'

Late in the afternoon my mother and Auntie Lorna and I walk along the beach to Surfers. The tide is out: our bare feet scarcely mark the firm sand. Their two voices run on, one high, one low. If I speak they pretend to listen, just as I feign attention to their endless, looping discourses: these are our courtesies: this is love. Everything is spoken, nothing is said. On the way back I point out to them the smoky orange clouds that are massing far out to sea, low over the horizon. Obedient, they stop and face the water. We stand in a row, Auntie Lorna in a pretty frock with sandals dangling from her finger, my mother and I with our trousers rolled up. Once I asked my Brazilian friend a stupid question. He was listening to a conversation between me and a Frenchman about our countries' electoral systems. He was not speaking and, thinking to include him, I said, 'And how do people vote *chez toi*, Rubens?' He looked at me with a small smile. 'We don't have elections,' he said. Where's Rio from here? 'Look at those clouds!' I say. 'You'd think there was another city out there, wouldn't you, burning.'

Just at dark the air takes on the colour and dampness of the subtropics. I walk out the screen door and stand my gin on a fence post. I lean on the fence and look at the ocean. Soon the moon will thrust itself over the line. If I did a painting of a horizon, I think, I would make it look like a row of rocking, inverted Vs, because that's what I see when I look at it. The flatness of a horizon is intellectual. A cork pops on the first-floor balcony behind me. I glance up. In the half dark two men with moustaches are smiling down at me.

'Drinking champagne tonight?' I say.

'Wonderful sound, isn't it,' says the one holding the bottle.

I turn back to the moonless horizon. Last year I went camping on the Murray River. I bought the cards at Tocumwal. I had to write fast for the light was dropping and spooky noises were coming from the trees. 'Dear Dad,' I wrote. 'I am up on the Murray, sitting by the camp fire. It's nearly dark now but earlier it was beautiful, when the sun was going down and the dew was rising.' Two weeks later, at home, I received a letter from him written in his hard, rapid, slanting hand, each word ending in a sharp upward flick. The letter itself concerned a small financial matter, and consisted of two sentences on half a sheet of quarto, but on the back of the envelope he had dashed off a personal message: 'P.S. Dew does not rise. It *forms*.'

The moon does rise, as fat as an orange, out of the sea straight in front of the unit. A child upstairs sees it too and utters long werewolf howls. My mother makes a meal and we eat it. 'Going to help Mum with the dishes, are you, Miss?' says my father from his armchair. My shoulders stiffen. I am, I do. I lie on the couch and read an old *Woman's Day*. Princess Caroline of Monaco wears a black dress and a wide white hat. The knitting needles make their mild clicking. Auntie Lorna and my father come from the same town, Hopetoun in the Mallee, and when the news is over they begin again.

'I always remember the cars of people,' says my father. 'There was an old four-cylinder Dodge, belonging to Whatsisname. It had –'

'Would that have been one of the O'Lachlans?' says Auntie Lorna.

'Jim O'Lachlan. It had a great big exhaust pipe coming out the back. And I remember stuffing a potato up it.'

'A *potato*?' I say.

'The bloke was a councillor,' says my father. 'He came out of the Council chambers and got into the Dodge and started her up. He only got fifty yards up the street when BA–BANG! This damn thing shot out the back – I reckon it's still going!' He closes his lips and drops his head back against the couch to hold in his laughter.

I walk past Biarritz, where globes of light float among shrubbery, and the odd balcony on the half-empty tower holds rich people out into the creamy air. A barefoot man steps out of the take-away food shop with a hamburger in his hand. He leans against the wall to unwrap it, and sees me hesitating at the slot of the letterbox, holding up the postcards and reading them over and over in the weak light from the public phone. 'Too late to change it now,' he calls. I look up. He grins and nods and takes his first bite of the hamburger. Beside the letterbox stands a deep rubbish bin with a swing lid. I punch open the bin and drop the postcards in.

All night I sleep safely in my bed. The waves roar and hiss, and slam like doors. Auntie Lorna snores, but when I tug at the corner of her blanket she sighs and turns over and breathes more quietly. In the morning the rising sun hits the front windows and floods the place with a light so intense that the white curtains can hardly net it. Everything is pink and golden. In the sink a cockroach lurks. I try to swill it down the drain with a cup of water but it resists strongly. The air is bright, is milky with spray. My father is already up: while the kettle boils he stands out on the edge of the grass, the edge of his property, looking at the sea.

THE MUNTA-GUTTA

HERB WHARTON

For a long time I've been going to tell a story about the Munta-gutta. It happened many years ago when all us Murris used to live in the old yumba, about a mile south of town past the cemetery. Sometimes, if we didn't catch a rabbit or shoot or snare a kangaroo or set traps, we'd be a bit short of meat. Then we'd go to our uncle, who worked at the slaughter yard. And sometimes us kids would get gingles and tripe and skirt and a bit of liver. We'd walk past the cemetery, then past the school to where the old wooden bridge spanned the big muddy waterhole of the Warrego River. Instead of walking over the bridge, we went down the steep bank and round the end of the waterhole across the sandy bottom of the creek – it was real wide, a hundred yards across. That's where the waterhole ended, just beyond the bridge. Then we walked up the bank past the big gum trees and

251

followed the fence where a Chinaman lived, a real ancient old bloke.

He was so frail and old he looked to me a thousand years old. He used to grow the most beautiful vegetables. We'd walk past his garden into the slaughter yard where the cattle and sheep and pigs were killed to supply the town. I used to give my uncle a hand, washing away the blood or tipping things out – probably making a real mess of myself. The blood that came out of the bullocks and sheep ran through the cement drain into a trap.

That old Chinaman would come over to the slaughter yard with two buckets hanging from a pole across his shoulders, and he'd fill them with blood. That was before the days of fertilisers: the blood was the fertiliser for his garden. I can still see him with those buckets – he had a real springy little walk, and he'd jog across from his little tin humpy that stood in the midst of his vegetables, on his acre or so of ground.

Anyhow, my uncle had finished his slaughtering for the day. The butcher's truck came to pick up the carcasses and my uncle told me to stay at the yard and not go near the water. He was always telling me that – 'Don't go near the river,' he'd say, 'the Munta-gutta lives down there.' I was only about six or seven, and I didn't know what he meant. My mother always said funny things about my old uncle, that he was 'one of them'. If he saw you scratching around drawing images in the dirt he'd thump you and make you rub it out – he'd say it was one of the old beliefs, that you had to wipe out everything you drew.

So he was gone and it was a real hot day. I knew it

was shallow at the end of the waterhole, with beautiful white sand like a beach at the edge of the brown, muddy water. I walked down past the old Chinaman's garden to the waterhole and sauntered over to the edge of the water. There was no one around. I decided to strip off. I was only wearing a pair of shorts and a shirt. I dog-paddled around in the cool water – it wasn't very deep and I couldn't have been far off the bottom.

Then my hand touched a log. I dog-paddled past it then put both my feet on it to rest them, hanging on with my hands. I was crouched down on the log with my head above water, blowing bubbles. Then I thought, if this is a log, it can't be far to the bottom. Hanging on with one hand, I tipped my head on one side and reached down with the other . . .

The log was thin, and bent up. And in the space between the arch of the log and the bottom, as I reached down with my hand, I felt something soft, damp and smooth. Something alive. It wasn't slimy, it was a damp, velvety sort of feeling. I traced along it with my hand and was amazed: I realised it was a bloody big thing, bigger than me. Three feet long at least. And there were two of those things, as I found out when my knuckles touched the second one, lying beside the other. The first thing I thought was – Well, this is it. This is the Munta-gutta!

I don't know how I got out of the water. I believe I sprang from the log and turned in mid-air – maybe I ran along the top of the water to get out! But I know now that it couldn't have been more than a foot deep. Anyhow, that was the fastest I ever made it out of the water in my life. Galloping over the soft sand, I reached down to pick up my shirt and trousers and I never stopped until I got to a big old gum tree. I got behind it with my clothes in my hand. I must have been really afraid, and I remember that I was gasping for breath.

Anyhow, after a while I finally calmed down enough to think properly. I put my trousers on and had a real slow sort of peek around the tree. It really was a huge tree – about ten little kids my size could have hidden behind it. I glanced towards the water. There wasn't a ripple in it. All I could see was the deep track I made when I ran out of the waterhole, especially in the wet sand near the bank. There was my trail in the white sand all the way to the tree. I was mystified. I thought, it's got to be the Munta-gutta. But then, the way the old people talked about the Munta-gutta, I thought it was a lot bigger than the thing I had felt. I hadn't felt its head, just its satiny smooth belly.

I don't know how long I stayed there, but finally I headed up the bank back to the slaughter yard, where I was supposed to be waiting. My uncle came back about half an hour later and yarded his cattle up and was ready to go home. I carried our little sugar bag, with our gingle and tripe and a bit of skirt in it. Everyone used to carry one of those sugar bags when they walked to town to get tucker. You could roll it up under your arm then use it as your shopping bag, put all your groceries in it and chuck it over your shoulder. If it rained you could punch a little hollow in it and use it for a cape that hung over your head and shoulders.

My uncle and me were heading home, and on the way
the old Chinaman sang out to us and gave us a cabbage
and a couple of tomatoes. Then we went down the bank
towards the water. Now my uncle was one of the best
trackers in that country. Whenever anyone got lost, people
would come to get him and he'd track for miles and miles
out in the bush. He taught me a lot about tracking horses
and cattle and other animals. He was a very smart man.
He didn't need to be told anything, he could read the facts
and see what had happened.

'Look, look at this,' he said to me and pointed to the
track. 'Must've been a kid playing down here on his own.
Looks like he been in the water ... looks like the Munta-
gutta must've frightened him. I see he come out of the
water and ran behind that tree there. I wonder ... you
never seen no kid down here, eh?'

'Nah, not me, I never seen no kid.' I couldn't tell him
that I'd touched the Munta-gutta, because then I'd have
got a flogging for going down to the river.

'Well, it's strange that the kid went back up the bank,'
my uncle said. 'His tracks don't come over this way.'

'I never seen no one, Uncle.'

We walked home across the river bed to the yumba.

It puzzled me for a long time. I kept to myself the secret
that I knew where the baby Munta-gutta slept in the
shallow end of the waterhole. I wasn't going to tell
anyone, not even my mates I used to play with. They'd
only say I was telling lies. I kept that secret for ages.

A few years later – I suppose I might have been twelve

by now – some of the old Murris from the yumba used to take us fishing for cod. We used drag-nets. When we got to the water we'd all have to be quiet, and if there was a log sticking out somewhere they'd say, 'That's where he lives, over there!' They'd slide gently into the water and dog-paddle silently across the water to set the net between the log where the cods were supposed to be and the deepest part of the waterhole. That was because when you disturbed the cod it always headed for the deepest water. After they'd stretched the nets out they'd stand there silently. Sometimes the water would be over their heads, and they'd dig poles into the bottom of the creek-bed and hang on to them, just dog-paddling there quietly. Then some of them would circle around silently until they got behind the log and the nets – and at that point they'd come into the water and make a lot of noise.

Sometimes those old cods wouldn't move, and the old Murris would tell us kids to dive right down amongst the logs. The first time I ever felt a cod down there, I thought it was another Munta-gutta. This is how it happened.

We were supposed to be hunting the cods into the nets, and they told me to dive down and feel around. You couldn't see anything, it was all brown muddy water. Well, I was feeling around and suddenly my hands rested on this thing. 'There's something down here,' I said. Of course, I was real game with a lot of people around. I dived down again and felt the same thing, this belly part – but it was the belly of a big cod. I kept giving him a few digs and he swam into the net. And when that old cod hit the net, them fellas lifted the poles from the muddy bottom and one bloke turned his stick clockwise and another turned his anti-clockwise. The cod was ravelled in the net and the two blokes swam along and put the poles together. Then, holding the poles at each end on their shoulders, they dog-paddled out of the water onto the bank.

On the bank they unravelled the net and out flopped this big cod, about thirty or forty pound. I just stood there stroking its belly, with the same mystified feeling I'd had when I touched the baby Munta-gutta years before. After keeping that secret for so long, I thought I had solved the mystery at last. I thought: so this is the 'Munta-gutta'. There's no bloody Munta-gutta at all. All those years ago it was only a big Murray cod!

Not far from the place where we'd caught this cod, upriver a bit, it was all steep banks on the western side, about thirty feet down to the water. There was a cave there – in the dry time you could see the top of it. Actually there were two caves, and if the water was real low you could see the top of the second one. This was supposed to be the place where the Munta-gutta lived. Of course, the old Murris told us to stay away and never go near the place. And most of them wouldn't go there either.

Well, I stood watching the men arguing amongst themselves. We'd already caught a few yellow-bellies and a couple of catfish. Even though there was a big mob of us, it would have been enough for a feed. They were arguing about whether we should try to catch another cod, or go home. Suddenly there was a big splash in the water, up near those caves.

'That's it, boy, we gotta go,' my uncle told me. He

began telling all those other fellas the same. 'We gotta go because that's him, that's the Munta-gutta telling us we've gotta go, we've got enough fish.'

You couldn't take too many – that was our law. You only took what you could eat. We had no fridges in them days, so we probably would have wasted it. There was another big splash – it sounded like a whale flapping about.

'It's only a tree limb fallen into the water,' I said.

'Don't be silly, boy. There's no tree over there big enough for that,' my uncle told me.

Then we heard this drumming sound, like an emu or something. And it came from near that cave as well.

My uncle said, 'That's him, come on, we gotta go!'

They picked up the cod and the nets and headed up the bank.

'That's only an emu,' I said.

'Don't be silly, boy,' they said. 'Emus don't live in the water.'

There was another big splash. Then I realised I was out on my own pondering this mystery. I thought I'd solved it when I thought of emus, but when I heard the next splash I was more confused than ever and bolted after the others. I could still hear this drumming, droning sound, just like an emu. Sometimes, in the winter time, out in the bush, you can hear an emu a great long distance away when he's drumming in the early morning and the female is laying eggs at nesting time. I thought: 'Well, I still don't know about this Munta-gutta.'

It wasn't far to where we had parked the old Ford truck

with its flat-top back and no cabin, just a windscreen and a seat. All us Murris used to jump on the back with the nets and the fish. When we got to the truck that day, I was looking back in the direction of the caves and they were all saying that there was no argument about this thing: the Munta-gutta ruled the river, he was the one who decided whether you could take fish, and saw that you didn't take too many and deplete the stock.

According to legend, that was no ordinary cave. It was connected to every other river system to the west and the east. There was another really big waterhole, perhaps fifty miles away, and the cave was connected to it through an underground passage. Sometimes you'd be sitting down by the river and you'd see old leaves and mud come to the surface. Not because the river was running – they'd just come bubbling up. That was supposed to be the Munta-gutta cleaning out its cave, and it was a sign that a flood was on the way. The old people said that if the Munta-gutta wanted to punish people, he'd dry all the water up, all those connecting rivers, and send a drought on the land. Then the people would go without water and without fish. The Munta-gutta would go to another waterhole, and then after a while he'd send floods. They always described the Munta-gutta as something like the Loch Ness Monster.

As kids, whenever we were told not to go near the river we used to say: 'Oh, that Munta-gutta, he can't catch us! We'll run out of the water onto the bank. He can't come out of the water and I'll beat him!'

But the old fella would reply: 'He don't have to come out of the water, he'll send a big whirlywind, spinning and spinning around to pick you up and dump you in the river. Or he'll send a big water spout, just like that. It'll grab you and dump you right back in the water.'

I used to say, 'I'll fix him! I'll get my father's gun on him. I'll shoot that Munta-gutta!'

And they'd say, 'You can't shoot the Munta-gutta, he's too smart for you.'

I still remember those caves, though they've built a dam there now and they are permanently under water.

The old men told this story about a fella who'd done something or other to the mob that lived there, and he was going to run away. He was going to head for another waterhole. Well, one of the old men called up the Munta-gutta, to punish this fella for taking the woman. And the Munta-gutta called up a big rain to come down, a vast flood. It caught that fella as he was going over the stony crossing at the end of the waterhole, and he turned to stone himself. According to legend, he's there to this day, just below the surface of the water. One of the old men told me when I was young that if that stone fella's head appeared, you would always get a big flood.

The Munta-gutta ruled, he set the laws. You could take enough fish to eat, but you could never waste or misuse the resources of the river or you'd be punished. The waters were probably the most important thing, more so than the kangaroo. For thousands and thousands of years everything depended on the water in that part of the country. Sometimes the creeks stopped running for a year at a time. Twenty or thirty miles apart there'd be these big permanent waterholes that always filled up in the wet season, and the people moved from one waterhole to another, so that they always had water. Yes, there was always water in that country. It seems, too, that those old Murris knew about the great underground reservoirs which we call the Artesian Basin today. Water was more precious than gold or gems: everything depended on it for life. And the stories about the Munta-gutta helped to keep order and preserve the resources of the country. I think that when the white settlers came, they heard those tales and so the Munta-gutta became the white man's Bunyip. There were, in fact, creatures that could fit the description of a Bunyip that the old people described – creatures like reptiles which have now been extinct for maybe ten thousand years, but which lived on in memory.

A few years later, I reckon I finally glimpsed the Munta-gutta. It was at the other big waterhole, west of where we caught the cod that day. By this time I was seventeen or eighteen, and I was working as a stockman on the station where the legendary stone man appeared when the river reaches its lowest level . . . after which the biggest floods always come. Some people used to describe how they had seen that Munta-gutta struggling to get up through the netting fence there when the floods came, trying to get upstream. A few miles away, at a big bend in the river, there was another permanent waterhole.

One day I was riding around on my own looking for a stallion near the river bend. There was no sign of the missing horse, but I heard these three terrific splashes, even bigger than the splashes on that fishing day years before. I rode up to the waterhole. It wasn't very wide, probably some seventy yards across. There was a steep bank on either side, and big coolibah trees all around. And there, right in the middle of the river bend, I saw a big long head sticking out of the water, with a lump behind it like a body. And just behind it was another head at about the same height, sticking out about two feet or more, like a giant duck, except it was brown. And it had a lump behind it, too.

The first thing that came to me was the thought: 'Oh, I've finally seen the Munta-gutta!' I looked again, and there was another of these things, swimming real fast towards the opposite bank. And as I sat there on my horse, gazing at this thing, I thought: 'I'm gonna be the first man to see the Munta-gutta come out on the bank!' I was that excited. It got bigger and bigger as it reached the bank and began to come out of the water ... and then I saw the long, scaly legs of an emu and all the water flying off him as he took off up the bank, his neck stretched out as he bolted away. Yes, it was a bloody emu! And the other two emus came swimming out too.

So I never saw the Munta-gutta after all.

HELLFIRE IN NEW HEAVEN

PHILLIP SCOTT

The island was 20 to 30 kilometres long, shaped like a half-moon with the main beach and new resort complex nestling inside the crescent. The terrain behind the resort was hilly and coated in dense subtropical forest. At one end of the island a mountainous plateau jutted unexpectedly out of the trees, its towering cliffs providing natural shelter to the beach. There was, apparently, another beach hiding around the back somewhere, but generally the island's coast met the ocean in sheer walls of rock. It was a two-hour trek to the second beach, through the bush, up over a thickly wooded ridge and down again.

The resort itself was virtually vertical. Built up the side of the hill in strata fashion were three levels of luxury motel-style apartments, linked by a steep road and two sets of stairs, one for guests and one for staff. There were no lifts or buggies. To get anywhere you had to walk.

The main reception area nestled at sea level, along from the wharf and past the communal swimming pool. Here, too, were the main bar, the dining room and a large activities area which could be used for everything from morning aerobics to a late-nite disco and dance spectacular. Tucked away behind it was the conference room. On the second level were the administrative offices, and at the very top, where the land flattened out somewhat, were the male and female swimming pools, a nine-hole golf course, a covered luncheon area and a fully equipped gymnasium. Each building was crowned by a tropical-style thatched roof, made from woven palm leaves and padding.

Right at the back, hidden as far away as possible, cringed two grey blocks of non-luxury staff quarters. (Their roofs were flat.)

By the time we docked I was feeling very hot under the collar, and not just because of the humidity. For once, it was a relief to see Paul. Clad in minuscule Aussie Boys swimmers, he was standing on the wharf, waving frantically – a ridiculous grin on his face. With him were two simply gorgeous boys wearing identical T-shirts, blue shorts and silvered sunglasses, the angelic uniform of New Heaven.

'Hello, hello, caro mio!' he cried, and hugged me, even though he was dripping wet. 'You must have a swim, it's bliss-in-a-pool. 'Specially in this humidity!'

'Let me get organised first,' I panted.

'I'll take you up to Newton's office,' said Claire, and glanced at her print-out once more. 'Boys, can you take Ms Scott-Merman to room 212, and Mr Petrucci's bags to 213. By the way, I'm in 216 if you need me.'

'We'll be next to each other,' I remarked convivially to Delia, though she didn't seem to hear. She stood mesmerised, staring up at the tiered levels of the resort. I had to admit, it was an imposing construction.

'Please, let's get moving, shall we?' Claire snapped. Without a word, the two boys picked up our bags and trotted off towards the stairs, with a silent Delia in tow.

'That's Darren and André,' explained Paul breathlessly. 'Aren't they cute? André's French-Polynesian or something. He's the one with the eyes. Darren's the one with the dick. Who's your mute girlfriend?'

'Just a journalist.'

'A pack of them got in yesterday. There's one or two can do an "in-depth" with me any time they like.'

'Shouldn't you be rehearsing your routines?' snapped Claire, evidently not The World's Number One Paul Fan.

'We're on a break,' he chirped. 'We're light years ahead of schedule. Besides, I'm thinking water. A swimming motif. I'm on the verge of a major inspiration!'

'I can't wait to see it,' she muttered. 'This way, Marc.'

'See you in your room, caro!' Paul called as he sprinted back to the pool.

Claire shook her head. 'Newton and his protégés!' she growled to herself.

As we strode along, passing reception and the bar area, I took stock of Claire. She was tall and greyish, probably in her mid-forties. Her face was unusual, with a high forehead and pointy nose. Deep-set lines had settled around the corners of her mouth, giving her a general air of determination. She wore little make-up, though I noticed two small, expensive-looking earrings. Her cotton suit was staff blue but well tailored. Her fingernails were long and painted a deep crimson, a blazing contrast to the rest of her business-like demeanour.

Our conversation was stilted, to say the least. We climbed a flight of stairs, popped through a 'Staff Only' entrance, dashed along a corridor and stopped outside a door at the end marked 'Newton Heath'. The door was slightly ajar, but Claire still knocked.

'Yeah?' came Newton's booming voice from inside.

'Marc Petrucci's here,' called Claire.

'Marc! Come in!'

Claire slapped me on the back, in an 'all yours' gesture, and strode away. I entered one of the most luxurious offices I'd ever seen. An enormous desk faced the floor-to-ceiling window, from which you could see right across to the ocean and all of the south end of the island. Immediately below spread the branches of a tree, thick with chattering parrots.

On the back wall hung a big black-and-white photo of a man wearing nothing but an elaborate Venetian carnival mask. The anonymous gentleman's penis was half in shadow but was still clearly gigantic.

An air-conditioner hummed in the corner. Newton was seated casually at the desk, which was covered in faxes and folders. Opposite were two comfy-looking office chairs, one of which was occupied by a muscular man in a mauve golf shirt and urban camouflage slacks.

'Newton,' I began, 'can you please explain –'

'Marc, am I glad to see you!' he interrupted. 'Have a seat. Allow me to introduce Hiram. Marc Petrucci, Hiram Hudson.'

The man shot out a hand, which I shook. He wore several chunky gold rings and a bracelet.

'Like the ice-cream,' I commented lamely.

He gave me a frosty smile. 'That's *Homer* Hudson. There ain't no similarity.'

Hiram's hair was reddish with streaks of grey still discernible in spite of his military clip. He flicked his head to one side and I was reminded suddenly of the American eagle.

'What's in a name?' said Newton cordially. 'Hiram here is practically Mr Gaytour International in person, Marc,' he continued, shooting me a conspiratorial glance. 'We're very honoured to have him here this week. Most unexpected, too.'

'It's a hands-on company,' enthused Hiram. 'Nobody's too big – or too small – to take an interest in the big picture. We are the big picture of the future, Mr Petrucci. Gays and lesbians. Lesbians and gays. It's about Pride, and it's about big bucks. You read me?'

I fought the impulse to say 'Loud and clear'. I lost. 'Er, loud and clear.'

Mr Gaytour International smiled. 'He's our boy,' he said to Newton.

'I knew you'd think so,' Newton grinned. 'Now if you don't mind, Hiram, I've got to brief Marc fully for this afternoon's session and we don't have a lot of time.'

'Go ahead,' said Hiram. He rose and crushed my hand again. He stood at least a foot shorter than me. 'I'll be there!' he barked encouragingly, and marched out of the room.

I sank back into a chair. Newton immediately opened a drawer in his desk and took out a half-empty bottle of whisky and two shot glasses. He filled them to over-flowing.

'Here,' he said. 'This might help.'

'Newton, what the hell is going on? What have you put me in for?'

'I know, I know, mate. I'm sorry, all right?'

It was serious. I'd never heard Newton apologise before.

'It's all because that shortarse prick arrived out of the blue.' Newton's voice had dropped to a whisper. 'I mean, he honestly does represent the entire American investment and he could pull out at the drop of a hat. It's not likely, so far down the track, but if he did I'd be saddled with a whopping big debt. The place cost a packet to build, as you can imagine. Without Gaytour's international connections we'd be up Shit Inlet. Trouble is, Hiram's so fucking hands-on. I had to think of a title for you, to make it look good.'

'Community liaison officer?'

'Yeah, well, we all make mistakes. See, I wasn't expect-ing the Murphy's Inlet crowd over here until the grand opening. You'd have been long gone by then, and I'd have gotten a real liaison officer. It's just a big pain in the bum they're coming today.' He suddenly laughed heartily. 'I'll be interested to hear what you say to 'em. Apparently some of them are pretty fuckin' shitty about the whole idea!'

'I'm no public speaker at the best of times!' I quavered. 'What will I say?'

'Tell 'em it'll be good for the area: tourism, money, youth employment. You know, bullshit. We've been careful with the environment, we've paid handsomely for the place so the previous owners have no complaints ...'

'What previous owners? I thought it was national park?'

Newton stroked his chin. 'I don't think I said that. We could never have got it if it was national park. No, it was privately owned, the whole island. The Murphy family bought it from the governor in 1899. Pre-Federation sell-off.'

'Murphy, as in the inlet.'

'Yeah. The name's everywhere. Except it wasn't called Murphy's Island, it was called Crab Island. That's another bloody problem, these fucking crabs are all over the place. Anyhow, there was only old Mrs Murphy left here. When she died, it came on the market and I swooped. If you see an opportunity, grab it with both hands, crabs and all! The old girl left no will, so the executors tracked down her closest living relative who turned out to be a phoney art dealer I defended ten years ago. He lives in London now, but we keep in touch. He put me onto it. Of course, he's no idiot. He drove a hard bargain, but how many islands are there for sale? Not too many! We're naming part of the golf course after the old lady: the Iris Murphy Memorial Ninth Hole.'

'How sweet.'

'Silly old bag. Now, let's work this out. It's one now – the Yanks are having lunch and they're pissing off to Murphy's Beach at two, all except Hiram of course. Our chef – who's sensational – has packed hampers and I'm hoping they won't be back before six. The Inlet gang get here around two; we'll give 'em drinks and mouthwatering delicacies, the grand tour at three, more drinks, and then your little Q&A at, say, five-ish? It shouldn't take more than half an hour. Get 'em on the ferry at six, and we can have a bloody good dinner and a bit of fun like the brochure says. Incidentally, I'll give you one of our brochures so you'll know what you're talking about.' He winked. 'I'm sure you won't let us down.'

THE WITNESS

AMY WITTING

This is something I've been carrying alone for forty years, something I wanted to say and never had the chance to say it. There's not much point in it now. Charlie's been long dead, Lilian died two years ago, and yesterday I saw that woman's death notice in the paper. *Dexter, Damaris, aged 68, at St Catherine's Hospital, after a long illness. Mourned by Peg and Bobby.* So she'd never married. Sixty-eight years old – older than she had looked, then, forty years ago, when it all happened.

That was the first thing I said about her, when I saw her crossing the home yard to the schoolroom with the children.

'Is that the new governess? A bit young, isn't she?'

'Yes,' said Lil. 'That's Damaris. Got that out of a book, I think. Christened Madge, I shouldn't wonder.'

A bit too young and a bit too pretty, is what I thought.

Seeing that moment again just as it was, the sunny day, the girl with the neat round head and the long neck – not so pretty, really, but neat, and there was something about the way she moved that took the eye – I thought, 'Why, nothing had happened then. The world was something it could never be again.' Somehow I felt as badly as I'd ever felt about it, after forty years. As if it was a whole world killed.

She wasn't so pretty when she left, poor wretch.

What's the point of talking about it now? As I said, they're all dead and who's interested? But I'm interested still, interested in getting it off my chest. I wanted someone to share it with then and I still have that same nagging feeling, resenting being alone with it.

From that first moment, when I ran into the wash house and found the poor creature screaming and writhing on the floor, clawing at her eyes, and Lil shouted at me, 'Get water! Get water!' I've been alone with it. They made great play with that at the trial, that Lil had screamed 'Get water!' but it wasn't like that. She was glaring at me as if I'd done it, as if she could hand the whole thing to me. 'This is your business, not mine,' she was saying.

I couldn't put that across in the witness box. I didn't want to, either. But I wanted Lil to know what I was doing for her.

The barrister, the counsel for the defence, said to me, very quiet and friendly, 'Now, Mrs Ferris, I want you to give the court your account of the events of that morning. From the moment you heard that screaming.'

'It came from the wash house. I ran in and I saw

Damaris rolling backwards and forwards on the floor, clawing like at her eyes. Lil was standing still, with an open tin in her hand. I think she was too shocked to move.'

'Objection!' said the other fellow.

'Upheld,' said the judge.

'You must tell us only what you saw and heard,' said our man, kind and regretful.

'Well, she was stock still and staring, and white as a sheet,' I said, and a bit of a smile went around. 'She yelled to me, "Get water! Get water!" She was standing in front of the washtubs, so I couldn't reach the taps, but the water in the copper was still cold and clean and there was a dipper on the edge of it, so I scooped water out of it, and sluiced it over her eyes, time and again, fast as I could.'

It's an odd thing that when you're doing something like that, you get a feeling for the person you're trying to help, that has nothing to do with right and wrong. Much as I hated that wicked girl I was handling her as if I was really fond of her, murmuring to her, 'Still now. Quiet now,' as if she was a little kid. She must have felt it, for she whimpered to me, 'Twice. She did it twice.'

Of course that settled it. Once could have been an accident – though I don't know what sort of accident gets caustic into somebody's eyes – but not twice. There was no doubt about it. That was how we saved the other eye. She had had time to shut it. She had shut it so fast that she couldn't open it herself and when I got a wet cloth out of the copper and kept rinsing and rinsing and then found another wet washcloth and held that over it – no use thinking about the other eye, I don't even want to think about it – but how I was praying that this left eye was all right, as much as if she was my own child. When at last I got the muscles relaxed and she opened the eye, there were little white lines of unburnt skin like a great white cobweb on the red flesh. That's a sight I'll never forget. And then it was nearly all undone, for she put her hand up to the eye and of course the stuff was on her hands too. I grabbed it just in time. Then I started to wash the stuff off her hands and I began to think I could do with some help.

'Give me a hand here, Lil,' I said.

After that first moment I hadn't looked at Lil. Now I did, and pretty sharply. Then I saw that she was in a very bad way. She hadn't stirred, was holding that tin still and staring in front of her.

I wasn't going to touch the thing with my bare hands. I wrapped the wet cloth round it and lifted it out of her hands. That was when I saw the state of the glove. I had sense enough not to speak. The other one was calmer now. She was sitting up, holding the washcloth to her eyes, but her ears were open. I looked at the glove, I looked towards the tap, and then at Lil. She got the message. I don't think she had the sense then to act without prompting. She turned on the tap, held the glove under it and rinsed it clean. Then I set the tin on the bench, found the lid sitting there and rammed it on.

It must take a while to realise that you've committed a crime. If Lil was used to it, she would have washed the stuff off her glove right away, while I was busy with the other one. The whole palm had been smeared; you could see that she had held a fistful, a real fistful. So much for her story that the lid was hard to shift, that she'd got it off with a jerk and lost control so that it spilled. The other one had been kneeling in front of the copper setting the fire under it. She had looked up unexpectedly and got the spilled stuff in her eyes.

The other one told her story first. She was wearing dark glasses. She took them off to show the jury the damage. I was glad I couldn't see that; the look on some of the jury was enough. She put the glasses on again and they looked relieved. She said she had been kneeling in front of the copper setting the fire. Mrs Harrison had been filling the copper with a dipper from the washtub. Suddenly Mrs Harrison had said, 'Look here!' She had looked up and got a handful of the caustic in her face, blinding her right eye. She had begun to scream from the pain and put her hands up, but it had happened again. She had thrown another lot. Funny, she wasn't allowed to say 'handful' and 'thrown'. Lil's man objected and the judge said he was right. Was 'handful' an estimate of quantity? She supposed so, though how the poor girl could estimate quantity when she was rolling on the ground screaming, I don't know. He brought that out, and she admitted she couldn't have known how much paste there was, so the word 'handful' had to go. The story that comes out in court is made up of your answers to the questions they ask, and they have the choice of that, so it's not like telling a story as it happens. Not that I wanted to, on that occasion.

They don't take much account of your feelings, either.

Lil's man wanted to know if she had been lying still and got out of her that she was shaking her head and rolling from side to side. The paste was semi-liquid? Yes. Was it not possible that the paste had spread from the right eye to the left? 'She threw it!' 'But your eyes were shut?' 'Yes.' You could see that reliving it was making her feel sick. She was white and trembling and perhaps she gave up easily on that account.

Then came the motive. Had she any reason to suppose that Mrs Harrison would wish to harm her? Yes. Mr Harrison was in love with her and had asked his wife for a divorce, which she wouldn't give him. Of course it wasn't Lil's man who brought that out. It was the other one, establishing motive. He asked very quietly, what her relations with Mr Harrison had been. Had they advanced as far as physical intimacy? So that's what they call it, I thought. Yes, she said, they had. But she didn't tell about moving into the bedroom, which was the thing that had maddened poor Lil to the point where she'd lost control. Perhaps she wasn't brazen enough to say it right out in court, and it seemed to me that in a way she was pleading guilty. You could see that there was something she didn't want to talk about, and that told on the jury. I suppose her man didn't bring it out because he wouldn't want to lose the sympathy of the jury – and maybe she hadn't even told him – and Lil's man wouldn't, because it would strengthen Lil's motive. But perhaps he didn't know, either. Lil wouldn't be saying what drove her to it while she was sticking to her story of accident. I knew then that Lil was safe.

I wondered if Lil was worrying about me. I wasn't going to tell about the glove, but I'd seen it and Lil knew that I had seen it.

I had said, 'I'd better get Charlie,' and when I added, 'Are you all right, Lil?' I meant, was it safe to leave the girl alone with her. I think she understood me, for she nodded. I said, 'We have to get her to a doctor.'

I helped the girl up. She'd be better able to look after herself standing. Then I ran to where the men were at the sheep run.

'You'd better come,' I said to Charlie. 'There's been an accident.'

They made a lot of play of my saying that straight away, that it was an accident. What was I supposed to say? Your poor wretched wife has thrown caustic into your floozy's eyes and blinded her and now I hope you're satisfied with what you've done. That's what I would have liked to say. I think perhaps he heard it in my voice, because he ran back with me in a hurry.

I'll never know what happened between Lilian and Charlie. He took one look and ran to phone for the ambulance. I said to Lil, 'I'll get the children and take them back with me.' I was thinking, That's the end of poor Lil. He'll never forgive her for this.

The children were doing their correspondence lessons in the schoolroom. They were good enough children, the boy Gavin seven and the girl Iris five, doing what they were told without fuss. They looked at me in surprise. I must have been a funny sight, drenched as I was with the water from the copper.

I said, 'There was an accident in the wash house. Miss Damaris got burnt.'

They thought it must be from the copper fire and they didn't ask any more. They weren't inquisitive children. I find with most children that they're interested only in what affects them. Everything that had been going on in the house had gone right over their heads, I think. They might have noticed that Lil was snappier than usual, that's all.

'Miss Damaris has to go away to hospital, so you're coming to stay with me for a while. Come and show me where to get your night things.'

I took them to the front of the house, away from the wash house. They fetched their things and I hurried them into the car and back to town.

I still think I was right not to tell about the smear on the palm of the glove or of her saying to me, 'Twice.' After all, I couldn't say, 'Yes, she did it, but she was driven to it.' Sometimes you have to tell a bit of a lie to get near the truth.

As for what drove her to it, I wasn't supposed to talk about that. Only what I had seen and heard myself.

'Had you ever seen any signs of discord between Mr and Mrs Harrison?'

Well, of course I hadn't. I never saw them together. Charlie was always out on the farm when I visited Lil. I heard plenty, though, but for some reason what Lil said to me didn't seem to count. But from the start of the affair I'd listened to poor Lil and tried to give advice. I think I gave the wrong advice. I told her to sit it out. I said Charlie would wake up to himself, he was just at the age when a man tends to make a fool of himself over a younger woman, but it never lasted.

'Have you talked to Charlie?' I asked.

'He doesn't hear me. He doesn't even see me. He's like a man asleep, having a lovely dream.'

'He'll wake up,' I said.

But Charlie didn't wake up. He asked Lil to divorce him.

'As bold as brass,' she told me with the tears running down her face. 'No shame in either of them. That wicked little bitch, I curse the day she came here.'

'She'll pay some day,' I said. I wish I hadn't said that.

Lil had said to him, 'You can't divorce me because I'll never give you grounds, and I'll never divorce you whatever you do. You'll never drive me to it.'

This is the only place where I think I might have done wrong. I encouraged her. I said, 'Don't let them drive you away from your home and your kids. Just wait them out.'

It might have been the wrong advice, but I don't think Lil would have gone anyhow. It's my opinion that she loved that land more than she ever loved Charlie. She was the one who kept it together through the bad times and she wouldn't let Charlie owe the bank when things were good and he got grand ideas about expanding. He had cause to thank her for that.

They took Lil at her word. She had to leave the house to go to a CWA meeting and when she came back she found all her belongings in cardboard boxes outside the bedroom door, which was locked. The other's room was stripped bare. She had moved in to Lil's place.

Lil swallowed it. She had no choice. She moved her things into the other's room. But when you think what it must have been like, seeing that locked door every night and knowing what went on behind it . . . you can forgive Lil a lot, if not everything.

Our man made a great play with the fact that the two women were working side by side in the wash house. Would that have happened if the two women were enemies? I looked at this gentleman who had probably not rinsed a shirt in his life and wondered if he knew how life was lived. Friends or enemies, the washing had to be done. It was too much for one. They could hate each other as much as they pleased so long as the men's work clothes got onto the line.

On the stand Lil was quiet and dignified, not showing much emotion. It was true that she had had words with her husband over his attentions to Miss Dexter. She thought it was harmless but it was easy for a young woman to make too much of such a thing. There had never been a question of divorce. If they had had a serious relationship, she hadn't been aware of it.

I couldn't help looking at the other woman. She sat calm and easy, as if this didn't matter to her at all. The dark glasses must have helped. I thought it was Charlie's words she was hearing, not Lil's, and she was hiding her feelings, out of pride. You couldn't but be sorry for her at that moment.

It had been a shock to me, too, that Charlie had changed sides. I had expected him to go with the woman in the ambulance or at least to believe her and turn on Lil.

I had said the word 'accident' and they both stuck fast to it and so, I suppose, to each other.

At first it had looked as if that was the end of it. I kept the children for two days, then Lil rang, as calm as you please, to say that she would call for the children to take them home. The other woman had been taken to Sydney to the eye hospital and they had got in touch with the insurance company. All the employees were insured against accident, which was fortunate.

I think she was taken aback when the police came. The other woman had laid charges. Lil had to go with them to the station in town to make a statement. Then she had to go before a magistrate who said there was a case to answer and she was committed for trial.

Lil's friends blamed the gossip for that. Of course everyone knew what had been happening and the talk, for and against, was ferocious. Lil's friends said she should never have been brought to trial. It was all the work of evil tongues.

This was when I began to think that I wasn't any longer one of Lil's friends. In a way I could understand it. You could never wipe out that moment when I had seen the smear on the palm of the glove. Our eyes had met and she knew that I knew. Better to keep me right out of it. But I was the one who could have done with a bit of support. She would know that I meant to stand by her, but it was a hard thing to carry alone.

That trial was a long time coming. It must have been a terrible time, like having a debt that had to be paid some-time and having it weigh on you. I'd like to have helped

Lil through it by letting her know that I was standing by her, but she never asked. Perhaps she took it for granted. I hoped so. Nobody else ever spoke to me about it either, though I believe they never talked about anything else to each other. They weren't supposed to. It was something called *sub judice*, but tell that to the gossips. Everyone knew I was bound to be a witness, so I had a kind of official position that cut me off from the rest. I don't think I've ever been lonelier.

Lil said, No, she didn't regularly use caustic in the copper. The men's clothes were particularly dirty because of the sheep dipping. The caustic hadn't been used for some time, so the lid was stuck fast.

If the other fellow had known his business, he would have asked why the paste was so loose then. Why hadn't it dried out? Any woman would have asked that. Of course the stuff dries out and the usual thing is to mix it up with water just before you use it and stir it in with an old spoon or something that you keep in the wash house. It's not stuff to take risks with, as we all know. So I asked myself that question, and I didn't like the answer. I could understand Lil losing control and throwing the stuff into the woman's eyes instead of into the copper, but getting the stuff ready beforehand, opening the tin and mixing in the water to make it the right consistency – that was hard to take. Lil said that the lid came off with a jerk so that she lost control and almost dropped the tin. She caught it but not in time to stop the caustic splashing out. She thought she must have made a sound when it slipped, so that Damaris had looked up and got it in the eyes. Saying

'Damaris' must have been the hardest thing about that.

Everyone who had turned up to watch was waiting to hear Charlie, but he didn't give evidence at all. The crowd was disappointed, and so was I. I knew he was going to support Lil and lie about the affair, but I wanted to hear him lying, and I hoped I'd at least see him squirm. Well, I did, not long after.

As for me, I didn't even have to lie. They didn't ask about the glove. If they had, I meant to say that I hadn't noticed, but I didn't need to. Well, they're the ones who ask the questions, and if they don't ask the right ones, that's their lookout.

So Lil was acquitted.

That was when I thought my lonely time was over. I went up to Lil and Charlie where they were standing by their car. There weren't any people around, congratulating them, I noticed. The general feeling seemed to be that it was a good thing Lil had got off, but nobody was going to stand close to her when she had a tin of caustic in her hands. They didn't seem to care, they were wrapped in each other, but I had been a true friend to them and I thought they might thank me for standing by them.

I said, 'Well, that went all right, didn't it?'

They turned round and looked at me and I've never looked into colder eyes.

Lil said, 'What do you mean?' and Charlie carried on for her. 'You heard what the judge said. Isn't that good enough for you?'

I could see that I was never going to be forgiven for what I had seen and heard. I was never going to share that dreadful moment with anyone. I turned away, feeling sick, and there behind me was the other one. I think she was showing herself to them with me on purpose, because she and I were the ones who knew. It was a kind of demonstration.

'The doctor said that it was you who saved my eye-sight, at least what is left of it. You saved the left eye and there's some residual vision in the right eye, though the eyeball is badly scarred. I thought you would like to know.'

'I'm so glad,' I said. 'Lucky I got there in time.'

We were ignoring the others. I suppose they were just waiting for us to go away.

'I'll always be grateful to you,' she said.

Suddenly, as quick as a snake striking, she was facing Charlie, wearing a neat little smile and taking off her glasses. It was an obscene gesture, and Charlie, all unpre-pared, jerked his head away like a frightened horse. So he had to face the moment, after all. She put the glasses back on and walked away. As I watched her go, I realised that she was the only one I could have shared that moment with and I'd cut myself off from her. I walked away too towards my own car, still alone with it.

I didn't see much of Lil and Charlie after that. Some-times I thought, they couldn't have hated me more if I had told the whole truth.

I've never liked secrets. I've never wanted to have one, but I was stuck with that one. Until now, when they're all dead, and who's to care? Except me.

NOTES ON THE CONTRIBUTORS

GLENDA ADAMS is the author of *Games of the Strong*; *Dancing on Coral*, winner of the Miles Franklin Award and the NSW Premier's Award; *Longleg*, winner of the National Book Council Banjo Award and the *Age* Fiction Book of the Year Award; and *The Tempest of Clemenza*. She was born and educated in Sydney and spent many years teaching in New York before returning to Australia.

GEORGIA BLAIN has worked as a journalist and a copyright lawyer. Her first novel, *Closed for Winter*, was published in 1998. Her second novel, *Candelo*, will be published by Penguin in 1999.

JAMES BRADLEY is the author of a book of poetry, *Paper Nautilus*, which was shortlisted for the National Book Council Banjo Award. His novel, *Wrack*, won both the FAW Literature Award and the Kathleen Mitchell Literature Award, and was shortlisted for both the Commonwealth Writers Prize and the Miles Franklin Award. His new novel, *The Deep Field*, will be published in 1999.

LARRY BUTTROSE was born in Adelaide. He began writing poetry in his teens, then moved to Sydney in the early 1980s as a singer with a cabaret group called Quietly Confident. He has since branched out into play- and screen-writing – he co-wrote the West End hit musical *Hot Shoe Shuffle* – and has published two books of travel writing. *The Maze of the Muse* is his first novel.

MATTHEW CONDON is the author of several works of fiction and has won two Steele Rudd awards for his collections of short fiction. His latest novel is *The Pillow Fight*. He currently lives in Sydney.

RAIMONDO CORTESE has written several books and plays. His plays include *The Room*, *Lucrezia & Cesare*, *Features of Blown Youth* and *The Fertility of Objects*. He has also written a collection of short stories, *The Indestructible Corpse*, and a novel, *The Bird Sickness*, is forthcoming.

LIAM DAVISON was born in Melbourne in 1957. He is the author of *The Velodrome*; *Soundings*, which won the 1993 National Book Council Banjo Award for fiction and was shortlisted for both the *Age* Book of the Year Award and the Victorian Premier's Award for fiction; *The*

White Woman, which was also shortlisted for the *Age* Book of the Year Award; and *The Shipwreck Party*. His new novel will be published by Penguin in 1999.

MATT DRAY lives in North Queensland. His debut novel, *A Day at the Races*, will be published by Penguin in 1999.

NICK EARLS is the author of the bestselling novels *Zigzag Street* and *Bachelor Kisses*. *Zigzag Street* won a Betty Trask Award in the UK in 1998, and is being developed into a feature film. 'Sausage Sizzle' is from his forthcoming book, *Headgames*, to be published by Penguin in 1999.

PENNY FLANAGAN is a Sydney-based musician and writer. Her short stories have appeared in *Meanjin* and *Picador New Writing*. Her first book, a children's novel, *Changing the Sky*, was published in 1994. 'The Last Days of Summer' is an extract from *Sing to Me*, her first adult novel.

HELEN GARNER has been publishing fiction since 1977 when her novel *Monkey Grip* appeared. Her fiction titles include *The Children's Bach* and *My Hard Heart*. Her two non-fiction books are *The First Stone* and *True Stories*.

NIKKI GEMMELL was born in Wollongong. She studied writing at the University of Technology, Sydney. Her short stories appear in a number of literary journals and she has written two novels: the bestselling *Shiver* and the recently released *Cleave*.

PETER GOLDSWORTHY graduated in medicine from the University of Adelaide in 1974 and has since divided his time between writing and medicine. His bestselling and critically acclaimed novels, including *Maestro* and *Honk if You Are Jesus*, have been translated into numerous languages. *Navelgazing*, published by Penguin, is a collection of his essays.

MARION HALLIGAN is the author of five novels, of which *The Golden Dress* is the most recent, a number of collections of short stories, several autobiographical narratives of travel and food, and a picture book for children. She also writes essays and reviews books.

ELIZABETH JOLLEY was born in the industrial midlands of England in 1923 and moved to Western Australia in 1959 with her husband and three children. She is acclaimed as one of Australia's leading writers, and has received an Order of Australia. Her novels include *Mr Scobie's Riddle* and *My Father's Moon*, winners of the *Age* Book of the Year Award; *The Georges' Wife*, winner of the NBC Banjo Award for Fiction; and *The Orchard Thieves*.

NICHOLAS JOSE grew up in South Australia, where he spent a lot of time on Yorke Peninsula, the setting for his novel, *Paper Nautilus*. His other books include *Avenue of Eternal Peace* and *The Rose Crossing* – novels that draw on his connection with China – and *Chinese Whispers*, a collection of essays. His most recent novel is *The Custodians*, shortlisted for the Commonwealth Writers' Prize (Asia–Pacific).

GERARD LEE has travelled widely in Australia, Indonesia and Europe. He is the author of *True Love and How to Get It*, *Pieces for a Glass Piano* and *Troppo Man*. He co-wrote the award-winning film *Sweetie* with Jane Campion, and is the writer–director of *All Men Are Liars*.

AMANDA LOHREY was born in Tasmania in 1947. Her novels are *The Morality of Gentlemen*, *The Reading Group* and *Camille's Bread*. She was a lecturer in writing at the University of Technology, Sydney, and is now writing full time.

PHILLIP SCOTT is a writer, musician and performer, well known from comedy programs on ABC television. His novels are *One Dead Diva* and *Gay Resort Murder Shock*, and he is currently working on a third detective novel featuring his 'heroes', Marc and Paul.

HERB WHARTON, born in Cunnamulla, Queensland, began his working life in his teenage years as a drover. His maternal grandmother was of the Kooma people; his grandfathers were Irish and English. His first book, *Unbranded*, published in 1992, told of his experiences on the stock routes of inland Australia. His second book, *Cattle Camp*, published in 1994, contains stories by Murri stockmen and women.

KRISTIN WILLIAMSON is the author of the novels *Princess Kate*, *Tanglewood*, *The Jacaranda Years*, and *Treading on Dreams*, as well as the non-fiction books *The Last Bastion* and *Brothers to Us*. She has an academic background in history, education and theatre, and spent many years as a teacher and journalist.

AMY WITTING was born in Annandale, an inner suburb of Sydney, in 1918. She has published four novels, *The Visit*, *I for Isobel*, *A Change in the Lighting* and most recently, *Maria's War*; two collections of short stories, *Marriages* and *In and Out the Window*; and three books of verse, *Travel Diary*, *Beauty is the Straw* and *Collected Poems*. She was awarded the Patrick White Prize in 1993.

ACKNOWLEDGEMENTS

Grateful acknowledgement is due to the following authors and publishers for permission to reprint stories in this collection.

GLENDA ADAMS, 'The Hottest Night of the Century', from *The Hottest Night of the Century*, published by Angus&Robertson, 1979. Reprinted in this collection by courtesy of HarperCollins Publishers and the author.

GEORGIA BLAIN, 'Candelo', from her forthcoming novel, *Candelo*, to be published in 1999 by Penguin Books Australia Ltd. Published in this collection by courtesy of Penguin Books Australia Ltd and the author.

JAMES BRADLEY, 'The Turtles' Graveyard', from *A Sea Change*, edited by Adam Shoemaker and published by Sydney 2000, 1998. Reprinted in this collection by courtesy of the author.

LARRY BUTTROSE, 'The Sea Breeze', from *Café Royale*, published by Flamingo, 1997. Reprinted in this collection by courtesy of HarperCollins Publishers and the author.

MATTHEW CONDON, 'Come Walk With Me, My Lovely', from *A Night at the Pink Poodle*, published by Arrow, 1995. Reprinted in this collection by courtesy of Random House Australia Ltd and the author.

RAIMONDO CORTESE, 'The Immolating Nun', from *The Indestructible Corpse*, published by Text Publishing, 1998. Reprinted in this collection by courtesy of Curtis Brown (Australia) Pty Ltd and the author.

LIAM DAVISON, 'The Swimmer', from *The Shipwreck Party*, published by University of Queensland Press, 1989. First published in *Australian Short Stories*, No. 5, Pascoe Publishing, 1983. Reprinted in this collection by courtesy of the author.

MATT DRAY, 'Anzac Day', from his forthcoming novel, *A Day at the Races*, to be published by Penguin Books Australia Ltd in 1999. Published in this collection by courtesy of Penguin Books Australia Ltd and the author.

NICK EARLS, 'Sausage Sizzle', from his forthcoming collection, *Headgames*, to be published by Penguin Books Australia Ltd in 1999. Published in this collection by courtesy of Penguin Books Australia Ltd and the author.

PENNY FLANAGAN, 'The Last Days of Summer', from *Sing to Me*, published by Penguin Books Australia Ltd, 1998. Reprinted in this collection by courtesy of Penguin Books Australia Ltd and the author.

HELEN GARNER, 'Postcards from Surfers', from *My Hard Heart*, published by Penguin Books Australia Ltd, 1998. First published in *Australian Short Stories*. Reprinted in this collection by courtesy of Penguin Books Australia Ltd and the author.

NIKKI GEMMELL, 'Dust Slapped', from *Cleave*, published by Vintage, 1998. Reprinted in this collection by courtesy of Random House Australia Ltd and the author.

PETER GOLDSWORTHY, 'The Booster Shot', from *Little Deaths*, published by HarperCollins Publishers, 1993. Reprinted in this collection by courtesy of Curtis Brown (Australia) Pty Ltd and the author.

MARION HALLIGAN, 'At Merewether Beach', from *The Golden Dress*, published by Penguin Books Australia Ltd, 1998. Reprinted in this collection by courtesy of Penguin Books Australia Ltd and the author.

ELIZABETH JOLLEY, 'The Fellow Passenger', from *Fellow Passengers*, published by Penguin Books Australia Ltd, 1997. First published in *The Travelling Entertainer*, Fremantle Arts Centre Press, 1979. Reprinted in this collection by courtesy of Penguin Books Australia Ltd and the author.

NICHOLAS JOSE, 'The Boy, Summer 1961', from *Paper Nautilus*, published by Penguin Books Australia Ltd, 1987. Reprinted in this collection by courtesy of Penguin Books Australia Ltd and the author.

GERARD LEE, 'Three Ways', from *Eating Dog*, published by University of Queensland Press, 1993. Reprinted in this collection by courtesy of University of Queensland Press and the author.

AMANDA LOHREY, 'The Ferry to Manly', from *Camille's Bread*, published by Angus&Robertson, 1995. Reprinted in this collection by courtesy of HarperCollins Publishers and the author.

PHILLIP SCOTT, 'Hellfire at New Heaven', from *Gay Resort Murder Shock*, published by Penguin Books Australia Ltd, 1998. Reprinted in this collection by courtesy of Penguin Books Australia Ltd and the author.

HERB WHARTON, 'The Munta-gutta', from *Where Ya' Been Mate*, published by University of Queensland Press, 1996. Reprinted in this collection by courtesy of University of Queensland Press and the author.

KRISTIN WILLIAMSON, 'River Picnic', from *Treading on Dreams*, published by Penguin Books Australia Ltd, 1998. Reprinted in this collection by courtesy of Penguin Books Australia Ltd and the author.

AMY WITTING, 'The Witness', published in this collection by courtesy of Margaret Connolly & Associates and the author.